THE GUILD CODEX: DEMONIZED / THREE

HUNTING FIENDS
FOR THE ILL-EQUIPPED

ANNETTE MARIE

dark owl
fantasy

Hunting Fiends for the Ill-Equipped
The Guild Codex: Demonized / Book Three

Dark Owl Fantasy Inc.
PO Box 88106, Rabbit Hill Post Office
Edmonton, AB, Canada T6R 0M5
www.darkowlfantasy.com

Cover Copyright © 2020 by Annette Ahner
Cover and Book Interior by Midnight Whimsy Designs
www.midnightwhimsydesigns.com

Editing by Elizabeth Darkley
arrowheadediting.wordpress.com

ISBN 978-1-988153-42-1

BOOKS IN THE GUILD CODEX

MORE BOOKS BY ANNETTE MARIE

STEEL & STONE UNIVERSE

Steel & Stone Series

Chase the Dark

Bind the Soul

Yield the Night

Reap the Shadows

Unleash the Storm

Steel & Stone

Spell Weaver Trilogy

The Night Realm

The Shadow Weave

The Blood Curse

OTHER WORKS

Red Winter Trilogy

Red Winter

Dark Tempest

Immortal Fire

THE GUILD CODEX

CLASSES OF MAGIC

Spiritalis

Psychica

Arcana

Demonica

Elementaria

MYTHIC

A person with magical ability

MPD / MAGIPOL

The organization that regulates mythics and their activities

ROGUE

A mythic living in violation of MPD laws

HUNTING FIENDS
FOR THE ILL-EQUIPPED

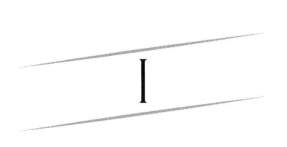

1

ADRENALINE FIRED IN MY VEINS, intensifying my senses. My pulse throbbed in my ears, jumping nervously, and air rushed through my nose with each deliberately deep breath. Tension infused my muscles as I held my stare on my opponent.

Lounging on the opposite side of the coffee table, the demon watched me with softly glowing red eyes. The living room lamp bathed his warm skin, toffee brown with a reddish undertone, and his long, thin tail coiled across the carpet, the barbed end twitching.

On the table between us were two stacks of playing cards—and the prize. The plastic container held four fat cinnamon buns from a nearby bakery, the tops drizzled with white icing.

I shifted my attention to my cards: the two of hearts and the queen of spades. To win, I had to play both before my opponent could empty his hand.

Zylas flicked his two cards as he studied me.

Entertaining a demon wasn't easy. He hated anything that involved a screen, and convincing him to try board or card games had been a losing battle—until I realized the missing ingredient. He didn't want to play games. He wanted to *win* games, and winning wasn't any fun without a prize to claim.

"It's your turn," I pointed out.

A corner of his mouth lifted, flashing a sharp canine. He brushed a finger across the top of his cards, then plucked one out and set it on the discard pile. The jack of hearts. He'd skipped my turn.

I gritted my teeth as he tossed down his last card, emptying his hand.

"*Vh'renith*," he declared smugly. "I win."

Clenching my jaw even tighter, I swept up the stock and discard piles. "That makes two wins for you, and two for me. The fifth will be the tiebreaker."

"The next winner gets the food," he agreed.

I shuffled the cards more thoroughly than necessary, just in case he'd come up with ways to cheat. He was a demon, so I couldn't rule out the possibility.

"I did not *cheat*, *drādah*."

"Stop reading my mind."

"Stop yelling your thoughts at me."

I froze in mid-shuffle. "Wait. You—" I gasped. "You *are* cheating! You can read my mind, so you know my cards and what I'm planning to do!"

He snorted. "I do not know your cards."

"But you can read my mind, so that means—"

"I do not know your cards."

At the hint of a growl in his voice, I snapped my mouth shut. Demons didn't lie—and could detect lies when others spoke them—and he hated it when I suggested he was being untruthful.

I dealt the cards. "If you can hear my thoughts, why don't you know my cards?"

He slid his off the coffee table and fanned them out. "If I heard every *ka'an* thing in your head, I would not be able to think."

"What does *ka'an* mean?"

"Turn the first card."

I flipped the top card off the stock to start the discard pile. "You know what I'm thinking all the time. You always notice when I …"

Trailing off with a blush, I cleared my throat and grabbed my cards.

"When you insult me in your head, *na?*" he asked slyly.

"See? You *do* know what I'm thinking."

He dropped the two of diamonds on the discard pile. "Only what you want me to know."

I plucked a pair of cards off the stock and organized my bulky hand, annoyed by his early advantage. "What do you mean, you only know what I want you to know?"

"Take your turn."

I played the jack of diamonds—skipping his turn—then the ace of diamonds and ace of hearts. With that, we had an equal number of cards again. Much better.

He scanned his hand. "Why do you think I know everything in your head?"

Frowning over his question, I almost missed him play a card. His ability to read my mind was something I tried not to think about too hard, but I *had* noticed he didn't react to my every thought. I'd assumed he was tuning me out so my inner dialogue wouldn't drive him crazy.

I discarded a card onto the pile. "You always seem to know what I'm thinking."

"Because I can hear you, or because I can guess?"

Guess? He couldn't be *guessing* what I was thinking. "You respond to my thoughts as if I'm talking to you."

"When you are thinking *at* me. Sometimes I hear other things, but I do not hear what you do not want me to know."

My mouth dropped open.

"Take two cards, *drādah*."

I looked down at the pile. A jack of hearts peeked out from behind a two of hearts. He had only three cards left. I drew two cards from the stock, added them to my hand, then slapped down an eight. "I choose spades."

He played the nine of spades. Two cards left in his hand.

"You're saying you *can't* hear my thoughts, but only when I don't want you to hear them?" I asked suspiciously as I rearranged my cards, planning my next move while simultaneously dissecting his expression. "How can you tell if you're *not* hearing things I think?"

He said nothing, waiting for my play, so I tossed down the two of spades and the two of clubs. His mouth thinned as he drew four cards, putting him at six and me at four.

After a moment's thought, he laid down an eight. "Diamonds."

I slapped my second eight down. "Spades again."

He scowled at his hand, then drew a card. I played another spade, leaving me with the jack and six of spades. As long as he didn't change the suit, I could play them both on my next turn and win our tiebreaker.

"You didn't answer my question," I accused as he scrutinized his options.

His scarlet gaze rose to me. "There are many things you think that I do not know. Like your face, *drādah*, and how it changes color."

My eyes popped.

"Your skin turns red," he mused as he leisurely drew a card from the stock. "Your breath grows quick. Your heart beats faster. Your scent changes …" He canted his head, observing my reaction. "You stare at me, and there are thoughts in your eyes, but I hear nothing."

My mouth opened and closed, and I could feel the telltale heat rising in my cheeks.

His voice dropped to a husky murmur. "What are you thinking now, *drādah?*"

"N-nothing."

His eyelids lowered, hooding his eyes. "Do not lie to me."

I gulped and stammered, "Wh-whose turn is it?"

"Your turn."

I snatched a card from my hand and tossed it down. As it hit the pile, I realized it was the six of spades. I was supposed to play my jack first to skip his turn! I would've won!

He fanned out his seven cards, watching me with calculating eyes, then played the six of diamonds over my six of spades, changing the suit.

I drew a card—the five of spades.

"What are you hiding?"

My attention shot back to him. "Wh-what?"

He played a diamond. "When your face changes color and your breath comes fast, is that because of me?"

"No!"

"Lying again, *drādah*."

Crap. Fighting my intensifying blush, I yanked a card off the stock. The last eight of the deck! Now we were talking.

He played another diamond, reducing his hand to four. "Why do you guard these thoughts? You do not hide other thoughts about me."

"It's none of your business," I declared as I slapped down my eight. "Spades."

And with that, I won. With no more eights, he couldn't change the suit, and on my next turn, I would play the jack and five of spades, emptying my hand.

As I clutched my winning pair, he fanned out his remaining four cards. Two jacks had been played, and the third was in my hand. Even if he skipped my turn once, I'd still win. The only way he could win was if he—

He placed the seven of spades on the pile. Then he put the seven of diamonds on top of it. Then he laid the seven of clubs on top of that. My eyes narrowed to slits as he held up his final card.

"No," I growled.

He dropped the seven of hearts on top of the pile, emptying his hand.

"No way!" I yelled, flinging my two cards into the air. With those four cards, he would've won no matter which suit I'd chosen.

He flashed a grin and pulled the cinnamon buns across the table. "*Vh'renithnās.*"

He'd only just learned the game, yet he'd beaten me three times in a row. Leaving the cards where they were, I pushed to my feet, fuming. Maybe I was a sore loser, but he was already bigger and faster and stronger and more cunning and he had an eidetic memory. He shouldn't be better at cards too. It wasn't fair.

As I stormed past him, he caught my wrist and pulled me backward. One arm flailing, I lost my balance and fell—landing squarely in his lap.

My blush reignited and I shoved away from him. He wrapped an arm around my waist, holding me down, and his warm breath stirred my hair.

"You missed it, *drādah*," he breathed in my ear. "Your moment of *dh'ērrenith*."

Dh'ērrenith—the demonic word for certain victory.

"If you can't read my mind," I muttered, fighting the urge to squirm against his immovable strength, "how do you know I was going to win?"

"Do not let your opponent distract you."

Had he brought up the mind-reading thing to fluster me? I swallowed the hysterical laugh bubbling in my throat and tugged at his encircling arm. "Let me go."

Instead of obeying, he slid the carton of cinnamon buns off the table and dropped it on my lap. "We will share the prize."

"You want to share?" Him? Mr. Selfish?

"We will share ... if you explain what makes your face change to red."

"What?" I shoved hard, twisting free from his arm. The cinnamon bun container tumbled to the floor. "What kind of offer is that?"

"You lost. I will share my prize, but I want something else."

"Then keep your prize," I grumped, straightening my sweater. I stalked to my bedroom, but as I stepped through the door, I couldn't resist glancing over my shoulder.

Zylas already had his teeth buried in an icing-drizzled bun. He angled his head, catching my eye. More heat rushed into my face and I fled into my room, shutting the door tightly behind me.

Breathing hard for no reason, I dropped onto my bed and rubbed my cheeks with both hands. Why was I so bashful? I shouldn't be blushing like this. Zylas was a *demon*—a demon with no respect for personal boundaries. The more his invasions of my space annoyed me, the happier he seemed.

I lowered my hands from my face, a smile pulling at my lips. This time, though, he'd overplayed his hand. What he'd revealed had been well worth the embarrassment.

He couldn't read *all* my thoughts.

How much sleep had I lost worrying about what he could hear in my head or how his demon brain interpreted it all? If he was in the dark about everything I preferred to keep private, that meant he didn't know why I blushed when he touched me, or why he sometimes caught me staring at him, or why I'd freaked out when he'd stripped us half-naked in a storm drain.

Especially that last incident. I really hoped he had no clue about that one.

Feeling newly cheerful, I fished under my bed and dragged out a thin metal case. Time to get to work.

"*Egeirai, angizontos tou Athanou, lytheti,*" I declared, my hand splayed across the cool steel top.

The box lit up with white runes, and I opened the lid. The Athanas Grimoire lay on top, its worn leather cover shiny from handling—though little of it recent. Carefully lifting out the book, I collected my notebook from underneath it, stacked it and the grimoire on my pile of reference texts, and carried everything into the living room.

Zylas had shifted to the sofa, lying sideways across it as he shoved half a fluffy cinnamon bun into his mouth.

"You're going to choke," I warned him.

Ignoring me, he swallowed his mouthful without chewing.

I tidied the deck of cards, then spread my books out and sat cross-legged behind the coffee table, using the sofa as a backrest. Zylas's tail hung off the cushions beside me.

Tucked inside my notebook were my mother's notes and translations, but I'd yet to figure out which pages of the grimoire they corresponded with. I shifted them aside to reveal my translation of the first page of the grimoire. Quiet awe slid through me every time I looked at the list.

Fourteen names stretching back over four *thousand* years, all belonging to my ancestors. Each sorceress had taken on the meticulous task of recopying the aging grimoire to preserve its knowledge, and I would be the fifteenth name on that list. The grimoire had last been recopied over three hundred years ago, the longest gap in its history.

As I scanned the list, my attention caught on a name: Myrrine Athanas. She was the fifth sorceress to have copied the grimoire, an ancestor from millennia ago.

Lower lip caught between my teeth, I flipped back to my mother's notes and read the top page.

Insertions from Myrrine Athanas — direct descendant of Anthea??

3 5 passages added to her grimoire copy, not from original book
   Journal entries?
   Could be more, need to check to end

Myrrine mentions Λευκάς - Leukás?
-> Leucadia, island in the Ionian Sea on the
    west coast of Greece
1000-700 BC?

Was she the first summoner to disobey
the 12 warning???

I reread the last line several times. When I'd reviewed her notes before, I'd assumed "12 warning" was supposed to be "12 warnings" and she'd missed a letter. Figuring I'd eventually find these warnings, I hadn't paid much attention to the note. But what if her quick scrawl didn't contain an error but was her shorthand?

12 warning ... twelfth warning ... *Twelfth House warning.*

Pulling the grimoire closer, I carefully turned the fragile pages. The ancient paper, cracked and stained, tore easily and I didn't want to add to the damage. Finally, I found the section I wanted—the demon Houses. I didn't need a translation to recognize the First House. The illustration of a winged demon, with long horns, a muscular build, and thick tail with a heavy plate on the end, looked eerily similar to Tahēsh, the escaped demon that had nearly killed me and Zylas three months ago.

I flipped past the first eleven Houses and stopped on the final one. An illustration of Zylas's doppelganger filled part of the page, and beneath the House name were two sentences written in precise strokes with an ancient pen. I'd translated them already.

Never summon from the Twelfth House.
For the trespass of this sacred covenant,
the sons of Vh'alyir will destroy you.

Could that be the warning my mother had referenced? Did she think Myrrine Athanas had summoned a Vh'alyir demon?

"Zylas?" I glanced over my shoulder. "Didn't you say no demon of your House has ever been summoned before?"

He sleepily cracked one eye open. "*Var.*"

"Are you sure? Could a Vh'alyir have been summoned a really long time ago?"

"I do not know." When I continued to look at him hopefully, he released a huffing breath. "Maybe. Most stories of our House are forgotten. Other demons say we are never summoned, but they maybe would not know if some few of our *Dīnen* disappeared long ago."

Only demon kings—the *Dīnen*—could be summoned to Earth, a fact which I suspected was unknown to most Demonica practitioners. I might be the only human on the planet who knew we were stealing demon leaders to enslave as fighting puppets.

I tucked my hair behind my ear. "Why have your stories been forgotten?"

"The old Vh'alyir demons are all gone. Dead." He gazed at the ceiling, his eyes seeing another world. "Our history died too. We are only what we are now."

"What are you now?"

He closed his eyes again. "I know no stories. My sire died too soon to teach me."

A memory pricked my subconscious, something else he'd told me, but before I could chase the feeling, he added brusquely, "All demons of my House are young and *zh'últis*. They do not know stories either."

If the Vh'alyir House didn't know their own history, maybe a *Dīnen had* been summoned and the current generation had forgotten about it. Myrrine had lived a very long time ago, even by demon standards—whatever those were.

I shuffled through my mother's notes to another page that referenced Myrrine Athanas. Returning to the grimoire, I searched for any mention of the ancient sorceress. Probably futile, considering the length of the grimoire and the illegibility of some pages, but …

In the back half of the book, I turned past an endless section of complicated arcane arrays and their accompanying instructions, full of crossed-out sections and notations—*that* would be fun to translate—and found a long list of incantations.

Was it just me, or did this page feel different?

I peered at the edge. Were two pages stuck together? I rubbed the corner between my finger and thumb, and the edges parted. With painstaking care, I peeled the pages apart and laid them flat. On one side was the completed array that went with the marked-up instructions, and on the facing page was an illustration of a medallion.

It vaguely resembled an infernus. The artist had drawn both sides, with a tiny but complex array filling one face. The medallion's other face displayed spiky markings in an outer ring around eleven sigils.

In the center was a twelfth sigil—Zylas's House emblem.

My heart beat faster as I leaned over the page. A line of text, four words long, titled the illustration, but I couldn't read it. It wasn't Ancient Greek, Latin, or any language I recognized. What did it say?

"*Imailatē Vīsh et Vh'alyir.*"

I jumped. I hadn't heard him move, but Zylas was sitting up. He reached past me, his arm brushing my shoulder, and touched the line of illegible text.

"*Imailatē Vīsh et Vh'alyir*," he repeated. "Magic Amulet of Vh'alyir."

It was written in demonic?

"A magical item of *Vh'alyir*?" I twisted to look at him. "What is it?"

"I do not know."

"But it's named after your House." The only other text on the page was a short line scrawled under the drawing—this one in Ancient Greek. Excitement fizzed along my nerves as I flipped to a blank page in my notebook and picked up my pencil. It didn't take me long to translate the line.

ὁ ὅρμος ὁ ἀπολωλώς ἀπάντων ἐστιν ἡ κλείς
Μυρρίνη Ἀθάνας

The lost amulet is the key to everything.
 — Myrrine Athanas

"The lost amulet," I whispered, "is the key … to everything? What does she mean, *everything*?"

Zylas frowned at the page. "How is it lost?"

"If Myrrine wrote this note, I guess the amulet went missing during or before her time." I slumped back against the sofa. "Key to everything or not, it's no use if it's been lost for millennia."

"But it is not lost." He pointed at the array-marked side of the illustration. "This *imailatē* was around Tahēsh's neck before I killed him."

2

"ALL RIGHT." Amalia paced the length of the living room, her hands clasped behind her back. "You're saying this ancient amulet, which was lost thousands of years ago, is the 'key to everything,' according to a medieval sorceress who may have summoned a Twelfth House demon despite it being forbidden."

"Not medieval," I corrected. "She lived during the archaic period, same as Homer. The earliest Greek poet," I added at her blank look.

"Sure, right." Amalia strode the other way across the room. "So this amulet, which for some reason has *his*"—she nodded at Zylas, who was sitting on the breakfast bar—"House sigil smack dab in the middle of it, was lost back in the archaic period, but *he*"—another nod at Zylas—"saw it a few months ago around the neck of a First House demon."

"Yes."

She raked her hands through her long blond hair. "And Zylas has no idea what the amulet is?"

"Not in the slightest," I told her.

Her face scrunched with bewilderment. "I don't get it."

"Neither do we." I swept over to the grimoire, which waited beside Zylas on the counter, open to the amulet page. "I translated the pages before and after this, but they don't explain what the amulet is."

"Why would it be in the grimoire without an explanation?"

"Myrrine knew something about it. My mom's notes suggest Myrrine added extra entries in the grimoire. Maybe she explains what the amulet is."

Amalia followed me to the counter. "I'm dying to know why it's *Vh'alyir's* Amulet. Why would something from the Twelfth House be so important?"

"And why did *Tahēsh* have it?" I looked up at Zylas. "Any ideas?"

He braced his elbows on his knees, his dark brows pinched above his red eyes. "He wore it when I saw him in the *kaīrtis*— in the circle. He brought it with him."

"He was *summoned* with it? But ... but if it's documented in the grimoire, it was here first. How did it get from my world to your world?"

Amalia squinted at Zylas. "Did it not pique your curiosity when you saw him wearing an amulet with *your* House emblem on it?"

Scowling, he jabbed a claw into the illustration. "I only saw *this* side. I did not see my House."

"Careful," I warned, sliding the grimoire away from him.

"Are you absolutely sure it's the same amulet?" she asked. "That's a complicated array. Maybe Tahēsh was carrying something similar."

"I did not see the other side. Maybe it is a different *imailatē*, but what I saw was this." He poked at the drawing again, more gently this time.

"Assuming Tahēsh had this amulet," I said, "how'd he get it?"

"He was *Dīnen* of the First House." Zylas brooded silently. "He was oldest of all male demons except *Ivaknen*. He knew much secret knowledge."

Tahēsh's superior knowledge was the reason Zylas had freed the powerful demon from his inescapable summoning circle. Zylas had hoped Tahēsh would know a way to get home without a soul.

"The First House is strongest," Zylas continued. "They have many treasures. They take things of power from other Houses."

"Do you think the First House stole the amulet from the Twelfth House?"

"*Var.* We are too weak to protect anything."

"You're not weak," I told him firmly. "You made them fear your House, remember?"

He flexed his fingers, unsheathing his claws. "I did this, yes, but it is too late."

"Too late?"

"I am oldest of my House. All others are younger and *nailēris*. I cannot help my House be stronger anymore."

Amalia looked at the demon with surprise. She'd never seen Zylas's regal side before.

"You can help them again," I reassured him. "We'll find a way to send you home. I promised, remember?"

"But I will not return as *Dīnen*." He straightened out of his slouch. "The *imailatē* is important, *na*? Should we find it?"

"Sure," Amalia said dryly. "That won't be difficult."

"It's less impossible now than if it'd been lost for millennia," I pointed out. "But is it worth the effort to find?"

"The 'key to everything' is pretty vague." Amalia drew the grimoire closer. "This array has elements of summoning Arcana in it. Maybe it's the very first infernus—the one Anthea created for the first demon ever summoned. That would make it ... well, not a *key*, but the infernus that started it all."

"But what about this other stuff?" I gestured to several tangles of lines and runes. "I've never seen Arcana like that before."

"Me neither. And this bit here doesn't even resemble Arcana."

"It is demon *imailatē*." Zylas leaned over the book too, our heads almost touching. "I do not know its purpose, but it is the *vīsh* of my kind."

"There are a few demonic runes used in summoning," Amalia said, "but nothing like that. Is it even possible to blend Arcana and demonic magic like that?"

Yes, it definitely was, but I hadn't told Amalia about my experiences combining magic with Zylas. It was just too weird.

"So, the array incorporates summoning Arcana, demon magic, and something else." I puffed out a breath. "In other words, we have no idea what the amulet is, what it can do, where it came from, or where it is."

"But we know Tahēsh had it last," Amalia mused. "The MPD took the demon's body, right?"

I nodded glumly. "If MagiPol has the amulet ..."

"I tore off his head."

I cringed at the memory before realizing what Zylas was getting at. "You think the amulet might've fallen off? It could still be in the park where he died, then."

"Unless some random person found it and carried it off," Amalia countered. "But chances are an object like that would end up back in mythic hands pretty fast. Maybe someone has been asking around about a weird infernus-type thing."

Perching on a stool, I pushed my glasses up my nose. "Our priority is the grimoire—translating it to see if there's a way to get Zylas home. Plus, Claude stole pages we need to get back. That said, I don't think we should ignore this amulet either. If it really is the 'key to everything' …"

I looked from Amalia's sharp gray eyes to Zylas's crimson stare. "If it's important, we need to find the amulet before it's lost for good."

I TUGGED MY JACKET tighter against the icy breeze. Mid-January was never a pleasant time of year, and not the season to be standing in an open field in the dark.

Zylas rose out of a crouch, his silhouette bulkier than usual. A baggy black sweater hung off him, the hood hiding his horns and the hem falling low enough to conceal his tail if he looped it around his waist. With the simple disguise, we'd only had to wait for darkness to search the park and not the dead of night when no one would be around.

Still, I fidgeted nervously as he cast back and forth across the winter grass, searching for a sign of the amulet. Our last visit to this park felt like a bizarre dream—Zylas carrying me on his back as he'd raced down empty streets; Tahēsh in battle with a strange collection of people; the short but violent fight that had followed.

Strips of churned dirt and dead grass marked the spot where a black van had peeled out of the park. The vehicle had belonged to two demon contractors and their champion. At the time, I'd had no idea who they were, but I'd since learned they were demon hunters who'd joined the hunt for Tahēsh.

"Nothing." Zylas glided across the grass toward me, his eyes glowing from beneath his hood. "It is not here."

"Are you sure?"

"*Var*. Not here."

I sighed, unsurprised. It'd been a long shot. "We—"

My cell buzzed with an incoming call. I pulled it out and lifted it to my ear. "Hello?"

"Did you find it?" Amalia asked without preamble.

"No."

"Damn. I haven't learned anything either. No one is trying to sell it that I can tell. But I remembered something."

"What?"

"There's this guy my dad worked with—a summoner. Dad always described him as 'cutting edge,' but I think that really meant this dude liked to experiment. MagiPol was breathing down his neck, so he retired to get them off his back. Dad always used the guy as an example of how MPD attention could ruin a summoner's career."

"Okay," I said slowly.

"But this guy, he also makes infernus artifacts. He's sort of an infernus expert, I think? If someone found an ancient infernus, they'd probably ask this guy for information."

Hope sparked. "Where is he now?"

"In Vancouver somewhere. I'll call Dad and find out."

"Good idea."

"Finding the amulet is only half the problem, though." She lowered her voice. "I don't think you should just hand over the 'key to everything' to a demon until we know what it does."

I glanced at Zylas. "He can hear you."

She muttered a curse. "You should come home and start translating. The grimoire is our best source of information."

"I'll be home soon. We're making one stop first."

"Suit yourself. Hey, bring me some Thai, would you?"

"Sure."

As I slid my phone back into my pocket, Zylas drifted closer. "The *imailatē* belongs to my House."

"I know. If we find it, it's yours." I rubbed my chilled hands together. "I don't want to get distracted from returning you to your world, but I have a feeling this amulet will be part of that. What if Myrrine meant it's the key to Demonica?"

Zylas's hands caught mine, enclosing my icy fingers in warmth. "You are too cold, *drādah.*"

"I'm fine," I squeaked, yanking on my hands. "I'm not hypothermic this time."

He pressed my fingers between his palms. "You will give the *imailatē* to me?"

Distracted, I frowned at him. "I don't need to give it to you. It belongs to you."

"Maybe it is powerful."

"It's still yours. I wouldn't keep it from you."

"Amalia would."

My frown deepened. Why did he use Amalia's name, but never mine? All I got were insulting nicknames. "Amalia doesn't trust you, but that's your own fault."

"*Na*, my fault?"

"If you were even a little bit nice to her, she would think better of you."

"Nice?" he scoffed. "*Nice* does not make trust."

I tugged on my hands again as I muttered, "It wouldn't hurt."

"Do you trust me, *drādah?*"

My gaze shot up to his. I opened my mouth but no words made it past my tight throat. Did I trust him? Of course I did, except …

I cleared my throat. "Do you trust *me?*"

He watched me silently—then suddenly pulled me closer. His hand cupped the back of my head, and he pushed his warm face into the side of my neck. His breath slid under my jacket collar, tickling my shoulder.

"Your heart is fast." He lifted his face. "You are not too cold."

I gaped as my very non-hypothermic heart galloped across my ribs. "I know. I told you that."

"You should go to a warm place."

"It's not that cold, Zylas, and I'm not soaking wet."

"Go to a warm place, *drādah.*"

I rolled my eyes. "Fine, I'm going."

A wolfish grin flashed across his lips, then his body turned to red light. His demonic spirit streaked toward my chest, and the infernus hidden under my jacket vibrated. His abandoned black sweater dropped to the ground.

Bundling the sweater under my arm, I stuffed my hands in my pocket and hurried out of the park. An irregular stream of cars zipped past as I headed west on Powell Street. After a few blocks, I turned. Waiting on the next corner, its windows glowing, was my guild.

Muffled noise leaked out of the building—sounded like it was busy—and I reached for the wooden door.

It flew open before I could touch it. A huge man burst out, almost bowling me over as I backpedaled.

"Oh, sorry," he said on his way by. Three more men and two women followed him, and all six looked ready to step into an MMA ring and kick ass. Definitely combat mythics.

A final woman walked out, long black hair fluttering behind her. She flashed me a smile before joining the others, who were climbing into a pair of vehicles parked at the curb. I blinked at the group. Was I supposed to know them? They didn't seem familiar.

With a mental shrug, I slipped through the door before it closed. The pub was crowded for a Wednesday night, and I slunk into the nearest corner and set Zylas's sweater on a table. After a moment, I unzipped my jacket and added it on top. Chatter filled the space, and I scanned the gathered mythics. Some familiar faces, some strangers, and—

My gaze reached the bar and stuttered.

Tori, the redheaded bartender, stood behind the bar, speaking to a pair of men across from her: blue-eyed, copper-haired pyromage Aaron and dark-haired, handsome electramage Kai.

The last time I'd seen those two had been in the Arcana Atrium. They'd stood on either side of Zora as she'd informed me that, from now on, she would be monitoring my every move to ensure I didn't break any MPD laws beyond my illegal contract. Aaron and Kai didn't know I was a rogue contractor, but they knew Zora was watching me.

My hand flew to my phone, nestled in my pocket, and I fought back a wave of panic. In the two and a half weeks since that encounter, I'd been holed up at home translating the grimoire, so I hadn't done anything that I'd need to inform Zora about. Should I have told her what I was doing tonight?

As all of that rushed through my head, I remembered something else: Tahēsh's body falling to the earth after Zylas had beheaded him, the demonic corpse landing at a woman's feet.

Tori's feet.

She'd been there. Her and Aaron and Kai and Ezra. They'd fled the scene right after, but Tahēsh had landed almost on top of Tori. Had she seen the amulet? Did she know what had happened to it?

I was moving before I could stop to think. Tori turned as I approached, and her jaw dropped as though the sight of me had blown her mind.

Maybe I should spend more time at the guild.

"Hi Tori," I began hesitantly. How was I supposed to broach the topic of that night in the park without raising her suspicions?

My skin prickled. My gaze darted sideways.

Kai and Aaron hadn't moved from their stools, but their expressions had drastically changed. Icy stares had replaced their good humor, and "back off" vibes radiated from them.

"How ..." I began haltingly, cringing away from the mages' hostility, "are ... you ... to ... night ..."

As Tori glanced at her friends, confusion crinkling her forehead, their glares intensified. They wanted me gone, and gone now.

"Good ... good to see ... you," I mumbled, stumbling backward. Forgetting about my jacket and Zylas's sweater, I rushed for the stairs and out of the mages' sights.

I didn't stop until I was pulling open the Arcana Atrium door on the third level. I flipped the "Arcana In Progress" sign over and hastily shut the door, my stomach heavy with a mix of fear and dismay—and a touch of humiliation.

Aaron and Kai had their reasons for mistrusting me, and I couldn't blame them for it, but they might as well have stamped "pariah" on my forehead. With two of the most powerful and popular mages in the guild openly rejecting me, the rest of the membership would never accept my presence. I'd be an outcast forever.

Nudging my glasses up to wipe my eyes, I dropped onto the bench and whispered, "Zylas."

Red bloomed from the infernus resting on my black knit sweater, and the demon materialized beside me.

"Did you pick up on all that?" I asked, pulling out my phone and opening the texting app.

"You think the female *hh'ainun* knows about the *imailatē*?"

"She might've seen whether it fell off Tahēsh, but I doubt she noticed it. I never did." I'd been too busy looking at Tahēsh's wings, tail, horns, terrifying muscles, and deadly magic to note his jewelry. "I can try to ask her when she's alone."

I paused halfway through typing a message to Zora explaining where I was. "Or maybe I shouldn't ask Tori anything? She and the mages ran away from the park after Tahēsh died. They didn't want MagiPol to know they were there."

"Because they smell like a demon."

"Maybe one has an illegal contract. Like Claude does." My thoughts turned to the third mage, who hadn't been at the bar with Tori. I hurriedly typed the rest of the message. "Claude had a printout on Ezra Rowe, but that could be a coincidence."

"If I get closer, I can smell which *hh'ainun* has the scent of *vīsh*."

"What, you want to sneak down there with all those people? That's not happening."

"Then you come," he suggested quietly. "I will pretend to be enslaved."

"Forget it. You can't act like you're contracted while *smelling* people. How would I explain why you're out of the infernus, even?" Shaking my head, I sent the text. "We'll have to wait for the right time. You'll get a chance to smell the mages eventually."

Zylas's head turned toward the atrium door. He snapped straight, arms at his sides, his face blanking.

The door flew open.

Adrenaline shot through me, and I whipped my phone, already in my hand, up to my ear as I whirled around on my stool.

Tori stood in the threshold, her face hard with suspicion.

3

I STARED AT THE BARTENDER in horror. She wasn't a sorcerer. She shouldn't have been able to open the atrium door—unless, while rushing and upset over Aaron and Kai's dismissal, I'd forgotten to lock it.

Crap. I *had* forgotten. How much had she overheard?

"T-Tori," I stammered. "Um. Just a moment, please?"

Her hazel eyes darted to the phone squeezed against my ear.

"I'm sorry," I said to a nonexistent caller, trying to sound natural while terrified she would see right through my lame farce. "Can I call you back? Thank you. Bye."

I dropped my phone into my lap, hiding the dark screen. Her attention drifted to Zylas, and I heaved a noiseless sigh. She wasn't laughing at my pathetic acting skills, so she must not have suspected anything.

"You startled me," I muttered, massaging my sternum.

"Sorry." She continued to stare at Zylas. "Who were you talking to?"

Another shot of adrenaline almost finished off my racing heart. "Amalia," I invented.

Barely paying me any attention, she stepped closer to Zylas. Instead of fear or scorn—the most common reactions to my demon—fascination lit her face as she examined him from head to feet. Zylas held perfectly still, maintaining his flawless impersonation of a demon slave. He was a much better actor than me.

"Do you dress him?" she asked unexpectedly. "Or did he come fully accessorized?"

I looked blankly between her and Zylas. Did she think he was a doll? "He—he came that way. Um. Can I help you with anything?"

"Yeah." She leaned sideways, her stare still fixed on my demon, and pursed her lips. "Damn, girl."

Bewildered by her marveling tone, I stammered, "P-pardon me?"

She pointed at Zylas's bare abdomen. "You can see this, right? I know he's a demon and all, but *those abs*."

I inhaled sharply and choked on saliva.

"They might be the most demony thing about him," she went on. "No man has abs that perfect."

Burning heat flooded my cheeks. Was she admiring Zylas's *physique*? Right here? Now? Or was she pranking me—trying to make me admit that I found my demon's body attractive? He was beautiful in his own way, and yes, his body was all but flawless, but he—he wasn't—and I wasn't—and why was she even bringing this up!

"I can't put clothing on him," I blurted shrilly. "Extra clothes can't go into the infernus with him. But—but it's fine. He's a d-demon, not a …"

Not a human. Not a male of my species. It shouldn't matter one iota that he was half clothed most of the time and barely clothed the rest of the time.

"… not a … *man*," I finished, almost choking on the word.

Tori arched an eyebrow, and I clamped my mouth shut, terrified I'd made things worse.

"Why've you got him out, anyway?" she asked, hands on her hips.

I gingerly prodded my cheek, suspecting my skin was redder than Zylas's. "I … I've been looking into …" I racked my brain for a lie. Someone else's grimoire, forgotten in the atrium, sat open on the worktable. "The magical properties of … demon blood."

Great cover story. Would she think I was conducting unethical experiments? I fought back a cringe, remembering the disgusting grimoire I'd found in a box destined for the MPD's Illicit Magic Storage.

"Hmm." With another arch of her eyebrow, Tori shifted to my other side and perched on the table. "So … I want to ask you something."

"Something *else*," I muttered irritably.

"Yep."

I flinched. I hadn't meant for her to hear that.

"Do you know anything about demonic artifacts?"

Surprised, I straightened. "You mean objects used for summoning and contracting, like the infernus?"

"I mean an artifact made *with* demon magic. Made *by* demons. Is that a thing?"

Tori was a witch, meaning she had no reason to ask those questions … except she was also best friends with three mages who smelled like a demon, had been in that park with Tahēsh and a team of demon hunters, and had fled the scene before MagiPol arrived.

"Why do you ask?" I inquired cautiously.

"Just some research I'm doing for a job."

"Oh."

I almost glanced at Zylas, certain he would confirm my suspicions: she was lying.

Demonic artifacts. I knew they existed only because Zylas had revealed that information to me. What would make Tori ask about it? She wasn't a Demonica mythic, as far as I knew—unless *she* was the source of the demon scent?

Swiveling toward Zylas, I tapped my knuckles against his chest plate. "This is a demonic artifact. It has magical properties, but I don't know more than that. Summoned demons might carry artifacts, but once contracted, they can't use them or create new ones."

I scrutinized her as she absorbed my words, but her bland expression gave nothing away.

"Any idea who might know something about these sorts of artifacts?" she asked.

"Short of discussing it with a demon"—like I had—"I don't know how anyone could learn much."

"Do people do that? Have conversations with a demon?"

"Well, summoners talk to demons before making a contract with them, but …" Trailing off, I organized my thoughts. "Even if someone has studied it, finding Demonica experts is difficult. Summoners aren't common, and experienced, knowledgeable ones are even more scarce."

Finally, Tori's expression changed. Frustration tightened her features, her freckled nose scrunching and lips pressing thin. I held my breath, arrested by the flash in her eyes—hopeless despair, quickly hidden.

Her questions weren't inane curiosity. She *needed* answers—though why, I couldn't imagine.

I straightened my glasses. "I'm also researching more obscure facets of Demonica. Not about that, specifically, but ..."

Doubts flitted through me. Was I being pathetically naïve? Was helping her dangerous?

"There's a mythic," I plowed on. "A retired summoner. He's an infernus maker now. I heard he's a collector of esoteric Demonica knowledge. I was planning to go speak with him but I ... didn't want to ... go by myself."

I finished in a mumble, all confidence lost. This was a dumb idea. I should've just kept my mouth shut.

"Can I come along?" Tori asked eagerly, her whole demeanor changing. "We can both see if he knows anything about our ... research topics."

Seeing her almost painful hope, my doubts faded. Whatever her motivations were, this was important to her. *Really* important. Was there any harm in helping her out? It would give me a chance to get to the bottom of her questions and learn what she might've noticed about Tahēsh's "accessories."

"That sounds good," I said. "You work most evenings, don't you? When's your next day off?"

"Saturday."

I nodded. "Okay. Let's meet here at seven."

"Seven it is." She gave me a swift, assessing look—then sighed. "Robin? Can I offer some advice?"

Nervousness flitted through my gut. "Yes?"

"When someone butts in on you and starts asking questions you'd rather not answer, 'get the hell out, you nosy asshat' is a good response."

I stared at her.

"You should try it," she suggested.

"Oh."

"See you on Saturday." With that, she hopped off the table and breezed out the door, gone as unexpectedly as she'd appeared.

I continued to stare, then slowly stood up. I crossed to the door, closed it tightly, and snapped the lock into place. A faint shimmer passed across the wood as the Arcana seal engaged. Brow furrowed, I turned around.

Zylas leaned against the table, arms folded. "She is not the one who smells like *vīsh*. The scent is on her but it is weak."

"So it's one of the mages," I mused.

"She lied. '*Just some research I'm doing for a job.*'" His accent vanished as he mimicked Tori's voice. "Not true."

"I figured. Did you notice anything else?"

"She smelled of fear and pain."

I sank onto the stool again. Tori was desperate for answers, and a witch's interest in demon magic only made sense if it was related to her friends and their secret—the secret that had brought them to the park where Tahēsh had been and sent them running shortly after.

"We need to figure out which mage smells like a demon," I sighed. "And why."

Zylas twitched one shoulder in a shrug. "It is *imadnul*. Not important, *drādah*. The demon is powerful. Better to stay away."

"Weren't you just saying you wanted to go downstairs and smell the mages?"

"I could smell enough *vīsh* on her to be sure. I thought before maybe this demon is Third House, but he is Second House."

"Is the Second House worse than the Third?"

"First House and Second House are allies. Their *Dīnen* are old and strong and smart." His tail lashed sideways. "More than other Houses, they kill Vh'alyir demons."

A chill washed over me. "Why?"

"We are weak. They hate us. They call us *karkis*."

"What does that mean?"

"Your word ... one who betrays?" His face hardened. "They say we are the House that is not summoned, so it is our fault."

"It's *your* fault other demons are summoned? That's ridiculous!"

"They decided this long ago, and others listened. They kill us everywhere. We have less numbers than the Houses who are summoned by hundreds and hundreds."

The horror infusing my gut deepened. The other demons were wiping out his House as punishment for what humans were doing? Demon society was blaming the weakest group for their suffering?

"My House is very few now. There are no old demons left to teach the young ones. They will never learn how to be strong."

"Is that why you need to go home?" I whispered. "So you can teach them?"

"*Na*, me? They do not want me to teach them. They hate me too." He straightened, pushing away from the table with the air of someone planning to change the subject. "*Drādah*, I want to know."

"Yes?" I asked cautiously.

"What"—he canted his head—"is *abs*?"

A blush burned through my cheeks. I'd really, *really* hoped he'd forget about Tori's comments—except he never forgot anything. "Abs are abdominal muscles … the muscles in your stomach."

He peered at his taut midriff. "How are muscles *perfect*?"

"Just ignore what Tori said."

"But your face changed color when she said it."

I abandoned my stool—which was much too close to his questioning gaze and *perfect* abdominals—and hastened over to the bookshelf. "Just forget about it, Zylas."

Of course, he followed me. "What did she mean?"

"Nothing."

"Are my *abs* better than a *hh'ainun*?"

"I don't know."

"Do you want to put clothes on me?"

"No."

"Why is your face changing color again?"

I grabbed a book about Arcana array calculations off a shelf. "I need to concentrate."

A long pause. Tension kinked my spine as I waited.

Warm breath brushed over my ear as he leaned in. "Am I *perfect*, *drādah*?"

I choked. Ducking away from him, I rushed back to the worktable. Focusing with single-minded determination, I opened the book to its table of contents and tried desperately to remember what I was supposed to be researching.

Zylas's quiet, husky laugh rolled through the room. Face flaming and teeth gritted, I cursed Tori and her big mouth.

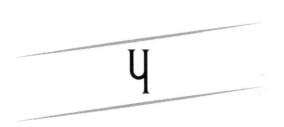

4

BRIGHT LIGHT STABBED through my eyelids, dragging me from sleep. I drowsily opened my eyes to find sunlight streaming through my drapes. For a moment, I was annoyed that Zylas hadn't closed them properly after returning from his nighttime wandering—then I realized. Sunlight. In *January*.

Flinging my blankets off, I scrambled out of bed. Cold air hit my bare arms and legs, my tank top and cotton shorts too thin for warmth, but I ignored the chill as I pulled the drapes away from the window. Blue sky dotted with fluffy clouds formed a cheerful backdrop behind the dreary buildings that surrounded my apartment.

Vancouver winters were mild, but in exchange for the lack of deep-freeze, its citizens had to endure a long season of perpetual overcast. Grinning, I hurried into the living room and threw open the heavy drapes that covered the balcony doors.

The morning sun hit me and I tilted my face into its golden light. Glorious. I couldn't wait for summer. Reading outside, listening to the breeze in the trees, enjoying the scents of sweet summer flowers and fresh-cut grass …

My happy smile still in place, I turned around. In my rush to the window, I hadn't noticed the room was already occupied.

Zylas was reclined across the sofa, head propped on a spare pillow. Our half-grown kitten, Socks, was lying on her back in the gap between his side and the sofa cushions, paws in the air and ears perked toward me.

The demon was watching me too, his limbs relaxed as if he were still napping, but there was no sign of drowsiness in his expression. His gaze moved across my face, intent, almost searching.

Searching for what?

My skin prickled, an odd nervous swoop in my gut. I hastily stepped away from the window—and my foot landed on something small and round.

The cat toy skidded across the carpet and took my foot with it. I hit the floor with a dull thud, my fall accompanied by the jingle of the plastic ball. Socks leaped off the sofa and streaked after the yellow toy, her black tail held high.

Stifling a groan, I sat up and rubbed my elbow.

Zylas folded his arms behind his head. "You were not even going backward this time, *vayanin*."

A new insult. Great. "You should clean up after your cat."

"*My* cat?"

I scowled at the kitten as she batted the toy into the kitchen. "She likes you the most."

"Does that make her mine?" His tail flicked. "How much do you like me, *vayanin*?"

"Ha. Nice try." I picked myself up off the floor. "What does *vayanin* mean?"

He smirked.

I crossed my arms. "You better not be calling me clumsy."

His smirk widened, and I bit the inside of my cheek against a furious growl. He was totally calling me clumsy—or a demonic equivalent. I hoped this new nickname wouldn't stick.

"How long have you been home?" I asked grumpily.

"Some hours. Before the sun came." He yawned, flashing his sharp teeth. "*Hh'ainun* sleep too much."

"Demons should sleep more." His leisurely naps didn't count—he always seemed aware of his surroundings. "Remember to close the drapes when you come in."

"*Hnn.*"

I stalked back to my room and dressed in fuzzy lounge pants and an oversized sweater. I wasn't going out today, so might as well be comfy. After a few minutes in the bathroom for my morning routine, I headed into the kitchen.

Socks had batted her toy into the gap between the fridge and cupboards, and she sat in the middle of the kitchen, staring at me accusingly.

"*I* didn't knock your toy in there," I told her as I fished it out. I tossed the ball over the breakfast bar and she tore out of the kitchen after it.

Sunlight filled the apartment, bright and warm. My good mood returning, I hummed as I poured a glass of strawberry-banana juice, then stacked yogurt, an apple, and a jar of peanut butter on the counter.

As I slid onto a stool at the breakfast bar and began slicing the apple into quarters, Zylas pushed off the sofa. He stretched his arms over his head, then kept arching backward in a feat of flexibility that even the fittest humans would have been hard-pressed to match.

When he straightened, I hastily returned my attention to my breakfast.

Amalia's door opened. Stumping out, with her hair tangled and a bathrobe hanging open over her t-shirt and leggings, she sagged onto the stool beside me.

"Why are you up so early?" she groaned. "Is that yours?"

Without waiting for an answer, she picked up my glass of juice and gulped half of it down.

"It's sunny today," I told her brightly. I circled the breakfast bar, and a moment later returned to my stool with a second glass of juice and another apple, which I set in front of her. I unscrewed the lid from the peanut butter. "Plus, I have lots of work to do. Better to start early."

"You mean translating the grimoire?" She moaned her way through a yawn. "That's not exactly a rush."

"No, but I want to find Myrrine's extra entries." I spooned peanut butter onto an apple slice. "I've been translating the grimoire for over two weeks now, and I haven't found a single thing related to summoning or demons. It's time to skip ahead. Searching for Myrrine's entries gives me a place to start."

She sipped her juice. "'Suppose."

As I bit into my peanut-butter apple slice, Zylas wandered over. He held Socks with one arm, her four paws dangling as she purred impossibly loud for such a small creature.

"Did you find out anything about the retired summoner?" I asked Amalia.

"Dad said his name is Naim Ashraf. He's a member of Odin's Eye now. Does consulting for them." She squinched one eye. "You sure you want to take Tori with you to meet him? You might need to get forceful with the guy."

I'd told her about my encounter with Tori last night. "You and I can always meet with him again later. I want to know what Tori is hiding—and why she's so desperate to learn about demonic artifacts."

Zylas watched me finish my apple slice. I picked up another one and loaded it with peanut butter.

"Maybe she saw the amulet on Tahēsh," Amalia suggested. "Or maybe she *has* the amulet. She was right there when he died. She could've—*ugh*. Do you have to do that?"

I held the slice out to Zylas. He lifted Socks onto his shoulder and took the slice, sniffing it curiously. The kitten head-butted his cheek and purred even louder.

"He doesn't need food," Amalia complained. "Why do you—"

"Tori seemed really upset," I interrupted. "I don't think she'd be that frantic over a random amulet she looted off a demon's body. Even if she has it, how would she know what it does or how important it is? *We* don't know and we have the grimoire."

"That's true," she muttered, observing with morbid fascination as Zylas swallowed half his apple slice whole. "It isn't even a demonic artifact, technically speaking. The array on the back is mostly Arcana."

I scooped a healthy dollop of peanut butter onto a third slice.

Amalia scowled. "That better not be for him."

Matching her scowl with one of my own, I stubbornly offered my demon the slice. "Why not? Does him enjoying something offend you?"

"That's not—it's just weird, okay?" She turned her glower on Zylas as he lifted the second slice to his mouth. "What about you? Don't you care that she keeps feeding you like a toddler?"

He bit his slice in half and swallowed. "I do not know that word."

"A child. She's feeding you like a child."

"I am not that young."

"Obviously, but she's treating you like you are."

His gaze flicked to me. "Giving food, this is a thing for *hh'ainun* young?"

"No." I glared at Amalia. "I'm giving you food because you enjoy it, not to be patronizing."

Socks jumped off his shoulder and onto the island. I shooed her away, angry with Amalia for casting such an unpleasant light on one of the few things I could do for Zylas to make his days in this unfamiliar world a little better.

"*Hnn.*" He considered his apple, then shoved the second half into his mouth. "I like it when you give me food."

"Good. That's—"

"It is not a thing young do in my world."

"What do you mean?"

A strange glint sharpened his eyes as they fixed on me. "In my world, males give food to females."

I blinked.

"They do this when they want to make young with the female."

My mouth fell open. Make … *young?*

He licked a smear of peanut butter off his thumb. "We do not need food if we have warm sun. Food is an extra thing to enjoy."

I couldn't react. My brain had frozen, gears locked.

"Males give a female rare or special food. If she eats it, she is thinking maybe he is a good sire." He paused thoughtfully. "Or she is luring him closer to kill him. But if she wants to make young too, she will—"

"Wait!" I gasped wildly. "No! No, no, *no*. That is *not* why I give you—I'm not—I wasn't—"

"I know." He wrinkled his nose in annoyance. "I am not *zh'ūltis*. I know *hh'ainun* do different things."

Faint relief cooled my embarrassment—until he leaned in, bringing his face close to mine, his hickory and leather scent tinged with the nutty tang of our breakfast.

"But it is fun, *na?*" His cocky grin flashed, revealing sharp incisors. "Keep giving me food, *vayanin*."

My jaw was still hanging open as he ambled away from the counter. I stared mutely as he disappeared into my bedroom, my eyes wide and glassy—and my face burning.

Again.

I FLIPPED SLOWLY through the grimoire, an unpleasant ache building in my forehead. With no idea what Myrrine's entries might look like, all I could do was skim the faded letters for her name.

Anthea had begun her career as a sorceress, though I had yet to figure out her specialty. I wasn't familiar with whichever branch of Arcana she'd focused on, and everything being in Ancient Greek only made it more difficult to pin down.

On top of that, Anthea had begun experimenting early on. A quarter of the way into the grimoire, she'd fixated on a particular type of spell, and by the halfway point, she'd been working on a single array—testing, revising, testing again. I wondered how long she'd worked on it—what timeframe the dozens and dozens of iterations represented. Had she spent months on it? Years? Decades?

She'd eventually begun a new array, the one that preceded the lost amulet's illustration. I turned past the drawing, chin propped on my hand and elbow braced on the breakfast bar. Another two dozen pages passed—more spell experimentation, the arrays marked with notes and corrections. Copying all this out would take me months.

As I turned over another fragile sheet of paper, the sketch of the First House demon appeared. Had Anthea begun summoning at this point? Were all those experimental spells her first attempts to summon a demon? I made a mental note to show them to Amalia when she returned this evening and see if they matched modern summoning arrays.

I flipped past the Twelfth House description, after which Anthea had begun inventing a new spell. I rubbed my aching temple as I skimmed a heavily annotated list of spell components. A short, dense set of paragraphs written in a cramped script filled the bottom quarter of the page, and I almost missed the two tiny words at the end.

Μυρρίνη Ἀθάνας

Myrrine Athanas.
Finally! I grabbed my notebook and woke up my laptop, the screen already open to an Ancient Greek dictionary. My pencil scratched across the page as I translated the paragraphs.

The minutes ticked past, my headache forgotten. Sitting back, I read over my completed translation.

Is it wrong of the scribe to add her thoughts to this book? I have dutifully copied every word as it lies upon the page, but I can no longer keep my pen from wandering.

I wonder: Why would Anthea forbid summoning of the Twelfth House? Why warn us of the retribution of their descendants, but fear not the vengeance of any other House? Why is the Twelfth House different?

And thus I wonder: Could it be a false warning with a deceitful purpose?

Perhaps I will discover the answers our brilliant and recondite foremother withheld when, tomorrow, I summon a son of the Twelfth House for myself. Should the warning be true, this will be my only addition to Anthea's legacy, and I pray you will forgive my foolish hope, sister.

— Myrrine Athanas

Breath held, I read over my translation again. Myrrine *had* tried to summon a Vh'alyir! She must've survived the attempt since my mom's notes said Myrrine had left at least five entries in the grimoire. Had she succeeded in her summoning?

I swiveled on my stool. "Zylas!"

Sitting cross-legged on the floor, he was pondering the five-thousand-piece puzzle I'd brought home for him yesterday. I'd hidden the box in my dresser, and without knowing what the finished puzzle was supposed to look like, it'd kept him occupied for the better part of the day—his slow progress helped by Socks, who was walking all over everything and batting the pieces around.

Uncoiling from the floor, he strode to me. I almost managed not to blush as he stopped beside my stool.

I pointed at my translation. "I found Myrrine's first entry, and she says she planned to summon a Vh'alyir demon."

"We are never summoned."

"It sounds like she tried, but maybe it didn't work." I studied my neat printing. "Myrrine wondered if the warning not to summon from the Twelfth House is deceitful. But in what way ... and why?"

His tail snapped against the floor. "Find her next entry so we will know."

I rolled my eyes and closed my notebook. "I can't right now. I need to be at the guild in a few hours to meet with Tori, and—"

His head turned sharply toward the apartment's door, then red light blazed over him. His power streaked into the infernus hanging from my neck.

A rap on the wood.

My stomach shriveled with anxiety. I minced to the door and put my eye to the peephole.

Waiting in the hall was a petite woman with short blond hair, a leather jacket, and a long, thin zippered bag hooked over her shoulder—which no doubt contained a very large sword.

I gulped. Unbolting the door, I swung it open. "Hi, Zora."

She slashed a mistrustful glare over me, then pushed into the apartment. My jaw tightened as I closed the door. Folding my arms, I watched her assess my home—my books spread on the breakfast bar and Zylas's half-completed puzzle. Socks cautiously stuck her nose out from under the coffee table.

Zora turned on me. "Why are you going to Odin's Eye with Tori?"

On Wednesday, when I'd messaged the sorceress that I was at the guild, she hadn't been pleased. For my planned outing with Tori this evening, I had let Zora know several hours ago—but it seemed that much warning wasn't good enough either.

"What reason do you have to go to that guild?" she demanded suspiciously. "How is Tori involved?"

I returned to my stool. "We're going to talk to an ex-summoner who's a member. Tori has a Demonica question, and I'm researching something from my family's grimoire."

Zora opened her mouth, then closed it. She strode to the counter and scrutinized the ancient grimoire. "This belongs to your family?"

"Yes. I'm working on translating it."

She glanced around. "Where's your demon?"

"In the infernus."

"And Amalia?"

"Shopping. Her favorite fabric store is having a flash sale on cotton blends."

"You haven't been out aside from visiting the guild on Wednesday, then? What were you doing there?"

"I was looking up some stuff from this grimoire in the Arcana Atrium books. That's when I ran into Tori and we made our plans for tonight."

The sorceress thought a moment, but couldn't come up with anything to complain about. "I want to know everything you do while you're with Tori tonight. I'll be checking with her too, so leave nothing out."

My gut tightened with anger and dismay, but I squashed it down. Getting angry wouldn't help me win her trust back.

"I have to go …" she muttered. "My team is waiting downstairs."

"Are you doing a job tonight?" I asked, thinking wistfully of my lone experience as a combat mythic on a job with her—not that I'd enjoyed it, but at least she'd liked me back then.

"We're helping with the SeaDevils investigation." At my blank look, she frowned. "You didn't hear?"

"Hear what?"

"About the guild attacks."

My eyes widened.

"I guess not," she said dryly. "Two nights ago, a group of rogues attacked the Pandora Knights. You've heard of them, right?"

"The mage guild?"

"That's the one." She tucked a short lock of hair behind her ear. "Rogues attacking a guild head-on is unexpected enough, but then last night, the same thing happened to the SeaDevils."

"The Pandora Knights are a bounty guild, aren't they?" I asked uncertainly. "But the SeaDevils …"

"Only do a bit of bounty work," she confirmed. "They weren't equipped for an attack. Their guild was leveled and two members died."

A small, sad sound escaped me.

Zora's face hardened with determination. "The other downtown guilds are teaming up to help with the investigation. We'll find the rogue group sooner or later, but until we do, be careful—especially at Odin's Eye."

I nodded earnestly.

She glanced over me. "By the way, are you going to your meeting like that?"

I looked down. My oversized sweater featured a cartoon Grumpy Cat dressed like St. Nick, with the text "*Feliz Navi-DON'T*" under it. It'd been Amalia's Christmas present to Zylas, but he wouldn't wear it.

"I was going to change."

"Good. No one at Odin's Eye will take you seriously in that. Wear your leather."

"My leather?" I shook my head. "I don't have any … leather."

"You *still* don't have combat gear?"

"I didn't know what to get," I mumbled.

"Get leather. Leather is better than just about anything." She headed for the door. "I need to go. Keep me posted on your evening."

"Okay. Good luck with your investigation."

"Thank—" She cut herself off, glancing back at me with a crinkle between her eyebrows, then swept out of my apartment. The door clacked behind her.

I looked down at my Grumpy Cat sweater again, then pulled out my phone to text Amalia. Guess I'd be joining her for a last-minute shopping trip before my meeting with Tori.

5

"SO …" TORI DRAWLED. "Tell me about this infernus maker."

I tried not to puff as we walked down Main Street, heading away from the guild. Tori was only a bit taller than average for a woman, but her stride far outstripped mine, and my thighs burned.

"I don't know much about him, to be honest." I tugged at the sleeve of my new jacket. *Leather.* Leather was not my thing. I hadn't liked any of the jackets from our impromptu shopping trip, so I'd let Amalia pick one for me.

That might've been a mistake. My new coat was tight, black, and didn't suit me in the slightest.

"He was an accomplished summoner until he retired fifteen years ago," I continued as we approached a crosswalk. "Now he makes infernus artifacts, but he's supposed to be well connected in the Demonica community. According to a rumor"—that rumor coming directly from Uncle Jack—"he was … cutting edge … when he was a summoner, and he's still very interested in new summoning practices and unusual Demonica knowledge."

The light changed and we crossed the street in front of a line of waiting cars, their headlights glaring.

"If this guy doesn't pan out," Tori said, "who else might have useful information?"

"Um, well, Demonica isn't a common class to begin with, and summoners are even rarer. It requires a lot of study, and summoning demons is quite tedious … and dangerous."

"Tedious *and* dangerous? Those two don't usually go together."

"It's dangerous when it goes wrong, and tedious when it goes right," I clarified with a shiver, remembering my first-hand experience with how badly summoning could go wrong. "Just setting up a summoning circle can take weeks, and you often have to wait weeks more for the demon to accept a contract."

Tori brushed red curls away from her face. "How did you become a contractor?"

Why hadn't I seen that question coming? I couldn't answer with either "completely by accident" or "sort of destiny"—even though both were true.

"I … fell into it, I guess," I said lamely. "Most of my family are Demonica mythics."

She absorbed that in silence, and my nerves prickled. Maybe this joint venture hadn't been a good idea, but we were already passing into Chinatown and it was way too late to back out.

"We're halfway back to my place," Tori remarked dryly. "I should've asked where we were headed before meeting at the guild."

"Oh," I cringed. "I'm sorry. I thought this would be easier."

Checking the street signs, I crossed to the opposite sidewalk and onto a main thoroughfare lined with commercial buildings. The raised SkyTrain tracks followed the center boulevard, and we weren't far from the spot where Zylas had leaped from a rooftop and onto a speeding train to escape Tahēsh.

"Um, so …" I peeked at the guild bartender. "How long have you been friends with Aaron and Kai and Ezra?"

"Since my first day at the guild, pretty much." A teasing smile quirked her lips. "Aaron is single."

I twitched. "What?"

"I know he's giving you the cold shoulder, but he's actually a really great guy."

She'd barely finished speaking when I snapped, "I'm not interested."

Her eyebrows rose.

"Why does everyone assume I want to date them?" I demanded. "Just because they're good looking? Ridiculous."

Ignoring her amusement at my outburst, I picked up the pace. How shallow she must have thought I was to suggest I date a guy who was actively shunning me? Tori didn't even know *why* he was being so cold to me—at least, I hoped she didn't.

After a few minutes of fuming, I remembered Aaron wasn't the mage I was interested in.

"I was wondering," I began, "about Ezra."

"What about him?"

How did one bring a polite conversation around to the topic of illegal secrets? "He seems nice."

Genius segue.

"He *is* nice," Tori replied shortly.

"He's an aeromage?" I prompted.

"Yeah."

"Is he strong?"

"Not as strong as Aaron and Kai, but pretty tough."

"Hmm." Was he weak enough to want to compensate with an illegal demon contract? I slid my phone from my pocket to check the directions, then led Tori off the main road and onto a narrow side street. "What happened to his eye?"

"Skiing accident. Ran into an unexpectedly aggressive pine tree."

Frowning, I glanced at her. Her response was flippant, but all friendliness had left her eyes.

We continued deeper into the commercial strip, the businesses and warehouses long closed for the day. Our conversation petered out, except for a brief exchange where she asked rather nervously if we were going the right way. I assured her we were, and that we could walk down all the dark, abandoned streets we wanted to. I was a contractor, after all; Zylas could handle any human threat.

Our destination was a small building—two stories, bright blue roof, and cheery lights shining from the windows—tucked beside a recycling depot and easy to miss. I checked my phone one more time to confirm, then veered toward the parking lot, Tori following me.

We passed several parked vehicles and approached the frosted glass door, marked with the Odin's Eye logo and "Private Security Services." A security firm was a much better cover for a guild than the Grand Grimoire's dusty games shop.

"Whoa, whoa, whoa." Tori gawked at the door like she'd never seen one before. "Is this *Odin's Eye?* As in *the guild?*"

I paused with my hand on the door. "Didn't I say that?"

"No."

"I thought I told you that the infernus maker is an Odin's Eye member? And his main role is Demonica consultation?"

"You did not mention that. At all."

Because I'd learned those details after inviting her along with me. Oops. "Oh. I … um … sorry."

She huffed. "Well, we're here now. Let's do this."

The brightly lit lobby featured four plush leather chairs and a glossy reception desk. No one sat behind the computer monitors, so I hesitantly tapped the button as instructed by a small sign. A buzzer went off, muffled by the walls.

Ten seconds passed. Twenty. Thirty.

"Is anyone coming?" I mumbled.

Tori cocked a hip, unbothered by the lack of a warm welcome. "Are they expecting us?"

"Well … no. I was worried that any advance warning would make it easier for him to avoid us."

"Fair point." Stepping up beside me, she smirked. "Let's find out who's home, shall we?"

She attacked the buzzer with reckless abandon. It blared over and over from deeper in the building, and I grabbed for her hand to stop her.

A door banged open with aggressive force, and a thickly muscled man with a dusky complexion and short black hair burst in, his heavy brows drawn over angry eyes.

It was the Grand Grimoire all over again. I should've sent Amalia with Tori. They were a matched pair.

"Who the hell—" The man's furious outburst cut off. "Tori?"

"Hey Mario. What's up?"

The Odin's Eye mythic grinned broadly. "What brings you out here? I can't remember the last time a Hammer came 'round to our guild."

"Because my guild has a charming pub and the world's best bartender," Tori joked easily. "What've you got?"

"Hey, we've got our own perks."

I looked between them, gawking in disbelief. Okay ... not a repeat of my first Grand Grimoire visit, but how did she know this guy? And how could she be so relaxed and casual and charismatic?

I told myself I wasn't jealous.

"You here to see Izzah?" Mario asked Tori. "Their meeting already started, but I can take you back there."

"Uh, no, I'm actually here to see ..." Trailing off, she shot me a pointed look.

I straightened, pulling myself together. "Is Naim Ashraf in?"

"Naim? Yeah, he's here." As simple as that, Mario gestured at us to join him. "Come on."

"You know people here?" I whispered to Tori as she followed Mario through the door and into a hallway.

"Yeah, they've been at the guild half a dozen times in the last few weeks."

I remembered the big, scary group that'd been leaving as I'd arrived the other night. Had they been Odin's Eye mythics?

Tori prodded me with her elbow. "Hang out with us more and you'll get to meet people too."

Yeah, like that would happen. No one would want to be my friend while their popularity ringleaders were ostracizing me.

Mario took us to the second level, which was similar to the Grand Grimoire's but ten times nicer, with clusters of furniture, work areas, a fireplace at one end, and a bar and mini kitchen at the other. I resisted the lure of their floor-to-ceiling bookshelves.

"Oooh, nice," Tori complimented Mario.

Grinning, he passed five guild members and headed toward an old man in a recliner. Deeply engrossed in a thick leather-bound tome, he scarcely looked up as Mario introduced us as "visitors" before heading off to join his comrades at a worktable.

Naim scrutinized us with dark eyes beneath snowy white eyebrows, stark against his chestnut skin. "Who're you two?"

I gulped at the sharp demand in his unpleasant voice.

"Can we ask you a few Demonica questions?" Tori inquired, her tone as formal as I'd ever heard it. "We'll keep it quick."

"Dunno what Mario told you, but I don't consult outside my guild."

"It won't take long."

"Doesn't matter." He took a sip of his drink, then returned it to the table beside him. "Go ask the Grand Grimoire if you need help."

Amalia had guessed correctly that Naim wouldn't be cooperative. Maybe he just needed persuading?

"The Grand Grimoire has contractors," I told him. "But MagiPol arrested their guild master and they don't have any other summoners—especially not ones with your experience and reputation for rare knowledge."

"I'm not wasting my time explaining the basics of Demonica to little girls. My scotch is older than you two, now leave me to drink it in peace."

Well, so much for the polite approach. Slipping past Tori, I unzipped my jacket halfway.

"I don't need help with the basics." I pulled out my infernus and held it up. "And if you're half the summoner I think you are, I shouldn't need to explain more than this."

Naim practically threw his book onto the side table to free his hands, his disbelieving stare locked on the pendant. His greedy fingers reached for it, and I quickly stepped back.

His mouth twitched behind his thick, frizzy white beard. "It's a fake. No way a girl like you—"

I tapped one fingertip against the center rune, silently asking Zylas for a light show. A swirl of his power roiled across the silver disc, the cool magic teasing my fingers.

"Real?" he gasped. "Then you must be Robin Page!"

I concealed a flinch. Had my reputation spread this far already? Why couldn't everyone just forget I existed?

"I heard rumors that a new House had finally appeared after all these years," he went on, "but I couldn't believe it. Your demon can only be the lost First House. Unless—unless it's the fabled Twelfth House?"

As the greed in his face deepened, I sank onto the coffee table in front of him. "We can discuss my demon after Tori and I ask a few questions, if that's okay."

"What would you like to know?" he offered eagerly.

I glanced at Tori as she sat beside me, and she nodded for me to go ahead.

"I'm researching an artifact," I began, wiggling a folded paper out of my pocket. "I believe it's an ancient infernus, and since you're an infernus maker …"

Hoping the slight tremble in my hands wasn't noticeable, I opened the paper to reveal my hand-drawn copy of the amulet illustration. Reproducing a page from the ancient grimoire had been risky enough. Showing it to someone, especially an untrustworthy ex-summoner, was nearly giving me a panic attack.

As Naim's gaze skidded across the sketch, I peeked to my right.

Tori was staring at the drawing. Her face had no expression, only a slight parting of her lips as though mildly surprised—but she was normally so expressive that her muted reaction was as good as a flashing sign. She'd seen the amulet before, I was sure of it.

"These sigils are House emblems," Naim observed, gesturing to the illustration of the amulet's front face. "I recognize most of them. Eleven sigils ... with a twelfth in the center. This represents *all twelve demon Houses.*"

He took a swipe for the paper and I snatched it away, my heart lurching. He couldn't summon a demon with only the House sigil, but I wasn't letting *anyone* touch this drawing.

"Have you ever seen or heard of an infernus like this?" I asked him.

"Is it an infernus? Where did you learn about this? Where did you get your demon? Your demon *must* be the First House." His attention swung between my infernus and the drawing. "The same sigil is in the center of the design."

I didn't like the heightening greed in his dark eyes. "You haven't answered my question."

"I've never seen an artifact like that before. But if you give me the drawing, I can certainly look into—"

I folded the paper with snappy motions. If he'd never seen it before—or wanted to pretend he hadn't—I wasn't giving him the chance to memorize any more of the drawing.

"Tori?" I prompted. "You had questions?"

"Uh." She squinted as though waking from a daydream. "Questions. Right. I'm investigating a series of unsolved bounties on demon mages."

As she flipped open her folder, I hid my chagrin. This time, Zylas wasn't out of the infernus and listening in. He'd warned me that he couldn't "hear" lies through my inner relay of the conversation.

"Certain sources and witnesses," Tori told an unenthusiastic Naim, "have suggested a summoner is creating demon mages using an artifact imbued with demon magic."

Wait ... did she say *demon mages*?

"What do you know about demonic artifacts?" she asked the ex-summoner, oblivious to my arrested stare.

"I've never created a demon mage. I don't know how it's done, or if it requires artifacts."

"Yes, of course. I'm just looking for information."

She flipped through a few papers in her folder. Black-and-white documents flashed past until she paused on an old photo of two men, one facing the camera and one in profile.

I gasped.

Tori glanced at me. I tore my attention off the photo.

"S-sorry," I mumbled. "Go on."

I scarcely heard her as she prodded Naim for more information about demon mages. My gaze dropped to the photo again, on display in her open folder.

The young man, maybe twenty-five, who faced the camera was a stranger. His skin and hair were equally pale, giving him a washed-out, almost phantomlike look. Speaking to him was another young man, and with his face in profile, his only defining characteristic was his dark hair.

I wouldn't have recognized him if not for the scar distorting his lower lip, the deep indent permanently twisting his mouth.

Claude.

It had to be him, twenty years younger. How likely was it that more than one person had a scar like that—or more than one person involved in Demonica?

With effort, I refocused on the conversation. Tori had just asked a question—which I'd completely missed—and Naim was considering her as though unsure whether he cared to answer.

"In regular summoning," he began, measuring each word, "the demon is summoned into a circle, the boundary of which is impenetrable to the demon. In demon-mage creation, the demon is summoned into a human body."

Thoughts of Claude evaporated from my head, replaced by disbelieving revulsion.

"The human body—or, some say, their soul—is the cage that traps the demon. It will either assimilate into its host or keep fighting to escape until it kills the fool that offered himself up for the ritual. When the human dies, so does the demon."

"That's horrible." As the words slipped out, I realized I had my hand pressed to my mouth.

"Wait." Tori leaned forward. "If the demon is summoned right into the human, is there even a contract? Or is the demon simply trapped and it just ... goes along with everything so it doesn't die?"

"I assume there's a contract, or at least binding magic involved." Naim shrugged dismissively. "As I said, if you want specifics, you need the summoner. No two demon mages are exactly the same—though they all meet the same end."

I swallowed my stomach down. Demon mages. I'd heard of them, of course, but they were a myth—the kind that spawned nightmares. They were the most illegal magic of all, according to the MPD, and unlike many other magical bans, I'd never seen a single complaint or argument against MagiPol's harsh treatment of demon mages and those who created them.

The snap of Tori's folder closing startled me out of my contemplation.

"'Kay, well," she told Naim, "thanks for nothing."

Sneering, he turned to me. "Now, girl, where did you get your demon?"

I shoved to my feet, my head spinning, stomach twisting, and patience gone. "If you learn anything about the artifact I'm interested in, or the demonic artifacts Tori asked about, let us know. You can reach us through the Crow and Hammer."

"Wait!" He scooted forward on his chair. "You agreed to tell me if I answered your questions!"

"You didn't have any answers, did you?" I gave him the same cutting stare Zylas gave me whenever I did something particularly *zh'ūltis*. "I expected more from a so-called expert."

Stepping past Tori's knees, I speed-walked across the room. As I pushed open the stairwell door, I replayed that last exchange in my head. Slow heat built in my cheeks.

Tori stepped through the door, letting it swing shut behind her.

"Was I too rude?" I blurted anxiously. "I should've been nicer. He was sort of helpful. I shouldn't have—"

She grinned. "That was perfect. He was a dick. You're one tough cookie, Robin."

"Me?" No way she was talking about me. I was the opposite of tough.

"You didn't let him intimidate you for a second."

"Was he intimidating?"

"Kind of, yeah. But still."

My brow wrinkled. Compared to Zylas in a temper, Naim was as intimidating as a toothless dog.

Tori started down the stairs. "So, what's that ancient infernus thing you're researching? It looked interesting."

"I ran across it in an old grimoire," I revealed, going with a version of the truth. "What about your demon-mage case? What got you started on an investigation?"

"I'm just doing some legwork for Aaron and Kai. It's their job."

Except it wasn't for a job; Zylas had already exposed that lie.

"Oh, I see," I murmured as we reached the bottom of the stairs.

She hesitated, glancing at me, and I returned the look, wishing I knew what she was thinking. She'd seen the amulet, probably on Tahēsh. Maybe she knew what had happened to it. On top of that, she was seeking rare Demonica knowledge likely connected to her mage friends' secret.

Giving nothing away, Tori shrugged and stepped into the hall.

"Oh!" she exclaimed. "Hi, Izzah."

As I squeezed into the hall with her, I spotted the group of people she'd almost collided with, headed by a vaguely familiar woman—the dark-haired one I'd seen leaving the Crow and Hammer on Wednesday evening.

"Tori?" The woman frowned. "*Wei*, what are you doing here?"

I leaned around Tori, curious about the woman's unusual accent, but the redhead was giving the whole group a jaunty salute.

"Nice to see ya. We're just heading out."

"What were you here for? Tori—"

Tori walked away while the woman was still talking, and I rushed after her with an awkward peek at the bewildered group we were leaving behind.

I caught up to Tori as we entered the lobby. "Is something wrong?"

"Nope. It's just that guy—the short, bald one at the back—is a famous bounty hunter and he was a dick to me at the pub the other day."

I hadn't noticed a short, bald man. "A famous bounty hunter? What's his name?"

"Shane Davila." She reached for the frosted glass door. "Have you heard of—"

There was no warning. I didn't have the slightest inkling something might be off until an impact like a cannonball hit the building.

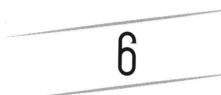

6

TORI FELL INTO ME. The floor quaked and I caught the back of her coat for balance as mythics elsewhere in the guild yelled out in shock. Tori faced the door, her complexion bleached of color.

Orange light exploded across the glass, and I recoiled. That couldn't be what it looked like. No way was there a literal *inferno* piling up on the—

The glass door shattered and fire blasted into the lobby.

Tori thrust her arm out. "*Ori repercutio!*"

The air shimmered and the raging fire bounced off nothing, splattering the walls instead of my and Tori's flammable bodies. In her hand was a tattered playing card—a sorcery artifact.

Seizing her arm, I gasped, "I thought you were a witch!"

"Yeah, well—"

Something metal clanked loudly. The sound came again, then again, almost like—like approaching footsteps. Smoke filled the lobby as flames climbed the walls, but even half-blinded, I couldn't miss the hulking shadow taking form in the open doorway.

With a clang, the steel beast stepped into the threshold. Four-legged, a metal mouth full of triangular teeth, its limbs connected with heavy gears. Glowing runes covered every inch of its body.

A golem? A golem *here?*

The metal beast charged us.

Tori hauled me sideways. The magically animated beast roared past us, its footfalls deafening, and she shoved me toward the door. "Out! Get outside!"

I wasn't quick enough getting my numb legs moving, and she beat me to the exit.

"What about the people inside?" I asked breathlessly, trying to think through my shock. Behind us, the golem was backing out of the desk it had demolished, and fire was spreading through the room. "They—"

"They're combat mythics!" Tori yelled as she jumped over the glass debris. "They can take care of themselves!"

She reached back and grabbed my arm again. Hauling me with her, she raced through the open doorway. As I stumbled onto the front stoop, she spun toward me—and flung us to the ground.

I struck the pavement, landing all wrong. Pain ricocheted through my hip and I felt a pop in my elbow. Blinding agony hit an instant later, the joint lighting on fire. Choking on a cry, I rolled onto my back—and saw why Tori had thrown us clear.

Hunks of debris tumbled down as a second golem pulled its massive fist from the guild's wall. It straightened to its twelve-foot height, humanoid in shape and glowing with runes.

Panic screeched through my head. The golem's huge fist, the size of a basketball and with a hundred pounds of crushing weight behind it, rose above its helmet-shaped head. Gears turned in its shoulder as it took aim—then that fist plunged toward me and Tori.

I screamed, and Zylas answered.

Crimson power streaked out of my infernus. The demon took form directly above me and Tori, one foot on either side of my waist and his arms raised as the golem's strike flashed down.

My scream rose in pitch, terror stopping my heart.

The golem's fist smashed into Zylas's waiting hands. He almost buckled, bracing hard, muscles taut and straining. The golem pressed into him, and he dropped to one knee, his greave slamming into the pavement inches from my thigh. He couldn't hold it.

My panic disappeared, and I shoved backward, sliding out from under him. "Tori, move!"

The redhead rolled sideways, getting clear.

Zylas, let it go!

He released the steel fist and it punched into the ground. As Tori and I bolted away from the golem, Zylas darted after us.

"A golem," I gasped, half incoherent. My left arm hung at my side, agony jarring through the limb with each step. "It's huge. How is it so huge?"

"Great question." Tori headed toward the parking lot, no doubt planning to get as far from that monster-sized golem as possible—a plan I wholeheartedly supported. "But let's worry about it later. We need to—"

She broke off, and a fresh wave of panic hit me.

The golems hadn't come alone. A group of men in mismatched combat gear stood in a line at the parking lot's edge, accompanied by three more four-legged golems.

One of the mythics pointed at me. "Take out the contractor first!"

Oh great.

The golems launched toward us, and a trio of mythics followed, preparing their attacks.

Tori reached for her belt, hidden under the hem of her leather jacket. Instead of another artifact, she pulled out a—a *gun?* The black pistol gleamed as she pulled the trigger with loud pops. Yellow splatters burst across two of the three attacking mythics, and they collapsed—but the third had blocked her shot with a water shield.

The hydromage conjured a liquid attack as the golems closed in.

Zylas! Take out the mage first!

He shot between me and Tori, sprinting at full, unbelievable demon speed. Springing over the golems, he leaped full tilt into the hydromage, smashing feet-first through his forming attack and driving the man into the ground—but the golems were still coming.

How was Zylas supposed to stop them without magic?

He sprang off the hydromage's chest and slammed his fist into a golem's side. I flinched at the loud bang of his knuckles impacting the unyielding surface. The beast's side dented inward, but it didn't even stumble. Whirling, it snapped its teeth at Zylas. He dodged away.

That won't work! I told him desperately. *They aren't alive. You can't hurt them!*

Silence answered me. I hadn't heard his telepathic voice since we'd defeated the darkfae Vasilii, and nothing I'd tried since had come close to reforging the mysterious connection between us.

The three golems turned on the demon, trying to surround him. They were too slow to pose much risk, but how was he supposed to—

"Knock it over!" Tori shouted. "Robin, use your demon to knock them on their sides! They have trouble getting up!"

What? She knew how to stop the golems?

Zylas didn't need me to relay the instruction. He vaulted toward the same golem and, with a neat twist, skidded under it—a breathtaking feat of timing and acrobatics that no one would believe I had orchestrated. He pistoned his powerful legs into the golem's underbelly. It lifted off its feet and crashed onto its side.

Beside me, Tori's mouth hung open. "Whoa. How'd you do th—shit!"

She seized my arm again—her fingers closing over my injured elbow. Blinding pain cleaved my limb and I almost crumpled. She dragged me away, and it was all I could do to stay upright, tears blurring my vision. She yelled something. Silver light flashed and a gust of wind blasted across us, whipping dust into the air.

Shouts. Pounding footsteps. Men and women streamed past us—the mythics from Odin's Eye. Armed and furious, they crashed into the other men. A dizzying racket of shouts, incantations, and clanging weapons erupted, but the loudest sound of all was a repeating bang.

The ground shook. The sound grew louder.

Pushing Tori's hand off my arm, I swiped the tears from my eyes—and gasped in terror.

The twelve-foot, two-legged golem was almost on top of us, its fist swinging.

An arm like a steel band hit me in the back. Zylas grabbed me and Tori around our waists and leaped into the air. The golem's fist flashed beneath us, and he landed lightly and sprang again, carrying us out of the golem's reach.

That one is too big to knock over, I told him woozily, sick with pain.

He skidded to a stop and released Tori. As she stumbled away, he gripped a fistful of my jacket, steadying me as I swayed. My glasses had somehow stayed on my face, and I almost knocked them off in a clumsy attempt to straighten them.

The massive golem turned, its helmet with its empty eye sockets pointed in our direction. It stomped toward us, ignoring the battling mythics nearby. Of course. Kill the contractor first. That was standard practice.

Why did I have to be the contractor?

Tori pushed the hem of her jacket up and unbuckled her belt—a heavy-duty combat belt loaded with pouches, a holster, and potion balls. "Robin, can your demon get me up onto the golem's head?"

Uh, what? Had I heard that right? "Its head? Why—"

"Can you?" she demanded, setting her belt on the ground. "Yes or no!"

I glanced at Zylas. "Yes, but—"

The golem's steel foot landed a yard away, vibrating the ground. As its arm drew back, I realized there was no time for "buts."

Zylas, let's do this!

I sprang in front of him and Tori, clutching the artifact hanging from my infernus chain, tucked behind the pendant. His warm hand snapped tight around mine, the slight shift of my elbow triggering more stabbing pain.

"*Ori eruptum impello!*" I cried.

As the golem's fist whipped toward us, pale light erupted from my artifact. It expanded in a silvery dome, blasting everything it touched away from me—except Zylas and Tori, who were connected to me through his grip on my hand, making them immune to the spell's effect.

The steel fist hit the expanding dome and stopped dead. Its limb creaked from the impact, but the force of its swing had been so great that the spell hadn't thrown its arm away from me.

With Tori held tight against his side, Zylas sprang onto the golem's stationary fist and ran up its arm like a ramp. The golem straightened, almost throwing them off, and reached up to grab the pests on its shoulder.

Releasing Tori, Zylas grabbed the incoming steel fingers with both hands, letting them push him down into a tight coil.

He launched off its shoulder, forcing the hand away from its body. The golem tottered, off-balance. He hit the ground and leaped again, catching me around the middle. Leaving Tori, he sprinted away from the golem and the battle.

I was only vaguely aware of him coming to a stop. I couldn't think through the agony radiating from my elbow. He lowered me to the ground, but my weak legs wouldn't take my weight. His hands bit into my waist, holding me up.

An eardrum-shattering crash split the night.

Gasping, I looked past him. The massive golem was lying face-down on the ground, and the glowing runes that had powered it were dark and magic-less. Tori stood on its back, holding a swath of amethyst fabric that rippled and danced, exuding magic in swirls of blue and violet light.

I was really starting to doubt that Tori was a mere bartender.

Zylas touched my sleeve over my elbow. I gasped again, tears flooding my eyes and blurring Tori and her unearthly artifact. The parking lot had quieted, the sounds of battle replaced by the scraping of the smaller golems' legs as they robotically attempted to stand. Calm voices called to each other; the Odin's Eye mythics must've defeated the attacking group.

"*Vayanin.*"

"I'm not klutzy," I whimpered pathetically. "I didn't fall. Tori knocked me down. Why are you so mean, Zylas?"

He chuffed. "You are injur—"

"Not now," I warned him, rubbing my good hand over my face and almost dislodging my glasses a second time. "People could be watching us. You have to act contracted."

His jaw flexed. He let his hands fall to his sides, his limbs unnaturally stiff. I wished we were alone so he could hold me up. I didn't want to pretend to be a strong, tough contractor with her mindless demon slave.

Sniffling, I reached for his wrist. His knuckles were split and thick blood dribbled down his fingers.

"I'm sorry," I whispered. "I should've warned you sooner that hitting the golems wouldn't work."

How could he have guessed? Human sorcery was an unknown to him. He might be the warrior, but I was his information source—his guide in any fight against mythics. I'd failed him.

Leaning over his hand, I carefully pressed down on each bone below his bleeding knuckles, testing for weakness.

"I don't think it's broken," I told him quietly. "The bones seem solid."

His fingers flexed slightly, a subtle warning. Tired, heavy footsteps came up from behind me.

"Can he feel pain?" Tori asked, stopping a step away. "Demons look so blank all the time, like puppets …"

Her solemn tone surprised me. Few people gave any thought to demons' suffering.

"Yes." I gently pressed on Zylas's thumb joint. "They all feel pain, contracted or not."

Tori stared at his injured hand, then gave herself a shake. "We need to go." She brushed at the layer of grit clinging to her pants. "We have to get back to the Crow and Hammer."

I reluctantly released Zylas's hand. "We do?"

"You should come with me. We might need you."

"Why?"

She glanced at the massive golem, lying on its face. "Because three combat guilds have been attacked in three days. That means the Crow and Hammer is probably next."

She started across the parking lot and I trailed after her, an inferno of agony building in my elbow. Zylas walked after me, keeping his steps wooden and his tail still. My gaze trailed across the destruction—the guild building, its front wall smashed in, smoke billowing from the holes and fire flickering from the interior; crushed pavement and crumpled cars in the parking lots; unconscious, injured, or possibly deceased men lying in heaps; the fallen two-legged golem; the four-legged ones on their sides, still glowing with magic; the Odin's Eye mythics, smudged with soot, their faces pale and furious.

Zora had described the previous two attacks, but I hadn't imagined anything like this—and now that I'd seen the violence for myself, I could all too easily imagine the same fate befalling the Crow and Hammer.

7

I SHUT THE DOOR to the Arcana Atrium with my good hand and turned the bolt. As a shimmer of magic ran across the door, the muffled voices from the pub below went silent; the sorcery that sealed the room was so strong it blocked out noise as well as magic.

Downstairs, guild members crowded the pub. They'd all heard about the attacks on the Pandora Knights, SeaDevils, and now Odin's Eye, and they'd gathered at their headquarters. I wasn't sure if they were here to protect the guild or merely for moral support.

I double-checked that the door was locked. *Okay, Zylas.*

With a flash of crimson light, he appeared beside me. I nodded toward the center of the room.

"You can heal your hand now," I told him. "No one will know you're using magic in here."

"*Vayanin—*"

"Don't call me that. I'm not clumsy. I only fall down when—"

His hand curled around the back of my neck, and he pulled my face into his shoulder.

I squawked in surprise, a leather strap from his armor pressing into my cheek. "Let me g—"

His other hand closed over my arm, just above my elbow, and agony speared the joint. A pathetic sound scraped my throat as a wash of cold magic shivered through my limb.

"Your arm is damaged. The bones are in the wrong spot and the other parts … I do not know your words … Other parts are being pulled wrong."

I turned my face sideways so I could breathe better, my glasses askew. "I'll be fine. You should heal your han—"

He pushed me back and before I knew what he was doing, the zipper on my jacket was undone. Holding my shoulder, he slid the jacket down my arm. The leather hit the floor and he kicked it aside.

"Don't do that," I protested, my voice trembling and tears streaking my face. He'd been careful, but getting the sleeve off had jostled my elbow. "That's brand new."

"Quiet, *vayanin*." He studied my fitted sweater. Wrapping one hand around my upper arm, he stretched the collar to his mouth and bit down. With the fabric between his teeth, he ripped the seam open with his other hand.

"Zylas!" I gasped. "Don't—"

Despite his efforts to stabilize my arm, the motion was too much. The room spun and my face smacked into his chest, my vision blurring. My glasses clattered to the floor.

He peeled my sweater off, leaving me in a tank top. I glanced at my arm—and he caught me as I slumped to the floor.

My jacket had been hiding it, but elbows were not supposed to look like that. Not like that at all.

While I hyperventilated, he calmly studied the joint. "I will straighten it first. I did this for your fingers, *na*? It will be fast."

Reminding me about the time a Red Rum rogue had methodically dislocated half my fingers wasn't helping my lightheadedness. "Okay."

A long pause. "Does it hurt too much?"

"I can handle it," I whispered faintly.

He tightened his hold on my waist. "I know *vīsh* … It makes pain less, but I have never used it on a *hh'ainun*."

I almost said I was fine, but the injury was excruciating and the healing would only make it worse. "Try the spell on me, please."

His warm palm pressed against my cheek. "I will use only small *vīsh* first."

I nodded against his hand. Magic tingled through my face, then flashed hot. The warmth rushed outward, filling my body—and the pain evaporated.

"Oh," I breathed. "This is good. I feel good."

I tilted my head back and smiled. Something rather like alarm flickered over his features.

"*Vayanin?*"

"You're mean to call me that. Can't you say something nice? Or you could use my name. I like my name. It's a good name. My mom called me little bird, because robins are birds and—"

"Can you stand?"

I pushed off him, swaying dramatically. "Of course I can stand. I feel good now. I'm fine. I don't think I'm even hurt, but you—oh, your hand is hurt, I remember—"

As I babbled, he grasped my upper arm and my wrist with each hand.

"—so you should take care of your injury because I'm fine, really, and—"

He pulled sharply on my forearm. A dull pop sounded and a disturbing twang ran all the way up to my shoulder.

"Oh." I blinked at my arm. "You fixed it. So I'm fine now, right?"

"You are not fine," he muttered.

"What's wrong with me?"

"Even that little *vīsh* made you *zh'ūltis*."

"Why would you use magic to make me stupid?"

He drew me into the middle of the room. "Sit."

I sat, my mouth turned down in a sulk. "You made me stupid on purpose."

"Not on purpose," he growled, crouching beside me. He handed me my glasses. "I told you I did not know how that *vīsh* works on a *hh'ainun*. Lie down."

Obediently, I lay back, returning my glasses to my nose. They'd survived their fall with no damage. "Does that *vīsh* make you stupid?"

"No."

"Then why me?"

"Because you are *nailis* to this *vīsh*."

"I'm not weak. You said so. When we were in the bathroom, remember? You said you thought I wanted you to die, and I told you you were stupid to think that—"

He straightened my arm out and prodded the joint.

"You know, I always thought that was extra stupid of you, because you can read my mind, so you should've known that …" I trailed off, frowning. "But you can't read all my thoughts. You said you can't hear the things I think about you."

"Except insults," he rumbled distractedly as a glowing red circle, filled with demonic runes, appeared beneath my arm.

"So you don't know anything that I think about you?"

"No."

"Really?"

"Yes."

"Why?"

"Be quiet. I am working."

I bit my tongue. Magic crawled over my arm, and the spell flared brightly. I waited for the burning pain the healing magic had caused me before, but nothing penetrated the feel-good haze blanketing my thoughts. Whatever that "little *vīsh*" had been, it was strong stuff.

"You are healed now," he told me.

Sitting up, I tested my elbow. Seemed fine, but I was starting to realize I had no idea what condition my body was in. All my nerves were tingling pleasantly.

"Zylas." I peered at him, surprised by his wary expression. "If you could know one thing I think of you, what would it be?"

His eyes narrowed.

I shifted forward onto my hands and knees, staring into his face. "If I tell you one thing, will you tell *me* one thing?"

"What thing?"

I frowned. I hadn't thought that far ahead. "I want to know … what does 'protect' mean? Our contract makes you protect me, but I don't know what that means to you."

His tail lashed. "You do not know this yet, *vayanin?*"

"No. You've never explained."

"I will keep you safe. That is what it means."

My brow scrunched. "But what does 'safe' mean?"

"Safe means you will not die. That is most important. For me, that is what safe is." He studied me. "But here, this world is different. Safe means more things. I am still learning them."

"Oh." On my hands and knees, I inched closer, as though being nearer to him would help me understand better. "What have you learned so far?"

"You do not feel safe if you are hurt or scared or alone."

Well, that made me sound like the biggest wimp ever. I scooched closer. "What do *you* want to know?"

"I will ask you later."

"Ask me now."

"You are *zh'últis* right now."

Pouting, I moved even nearer, bringing us nose to nose. "Why are you mean to me, Zylas?"

"I am not mean."

"You call me names."

"They are true things."

"Then say something true that's *nice*."

He smirked. "You are *vayanin*."

"Ugh!" I threw my hands up in my best Amalia imitation, almost smacking him. My head spun, balance gone, and I tipped over backward.

He caught my arms and tugged. I pitched forward, sprawling onto his lap with my face somehow mashed in the crook of his elbow.

"You're so aggravating," I muttered.

"You are so *mailēshta*."

I flopped onto my back, my head and shoulders pillowed on his legs. I squinted up at his face, then pressed my hands against his cheeks, his skin delightfully warm. "I wish I could see in your head again."

"What if you see I am something different than you want me to be?"

I stared up at him, my heart pounding in my throat. "I … I don't know."

"*Hnn.*" His hand closed around mine. He turned his face, nose pressed to my inner wrist, and inhaled. "You smell like my *vīsh.*"

My gut flipped twice and twisted straight into a knot. "What … I mean … is that bad?"

He slid his nose across my wrist, then paused. Angling his head, he peered at the back of his hand. "Bleeding again."

I jolted, then shoved up off his lap. "I forgot! You should heal your hand. Go on, take care of it."

I shooed him into the center of the room. As crimson magic lit up around his split knuckles, the cuts trickling blood, I backed into the far corner and took several deep breaths—then realized I was holding my wrist where he'd breathed in his scent on my skin. My stomach reknotted itself.

As Zylas carefully adjusted the healing spell, I marveled at the complexity of the magic. I could vaguely grasp what made healing so much more difficult than the battle magic he and other demons wielded. He couldn't just call up a spell and use it. He had to cater the spell to each individual wound, sometimes using multiple variations to heal different aspects of an injury.

The red light of his *vīsh* reflected off the glossy floor, flaring brighter as he cast the spell. I leaned against the bookshelves, watching the splits in his skin close up. The weird, tingly feeling faded from my body, and as my head cleared, I tried not to think of how idiotic I'd sounded a minute ago.

"You would've had no problem with those golems if you could've used magic," I murmured. "If they attack the guild, there will be mythics everywhere. You still won't be able to use magic."

The healing spell disappeared and he opened and closed his fingers. "What are *golems*?"

"I've only read about them. They're metal creatures that move around because of a spell. They aren't alive and can't think … They're like robots with really simple programming. Uh, I mean—" I racked my brain for a comparison he'd understand. "They're like vehicles, except with no driver and really stupid."

He rose to his feet. "These are made with *hh'ainun* magic?"

"With sorcery, yes."

"Do they bleed?"

"No, they're made of metal."

"Why is there demon blood in them?"

My brow furrowed. "There isn't. Blood is rarely used in sorcery."

His tail snapped sideways. "I could smell demon on the golems. The large one had demon blood coming out after it fell."

"Demon blood coming out of it?" I stared at him. "Are you sure?"

"Stop asking me that."

I absorbed his revelation, then hurried to the bookshelf and scanned the titles. Golems were black magic, so I doubted the Crow and Hammer would have instructions on how to construct one, but they might …

"Aha!" I pulled a book out and flipped to the index. "Page three hundred and forty-two."

Zylas came to stand at my shoulder as I turned to a subheading labeled "Animation Magic – Golems" and skimmed through a page and a half of description and history. The reference book included nothing specific, but it gave me a general idea.

"Golems are constructed using metallurgic and astral sorcery," I summarized. "Blood doesn't fit with those. I don't think it's supposed to be part of a golem, especially not *demon* blood."

My churning thoughts brought an image of a stained book into my mind's eye: the grimoire of David Whitmore, a deceased sorcerer who'd experimented with incorporating demon blood into Arcana spells.

"Demon blood combined with Arcana." I looked up at Zylas. "Claude used demon blood to make vampires more powerful. Could he have created the golems? Who else would be experimenting with demon blood?"

"I did not smell him, but there were many scents."

I closed the book. "If Claude is behind these attacks … but why would he attack guilds? His interest is in Demonica, isn't it?"

"He uses others to get things he wants."

Shoving the book back into its spot on the shelf, I threw my torn sweater in the garbage and picked up my leather jacket. "Darius needs to know that Claude might be involved in these attacks. The last thing we want is anyone from the guild going up against Nazhivēr."

"They would die," Zylas agreed—though not in a tone that suggested the idea bothered him.

I rolled my eyes. "Back in the infernus."

He scrunched his nose in annoyance, then dissolved into crimson light. As he streaked into the infernus, I unlocked the door, the motion of the bolt disabling the spell that sealed the room off from the rest of the pub. At least no one had burst in on us this time.

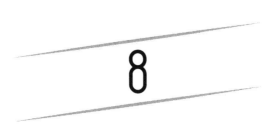

8

I SAT IN DARIUS'S OFFICE, a thick book propped on my knees. Two more texts rested on the edge of his desk. I'd spent the last few hours reading up on golems—mostly a bust—and trying to identify the sorcery on the back of the Vh'alyir Amulet.

Darius was a level below me, in the middle of a big meeting about the guild attacks and the danger to the Crow and Hammer. I'd considered interrupting, but there were a dozen other people in the room with him. I'd also spotted a short, bald man at the head of the table—likely the famous bounty hunter who'd given Tori trouble—and I'd rather keep my distance from all bounty-hunter types.

I paged through the thick Arcana text, idly hoping I might recognize an array design in one of the many diagrams. Noise rumbled up through the floor, carrying from the pub two levels below. I could've gone downstairs to mingle with my guildmates and find out more about what was happening—and why Shane Davila had shown up—but I wasn't in a socializing mood.

It was hard to be social when you couldn't stop thinking about your parents' murderer.

I hadn't seen Claude since shortly after Red Rum had kidnapped me, when he'd smilingly offered me a place as his valued protégé and partner in translating my mother's grimoire. How he could have made that offer knowing he'd killed my mother was incomprehensible. Who was that cold and unfeeling?

He was the reason I was translating the grimoire alone instead of with my mom, a mother-daughter project she'd talked about since I was a little girl. Because of him, my mother was gone forever.

Amalia and I hadn't given up on finding Claude, and Uncle Jack had been putting out feelers too. We'd revisited both Claude's townhouse and his condo over the last couple weeks, but between vampires and the MPD, not a single clue had been left behind. We didn't know where he was, where he'd come from, or his real name.

But finally, I had two clues—the old photo in Tori's folder, and the demon blood in the golems.

I continued perusing my book. Another forty minutes passed, and the noise in the pub gradually quieted. I finished the Arcana text and started skimming a shiny book titled *So You Want to Study Sorcery*, which included a beginner-friendly breakdown of all Arcana specializations.

As the clock struck midnight, the door behind me opened. Darius paused in the threshold, his eyebrows high in surprise and his salt-and-pepper hair ruffled as though he'd run his hand through it a few times.

"Robin," he murmured. "What brings you to my office so late?"

I closed the book. "I have information about the attack on Odin's Eye."

"We just finished our meeting. Is this something you couldn't share with the group?"

"It, um ... it would've been difficult to explain how I know."

He closed the door and circled his desk. Sinking into his chair, he steepled his fingers. "What did you learn?"

"Zylas figured out that those golems were made using demon blood."

"Demon blood?" His expression shifted from surprise to contemplation. "I see. That explains some things."

"It does?"

"We debated whether the golems had been altered to be longer-lasting or more powerful, and others noted that blood may be a component—but we didn't realize it was demon blood."

I leaned forward in my chair. "I think Claude is behind these demon-blood golems."

"The summoner Claude Mercier?"

"He was using demon blood to make vampires stronger. I think he's been experimenting with combining demon blood and Arcana."

Darius rested his chin on his hands. "I recall several reports last month about unusual vampire activity—none from you, though."

I winced. "Uh ... I ... well, it's hard for me to report things because—"

Crimson light blazed across my infernus. The power streaked out of the pendant and pooled on top of Darius's desk. Zylas materialized on the desk, crouched atop the GM's paperwork.

"Ah," Darius murmured. "Zylas."

My demon swept his tail sideways, sending a cascade of papers onto the floor.

"Because of my demon," I finished with a heavy sigh. "Zylas, why are you out of the infernus?"

"You are talking about pointless things." He rocked forward on the balls of his feet, getting in Darius's face. "Tell us what you know about the golems, *na*?"

I grabbed the demon's wrist and yanked him backward. He shifted maybe two inches, but at least he straightened so he wasn't obnoxiously close to the GM.

"The golems aren't Claude's," Darius told us bemusedly. "They belong to a dark-arts sorceress named Varvara Nikolaev, who's in the midst of a power-grab here in Vancouver. She orchestrated the guild attacks over the last three nights."

"Varvara Nikolaev?" Disappointment sank through me at the unfamiliar name. "So ... not Claude?"

Zylas sat on the desktop, one leg folded and a knee propped up. "The summoner does not fight. He is the *ūdrash* that builds a trap in the night and waits for *zh'ūltis* prey to walk into it."

"*Ood-rash*?" I repeated. "What's that?"

"It is ... an animal with ..." He raised his hands in a gesture that indicated something about the size of a car, then grimaced. "Not important."

"Good point, though." I looked back to Darius. "Claude spent years pretending to be my uncle's friend for a chance to steal more demon names, and with the vampires, he was manipulating them into becoming his personal bloodsucking army. His plan only failed because he didn't realize one of the vampires was actually a darkfae."

Darius's eyebrows shot up.

"Claude had his demon watching everything while he stayed out of danger," I continued. "Do you think Claude could be using Varvara in the same way?"

"Varvara is too experienced and cunning to be used. I think it's more likely that, if Claude is involved, he and Varvara have some kind of arrangement. He's providing her with a more powerful form of golem, and she's providing him with something in return."

"But what would Claude want from her?"

"That is the crucial question." Darius rubbed his short beard. "Tomorrow night, combat teams from the Crow and Hammer and Odin's Eye will ambush Varvara and her followers before they can ravage another guild. We have a plan for disabling her golems, but Claude could provide further assistance to protect his interests ... whatever they may be." His gaze shifted to Zylas. "I'm particularly concerned about his demon."

Darius, Girard, and Alistair had fought said demon, and though they'd inflicted some damage, they hadn't come close to defeating him.

Zylas smirked. "Nazhivēr will crush all the *hh'ainun*."

Before I could admonish Zylas, Darius nodded.

"Which is why you two will join us tomorrow night." The GM leaned back in his chair. "While our teams deal with Varvara and her rogues, you can ensure that Claude, his demon, or any other pawns don't join in."

"I'm not sure we can do that," I admitted. "Even Zylas is no match for Claude's demon."

"Could you distract the demon, giving us time to withdraw?"

"Uh, yeah, I guess we—"

"No."

Darius and I looked at Zylas.

"Hunt the summoner, yes. Fight Nazhivēr to protect stupid *hh'ainun*? No. I promised to protect Robin. *Only* Robin."

A thrill ran through my center at the sound of my name in his accent, but the rest of his declaration made me frown. "Zylas—"

The office door flew open and hit the wall with a bang.

Zora stood in the threshold, dressed in combat gear, her sword strapped to her back. Her wide eyes flashed from me to Darius, then to my demon sitting on the GM's desk. Her face paled.

"Good evening, Zora," Darius said calmly.

"Tori said Robin was here somewhere and—Darius, you— that—" She shook her head, then shot me an accusatory glare. "Why is your demon out? Are you threatening our guild master?"

"No!" I exclaimed, my anger swamped by rapidly increasing alarm.

There was no obvious reason for my demon to be in the office, and I didn't know what possible excuse I could make. As far as Zora was aware, my illegal contract allowed my demon to use magic; she had no idea Zylas could let himself in and out of the infernus at will.

Silence stretched through the room as everyone waited for my response, Zora with suspicion and Darius with subtle warning. He'd promised that if anyone from the Crow and Hammer found out I was an illegal contractor, he'd turn me in to the MPD to protect his guild. I needed to say something—a plausible explanation for why Zylas was sitting on the GM's desk.

I opened my mouth, but my mind was blank and buzzing with panic.

"*Ch.*" Zylas propped an arm on his raised knee. "*Hh'ainun* are so stupid. It would be easier to kill you all."

Silence answered his pronouncement. A heartbeat passed where I wondered if I'd hallucinated him speaking, then my heart deflated with sickening dread.

I was a dead woman. Officially dead.

Zora's face blanked with disbelief. Darius's mouth thinned, his expression grim.

Zylas hopped off the desk in one fluid motion. His prowling steps carried him toward Zora, and she skittered away from him with a quiet, frightened gasp. He grabbed the door, swung it shut, then turned to the three humans trapped in the office with him.

"I will explain with small words." His tail snapped impatiently. "You three want the same thing. You want this place and its humans to be safe."

We all stared at him.

"I will kill the things that put Robin in danger. I will protect the things that keep Robin safe." He focused on the guild master. "Is this a safe place for Robin?"

Darius's eyes narrowed. "If I make the guild a safe place for Robin, you'll protect the guild? Is that what you're saying?"

Zylas bared his teeth in a wolfish grin.

"And"—the GM's gaze sharpened—"you'll protect the guild against Claude and his demon?"

"One thing for another thing, *hh'ainun.*"

"I see." A faint smile curved Darius's lips. "I believe I've been outsmarted. This is not my night." Pushing to his feet, he nodded toward the door. "Robin, could you please give me and Zora a minute alone?"

"Sure," I mumbled, feeling sick. Grabbing Zylas's wrist, I pulled him into the empty room beyond. Closing the door, I sagged against the wall. "I can't believe you did that, Zylas."

He gazed intently at the door. "Better this way, *vayanin*. The female *hh'ainun* was too dangerous. Now she will do what her leader tells her."

"You've been waiting for something like this to happen, haven't you?" I wasn't sure how comfortable I was with that level of scheming from my demon. "How many plans did you have for keeping Zora from blowing our secret?"

"Too many for your *hh'ainun* mind."

"Ha ha." Sighing, I let my head fall back against the wall. "You're putting more thought and effort into my safety than I am."

"I know. You need to make me more food, *vayanin*, or I will think you do not want our contract."

My cheeks heated. I hadn't given him any food, let alone baked for him, since the whole "sharing food is a courting ritual" conversation. Any thought of how my end of our binding contract was the demon equivalent of hot and heavy flirting ... it made me want to crawl under a rock and die.

The office door opened. Cheeks still warm, I minced back into the room, Zylas behind me. Zora stood beside the desk, warily eyeing the demon as Darius returned to his chair.

"Well," he said, his tone a mystery; I couldn't tell if he was amused, angry, or resigned. "We're all agreed, then. Zora will keep your secret, Robin, and in return, you and Zylas will protect our combat teams from Claude, his demon, and any additional threats he might introduce tomorrow night."

I nodded.

"And I'll be going with you."

My gaze jerked to Zora.

She folded her arms. "Illegal contractor or not, you can't go out there unprotected. You need a champion."

"You … you're going to …"

She glanced at Zylas, her expression a mix of wariness, determination, and a hint of curiosity. "If nothing else, it should be interesting."

9

"STEALTH IS CRUCIAL for this mission." Crouched in the shrubs beside me, Zora kept her voice low. "At this very minute, we have five teams moving in on different locations. They have to simultaneously disable Varvara's golems, ambush her rogue soldiers, and capture the sorceress. If any one part fails, the whole mission and all our guildmates will be in severe danger."

I nodded earnestly, my gloved hands tucked in my leather jacket's pockets for warmth.

"So why," she asked, her voice roughening, "did you just let your demon run off *by itself?*"

"Himself," I corrected. "He's not an 'it.'"

"Why did you let *him* go off alone? He could be doing *anything*. If he's seen—if he attacks anyone—"

"He won't do anything like that. He's scouting around for any traces of Claude and his demon. No one will see him. He's very sneaky."

Pressing her lips together, she adjusted her sword baldric. We'd hidden ourselves in a strip of trees and bushes bordering a road, but aside from that, this area was solid concrete—an industrial complex that edged the harbor where massive quantities of cargo were moved between huge freighters, long trains, and endless trucks. It was called a stevedoring operation, and I'd had to look up the term. It had evolved from the Portuguese *estivador*, the original name for dockworkers who loaded cargo on ships.

"How can you just *trust* that demon to wander around alone?" Zora demanded. "You didn't even give him a command before he went."

"He already knows the plan," I said with a shrug.

A quiet snort sounded from my other side. Amalia, sitting with her back against a tree, rolled her eyes at Zora.

"You're used to brainless contracted demons," she told the sorceress. "Zylas is an asshole, but he's a goddamn smart one. Don't make the mistake of thinking he doesn't know *exactly* what's going on."

Zora rubbed her hands over her face and into her short blond hair. Huffing, she sat back on her heels and checked her watch. "We still have a few minutes. Why don't you give me the whole story?"

"You want to know now?" I asked cautiously. I reached up to adjust my glasses only to remember I was wearing contacts. "I offered to tell you a bunch of times ..."

She looked away, her face in shadow. "I've made mistakes before about who to trust. I was afraid if I heard your story ..." She huffed again. "You seem like a good kid, and I didn't want to fall for someone's innocent act again."

"Oh," I said, my defensiveness softening.

"Darius trusts you, and I trust him." She was quiet for a long moment. "I'd like to know, if you're still willing to tell me."

I settled down beside Amalia. "I guess it all started with Claude."

Zora listened attentively as I gave a highly abbreviated version of my accidental contract with Zylas, how I'd come to join the Crow and Hammer, and Claude's role in my parents' murder and the vampire outbreak last month. The only thing I left out was the true nature—and value—of my family's grimoire.

When I finished, Zora pursed her lips in a silent, wowed whistle. "Demon-blood-enhanced vampires. *That* explains a lot." She drummed her fingers on her knee. "What would he want from Varvara in exchange for the enhanced golems?"

"He wants all the demon names for himself, but Varvara can't help him with that."

"Claude Mercier is an alias, right? Have you uncovered anything about his true identity?"

"Um, well, we searched his house and apartment. That's … about it. All I found was a printout of Ezra Rowe's mythic profile."

"Ezra? What does he have to do with Claude?"

My stomach gave an unhappy twitch.

Naim Ashraf, the ex–summoner, hadn't provided any useful information about the Vh'alyir Amulet, but he and Tori had inadvertently given me a different clue: demon mages.

After my first bizarre encounter with Tori and her mage friends on Halloween, Amalia and I had debated over a dozen possible explanations for why they smelled of demon magic, but we'd never considered a demon mage as an option. Why would we? The MPD had stomped out the already rare practice so thoroughly that it'd become an urban legend.

On top of that, I couldn't imagine a demon mage hiding in a guild and passing himself off as a regular mythic. Madness was a notorious symptom of demon magery. After all, how could a human with an unwilling demon stuffed into their body for the sole purpose of giving them access to the demon's powerful magic not descend into some level of derangement?

None of Tori's friends struck me as power-hungry, demon-harboring madmen, but I wasn't ruling out the possibility—especially when it came to the quiet, unusually scarred Ezra Rowe.

"Have you asked Ezra?" Zora prompted.

"Not yet."

"Hmm." She slid her phone out of her pocket. "He'll be busy disabling golems right about now, but ..." Her thumbs flashed across her phone screen. "There. Sent."

"Sent?" Alarm shot through me. "What's sent?"

"An email." She grinned. "Don't worry, I wouldn't text him in the middle of a dangerous raid."

Something close to terror flitted through my chest. Not good. Not good at all. The last thing I wanted was Ezra's attention before we figured out what was going on with the three mages.

Glowing red eyes appeared between two trees, then Zylas slunk into the faint moonlight leaking through the bare branches overhead. Zora's hand inched toward her sword hilt, but she caught herself and lowered her arm.

He dropped into a crouch, joining our small circle, his gaze fixed on the sorceress. "Your fight strategy, it is to *disable* the golems first?"

It took her a moment to react to his question, disbelief wrinkling her forehead all over again. A demon speaking took some getting used to.

"Yes," she belatedly confirmed.

"You said the golems are in one place."

She nodded.

"They are not in one place."

A pulse of confused silence.

"What?" she demanded. "What do you mean?"

"I went all over." He waved at the stevedoring operation, which spanned twenty city blocks. "I could smell the demon blood in the golems. I found them in *lis* places. Five places," he corrected. "Most are close to a building with many *hh'ainun* in it."

Zora's face went ghostly pale in the silvery moonlight. "Are you sure? Absolutely sure?"

"Of course, *talūk*," he growled irritably.

I squinted at him. "What did you just call her?"

His tail snapped against the ground. "It is a mean word. You would not like it."

I started to apologize to Zora for my demon's bad manners, but she already had her phone to her ear. I could hear faint ringing, then a male voice answered.

"Andrew," she replied, biting off the words in her urgency, "contact the team leads and tell them the golems are not all in the warehouse. Do you copy that? At least part of the golem supply has been moved."

She listened. "Yes, tell them it might be an ambush. They need to be ready for the worst. Can you reach Darius?" A pause, then she bit off a curse. "If phone signals are poor, get Bryce on it. You have six"—she checked her watch—"five minutes. Start with Kai, Aaron, and Tabitha."

Ending the call, she turned back to Zylas. "Where is the largest collection of golems?"

He considered her, then pointed over her shoulder. "By a building. That way."

"Can you get us there unseen?"

"*Var.*"

She looked at me, brow scrunched.

"That means yes," I translated. "But Zora, we're supposed to be looking for Claude."

"We're supposed to ensure our guildmates survive," she retorted, pushing to her feet. "If the golems have been moved, that means the enemy knows we're coming. It's a trap. We have to help."

I nodded. "Amalia, you should go, uh, get in position." The words seemed silly, but that was the proper terminology, wasn't it?

She hefted the pair of binoculars hanging around her neck. "You got it. Don't forget your earpiece so you can actually hear me if I spot anything."

With a quick wave, she hurried out of the trees and toward a high fence topped with barbed wire. Beyond it, cylindrical reservoirs, three stories tall, rose above everything else, a metal staircase running along the side of each one. She started to climb the fence, her feet slipping on the post, and Zylas snickered.

I nudged him with my elbow and shot him a pointed look. He scowled at me. I gave him an even firmer stare.

Growling under his breath, he shoved up and trotted out of the trees. He grabbed Amalia by the waist, yanked her off the fence, and threw her over his armored shoulder. One impossible jump later, he dropped her on the other side. Her faint cursing carried back to Zora and me as he vaulted over the fence again and headed straight into the trees.

"Follow him," I whispered to Zora. "He'll lead us to the golems."

She loosened her sword in its sheath. "I'm getting a better idea of how you survived the storm drains last month."

Zylas ghosted ahead of us, and as I trekked after him, I slipped a plastic earpiece into my ear and checked the app on my phone. Zora had shown me how to use it earlier this afternoon, and it would allow us to stay in contact with Amalia. I flipped on the mic.

"Amalia?" I whispered.

"*Almost … at the … top.*" Her voice puffed from the tiny speaker. "*Damn, I'm out of shape.*"

"Let me know if you see anything suspicious."

"*Yep.*"

The tree line ended, and Zylas darted across a street and into a dirty alley with a fence on one side and a long, dark building on the other. Zora and I rushed after him, closing the gap. The demon paused to listen, his tail twitching as he concentrated.

"That building there," Zora breathed, pointing to a three-story gray rectangle with a few glowing windows—the only structure in this part of the complex not closed for the night. "That's where the rogues are. Any moment now, our first team will—"

The lights in the windows flickered, then all went out at once. A moment later, firelight flared somewhere inside the building.

"It's started," Zora muttered. "I hope Kai got the message. Let's hurry!"

Zylas continued down the dirt road, me and Zora a few paces behind. More light—fire, along with colorful flashes—emanated from the rogues' building, and muffled bangs and crashes became audible. My nerves tightened. The golems had been moved, the enemy might know we were here, and if Claude was nearby, that meant we had Nazhivēr to worry about.

"Any sign of a flying demon?" I whispered into my mic.

"*Nope.*" A rustle as Amalia shifted position on her high perch. "*But people are running out of that building now and—oh shit! There are the golems. Someone just got trampled.*"

Orange light flared from the other side of the gray structure.

"Hurry!" Zora barked.

Zylas broke into a fast jog, forcing me and Zora into a run. He raced to a dead end, where a collection of rusting tractor-trailers was parked. As I reached him, he scooped an arm around my middle, lifting my feet off the ground, then caught Zora in the same grip.

She was still gasping in surprise as he sprang on top of the nearest trailer. With three lightning-fast leaps, we were over the fence, into a parking lot, and streaking toward a gap between the rogues' building and a storage bay—a long strip lined with overhead doors.

As though a volume switch had been slammed straight to max, noise erupted—shouts, screams, bangs, thuds, crashes, and bizarre reverberations that could only be magic. Light blazed and flickered from the front of the building as Zylas sprinted toward it, only marginally slowed by his two passengers.

Ahead of us, a new racket erupted—metallic banging like off-kilter pistons. A dog-like golem, identical to the ones that had attacked the Odin's Eye guild, charged out of the storage bay's nearest door toward the unseen fight.

"*Shit!*" Amalia exclaimed in my ear. "*Robin, there are golems closing in on them from all sides. Our guys are about to be trapped in the middle.*"

"We're on it! Zylas—"

Before I could say more, he swerved toward the storage bay, where three more golems had appeared, pinkish runes glowing over their metal bodies as they ran with lumbering gaits.

Zylas's slowing stride was my only warning, and I braced myself as he let go. As Zora and I dropped to the ground, he launched toward the lead golem and slammed both feet into its front legs. The steel limbs went out from under it and the golem collapsed onto its side with a hideous metallic shriek.

Zylas rolled clear, shot to his feet, and leaped again as the second golem belched a jet of fluid at him. It sprayed across the pavement, bubbling and hissing.

"Zora," I shouted over the cacophony. "Can you distract one?"

She nodded and drew her sword. Gulping back a wave of panic, I pulled my infernus chain off my neck and sprinted toward the last golem in line. As I closed in, it turned in mid-charge—and headed straight for me.

Zora shot across its path. Jaws spewing fire, it lurched after her, and I dove toward its exposed side.

I stuck my hand under its belly and shouted, "*Ori eruptum impello!*"

Silver light ballooned out from the artifact in my hand. The spell expanded under the golem, heaving the beast upward. It crashed onto its side.

Zora leaped in front of me, her sword held crosswise and her hand braced against the blade. "*Ori gladio reflectetur!*"

A semi-transparent purple wall the width of the blade whooshed out of the steel, and the acid spouting from the next golem's mouth splattered all over the barrier instead of us.

The spell faded almost as fast as it had appeared, but it'd been enough. Zora grabbed my hand and sprinted away from the golems. I looped my infernus back over my head as I ran.

Another booming crash—Zylas knocking his second golem over. Three down and three more to go, one charging after us and the other two hopelessly chasing the agile demon.

"Nice work with the *impello* spell," Zora congratulated with a quick grin. "Don't suppose you have another one?"

"No, sorry."

"Then this way. Come on!"

With a golem in pursuit, she raced toward an abandoned flatbed trailer. Seizing the hooked end of a rusted chain hanging from the bed, she tossed it to me. "Get ready!"

I caught the heavy chain, already panicking. Ready for what?

The golem barreled toward us, and Zora stretched the chain out. Catching on, I locked my limbs. As the golem reached us, she jumped aside. The golem ran into the chain, almost tearing it from my gloved hands.

I threw the end of the chain to Zora. Dodging its snapping jaws, she looped the chain around its neck and lobbed the end back to me. I shoved the hook into a gap in the golem's shoulder joint, and we both ran for it.

The golem hammered after us, hit the end of the chain, and jolted to a stop. Straining forward, its feet scraping the ground, it struggled to break free. The chain held.

"Yes!" Zora yelled. "Now let's get the last—"

She broke off with a surprised grunt. The final golem was lying on its side, and Zylas stood over it, holding its steel skull. He dropped the dismembered head to the ground.

An explosion boomed from around the corner of the building. A fireball burst outward, orange-tinted smoke billowing into the sky.

"No!" Zora sprinted toward her battling comrades, shouting over her shoulder, "Come on, Robin!"

As I took a frantic step after her, Amalia's voice crackled in my ear.

"Robin! A dude with a supersized golem just left the far end of that long, skinny building. He's heading away from the fight."

"Claude?" I gasped.

"Who else could it be? He's moving quick—go after him!"

Zylas! I called silently, then asked Amalia, "Any sign of Nazhivēr?"

"Not yet. I'm watching, though. Hurry before Claude gets away!"

Zylas scooped me off the ground. I grabbed his shoulders as he slung me onto his back without breaking stride. He streaked the length of the storage bay, then leaped from a car roof onto a building.

"Can you see him? He's straight ahead of you, moving west."

"I see," Zylas growled, either overhearing Amalia or picking up on my thoughts.

Eyes watering from the cold wind, I squinted across the labyrinthian stacks of industrial piping that filled the huge concrete lot. Fifty yards away was a faint glow—runes covering the surface of a huge bipedal golem.

Zylas sprang off the building, hit the ground, and shot into the steel maze. The golem, the same model as the twelve-foot-tall one Tori had knocked down with her mysterious artifact, strode among the stacks, its head and shoulders visible above the piles.

Was it Claude? Had he come here to prepare the golems for Varvara? Would I finally see my parents' killer again?

If it was him, what would I do?

My throat closed, rage, panic, grief, and determination filling my lungs in place of air. As we closed in on the lumbering golem, Zylas vaulted onto a pile of steel pipes. He slid to a stop, the metal shifting under his feet with a soft clank.

The man walking a few paces in front of the golem paused. As the steel brute halted as well, he turned toward me and Zylas in plain view atop the stack.

Somewhere behind us, another fireball exploded skyward. The orange light washed across the man's face, illuminating every detail.

"*You?*" I gasped.

The man wasn't Claude, but I'd seen his face before. Pasty pale skin, hair more white than blond, hollow cheeks with sharp cheekbones, and pale eyes without visible eyelashes to frame them.

It was the man from Tori's photo—the pale man young Claude had been speaking to. The *exact* same man, identical in coloring and features … and age.

But that photo was at least twenty years old. The man peering up at me and my demon with mild surprise was only a few years older than I was.

What the hell was going on?

10

"DO I KNOW YOU?" the man asked.

"Who are you?" I demanded shrilly. "How do you know Claude?"

"Claude? I don't know anyone by that name." He stepped toward Zylas and me. "Who are you—and what is that unusual demon?"

Zylas squeezed my thigh and I slid off his back. My feet thumped against the foot-wide pipes we stood on as another burst of green magic lit the area.

Zylas, can you take him alive? We need to know who he is.

The man took another step closer, staring up at us. "I've never seen a demon like that before."

Zylas's tail twitched, then he launched off the stack of pipes. He hit the ground and lunged at the man. The golem turned, its arm swinging, the motion so slow compared to Zylas it was almost comical. He flashed for the unprepared mythic.

"*Ori unum!*"

The air shimmered blue and Zylas's hand slammed into a faint barrier. He lurched back and darted away.

"My," the man remarked, perfectly calm as though a demon hadn't just attacked him. "You're a fast one."

As the golem took a thundering step toward its new adversary, the man placed a hand on its leg. He murmured something and the runes covering the golem dimmed to the faintest glow.

"We don't need that thing getting in the way," he said as he unzipped his leather coat and let it fall to the ground. His sleeveless shirt bared his muscular arms, covered from wrists to shoulders with half-inch-wide steel rings—dozens of them, perfectly fitted to the contours of his limbs.

Grinning, he sank into a half crouch, his intent stare on Zylas.

Trepidation sparked through me. No mythic, no matter how skilled, was a match for a demon. This man was either exceptionally dangerous or exceptionally stupid.

Be careful, Zylas.

My demon curled his fingers, claws unsheathing, but he didn't summon his semi-transparent talons. He studied his opponent—then vaulted forward.

"*Ori—*"

Zylas dug a foot into the concrete and changed direction. He sprang again, coming at the man's flank.

"*Ori duo!*"

The air shimmered and Zylas was flung backward without ever having touched the sorcerer. He landed on his feet and attacked again.

"*Ori unum!*"

Zylas's kick hit a shimmering blue shield.

"*Ori unum! Ori duo!*"

His claws, slashing for the sorcerer's lower back, bounced off another shield, then a shimmer of air hit the demon and he flew backward.

My fingers tightened into fists. So fast—the sorcerer's incantations were incredibly short and he spat the syllables so swiftly Zylas couldn't land a strike.

The demon's lips peeled back from his teeth. Ten paces from the sorcerer, he raised his hand, fingers outstretched.

Zylas! I protested in alarm.

Crimson veins crawled up his wrist. As the glow spread over his hand, a spell formed in front of his palm, spiky runes coiling through a pentagram. A bright flare blasted toward the sorcerer.

The sorcerer flung his hand up. "*Ori tres!*"

A wave of sparkling green light erupted from his hand and met the incoming missile of power. The two magics collided a foot from the sorcerer's fingers.

Zylas's crimson power, the deadly demonic magic all mythics feared, evaporated like smoke the moment it touched that shimmering green magic.

The sorcerer raised his other hand toward the shocked demon. "*Ori quattuor.*"

A band around the sorcerer's arm lit up with indigo light and he slashed his arm sideways.

Watch out! I cried helplessly in my head.

Zylas darted away as a wild barrage of six-inch-long spikes shot out from the artifact. They flew in a random spray, and Zylas couldn't avoid them. He ducked, arms shielding his head. They bounced off his armor—but three speared his right shoulder, left thigh, and midriff. The glowing barbs stuck in him, pulsing strangely.

The sorcerer raised both hands. "*Ori—*"

Crimson magic rushed up Zylas's arms. Snarling, he shot forward, spells forming over his arms.

"*Ori tres! Ori unum! Ori duo!*"

As fast as Zylas attacked, the sorcerer countered, the dozens of artifacts around his arms flashing with each rapid incantation.

Zylas jolted backward, recovered, and struck at the man's throat.

"*Ori unum!*"

The demon's fist bounced off the blue shield—and the sorcerer pitched over backward, Zylas's tail hooked around his ankle below his shield. The man was still falling when the demon grabbed him by the throat, cutting off his air—and his ability to cast spells.

The sorcerer hit the ground on his back, Zylas's greave on his chest and fingers squeezing his throat. I scrambled down the stack of pipes, my heart thudding loudly. Glowing spikes were still sticking out of Zylas, and the sight made me ill.

As I jogged over, my earpiece crackled.

"*Ro—hear me?—do—see—*"

"Amalia?" I pressed the earpiece, frowning. Had my phone lost signal?

"*—there! Please—*"

"What? I can't hear you."

The speaker crackled, then Amalia's shriek burst across my eardrum at full volume.

"*Look up, goddammit! He's above you!*"

My head snapped back—and a demon dropped out of the sky.

Zylas slammed into me and the world spun as I was wrenched off my feet. He landed in a skid and I glimpsed a flash of movement—the dark shape of wings and glowing crimson.

A magic attack shot at us. Zylas dove for the ground, the blast flying over our heads, then caught himself on one hand and flipped back onto his feet as he whirled to face the enemy. My head spun sickeningly from the rapid changes of direction.

Dusky lips pulled back to bare pale fangs, Nazhivēr landed neatly, his wings arched. His clothing and armor were more substantial than Zylas's but still lightweight. His long black hair was tied back, making his sharp features more severe. Behind the demon, the sorcerer climbed to his feet and rubbed his throat.

"*Dīnen et Vh'alyir,*" Nazhivēr rumbled.

"*Dīnen et Dh'irath,*" Zylas snarled back. "*Kir aditavh'anthē hh'ainun?*"

"*Kir anthē?*"

"Nazhivēr," the sorcerer said, moving to the demon's side. "We're taking the demon alive, correct? And the girl?"

Nazhivēr sneered. "*We* are doing nothing, *kanish*. I will deal with them. Take the golem and go."

"But …" The sorcerer eyed the six-and-half-foot demon, then shrugged. "Fine."

My skin prickled. Nazhivēr was in command—and that couldn't be a good thing. Panic simmered in my gut.

"*Rēdirathē payilasith,*" the demon rumbled, ice frosting the ground around his feet. "*Thē īt nā, Vh'alyir.*"

Zylas growled softly, then loosened his arm. He pushed me away from him and muttered, "*Drādah ahktallis.*"

Smart prey. He was telling me to escape danger. *But Zylas—*

He shoved me again. As I fell, Nazhivēr slammed into him. Zylas twisted free. Glowing talons blazed over his fingers, and the two demons met with slashing blades of magic. I scrambled backward on the ground, Nazhivēr's sweeping tail just missing my face.

He drove into Zylas, forcing the smaller demon back. Zylas darted side to side, lightning-fast, but Nazhivēr wasn't much slower. Second House, Zylas had told me. Like Tahēsh, Nazhivēr belonged to a House that had made a hobby of killing the weaker Twelfth House demons.

The pair crashed together again and broke apart, blood splattering the ground. Zylas skittered back a few steps, then made another sideways evasion. As I sat up, he vaulted over a stack of pipes and dropped onto the other side.

Nazhivēr leaped over the obstacle after his opponent.

Zylas was leading the demon away to give me a chance to reach safety. But should I go back and find Zora, or should I stay to help Zylas? Was he any match for Nazhivēr? This battle was all wrong—Zylas needed to strike when his more powerful opponents were weak or unprepared.

Zylas, what should I do?

Nothing. Was our telepathic connection that broken? Even in a situation this desperate, I couldn't hear him? I braced my hands on the ground, paralyzed by indecision.

A shadow fell across me, blocking the moon's silvery light.

The sorcerer crouched, smiling pleasantly. This close, I could see he wasn't merely pale; he had albinism. His skin was almost translucent, his pale blue eyes framed by lashes as white as his hair.

"I heard rumors about a teenage girl who showed up out of nowhere with a demon from a new House. That must be you."

I was almost twenty-one, not a teenager. They couldn't even get my age right?

His pale gaze slid over me. "You have the look, don't you?"

"Wh … what?" I whispered.

"You *really* have the look," he breathed, licking his lips. "It's almost too perfect, isn't it?"

A reddish glow lit the sky, the battling demons out of view among the stacks of pipes. I slid back a few more inches. *Zylas? Are you okay? Please answer me!*

As nearby magic detonated with an ear-splitting boom, the sorcerer reached for me.

"*Ori eruptum impello!*" I screamed.

The silver dome whooshed out of my artifact, but the spell hadn't had enough time to recharge. Instead of blasting the sorcerer ten feet, it knocked him on his rear.

I leaped up and sprinted away.

Footsteps pounded after me, the man chasing me down with his much longer stride. A hand grabbed the back of my jacket and yanked me off my feet. I smacked into his chest. Ripping my glove off, I raked my fingernails across his face.

He shouted and released me. I dove away, slipped, and crashed down. Gasping, I rolled sideways.

His foot landed on my stomach, pinning me to the concrete. He towered over me, shallow scratches on his cheek leaking blood.

"Fierce," he crooned, grinning in a way that made my whole body turn to ice. "Exactly how it should be. You'll be the closest yet. Almost the real thing."

He extended his hand toward me, moonlight gleaming on the metal bands encircling his entire arm. He opened his mouth.

"*Ori defendatur!*"

The feminine voice rang out, and a blast like a sparkling pink beachball hit the sorcerer in the chest, hurling him away.

Zora shot out from between stacks of steel and slid to a stop beside me, her sword angled toward the enemy. "Robin, are you okay?"

"I'm—I'm fine," I panted, shoving to my feet. "Are you—"

"Who is he?"

Standing again, the sorcerer brushed the grit off his shirt.

"I think he—" I began.

"*Robin!*" Amalia's voice burbled through the speaker, distorted and almost unintelligible. "*What—you need—Zylas!*"

I didn't know what she was saying, but I could hear her panic as she yelled my demon's name. Terror shot through me.

Daimon, hesychaze!

At my silent command, the infernus buzzed. Red power streaked across the lot, faster than a demon could run, and hit the pendant. It vibrated, then the light burst back out. Zylas took form again—and his fist struck the sorcerer in the gut so hard the man lifted off the ground.

He slammed down, mouth gaping and eyes rolling back in his head.

Zylas staggered and caught himself. Blood ran down his right arm and dripped off his chin. Wounds lashed his body from Nazhivēr's claws, and he couldn't straighten all the way.

"Zylas," I whispered in horror.

"He is coming."

With a sweep of his wings, Nazhivēr appeared on top of a stack of pipes. White teeth flashing, the demon extended both hands. Glowing hexagons materialized out of nothing, two feet wide, ringing his arms and overlapping each other.

"*Kasht*," Zylas spat, thrusting his palm toward the ground. A circle filled with spiky runes formed beneath him, spreading outward until we were both standing among the glowing lines.

The temperature dropped, the faint light of the full moon dimming as the two demons drew in all the power from nearby sources. The heat rushed from my body, my breath puffing white.

Three seconds to build out their spells. Two. One.

A blast of spiraling magic erupted from Nazhivēr's palms. It screamed across the distance. Crimson flashed as Zylas's barrier coalesced in front of us.

The attack hit the barrier and exploded.

Zylas's spell shattered and concussive force threw me backward. He caught me in midair and we slammed down together, his arms shielding my head and shoulders. His blood splattered my face.

Nazhivēr jumped off his perch and strode toward us, his tail snapping side to side. Zylas pushed off me, moving too slow, dark blood running from the corner of his mouth. He staggered to his feet, listing sideways.

Nazhivēr grinned. He could sense it: *dh'ērrenith*. We were defeated. Zylas wouldn't last much longer.

"*Ori sol videatur!*" Zora shouted.

Light as bright as the sun flashed. Agony speared my eyes, and I shrieked at the sudden pain. Zylas yelped—and so did Nazhivēr.

All I could see were bright spots. I was blinded—but were the demons? They had infrared vision, but would it work while their normal vision was excruciatingly white?

Scuffing footsteps, and Zora's voice rang out in another incantation. A smear of green blazed among the spots crowding my vision. She was fighting Nazhivēr? Alone?

I reached out blindly and my searching hand hit Zylas's leg. I grabbed his wrist and hauled myself up, clinging to his arm.

Zylas, we can fight too! We can use my cantrips!

His hand closed around mine, blood-slick fingers digging in. His shadowed face appeared among the spots as my vision recovered.

Zora shouted another incantation. Her sword struck metal with a ringing clang.

Like we defeated Vasilii. We can do it.

I pulled his arm up, pointing our hands toward the sounds of battle. My vision cleared a little more, and with a final blink, my sight returned.

So did Nazhivēr's.

He swept his powerful arm out. Zora was already swinging her sword, the long blade giving her more reach than Zylas's claws, and the point cut across the demon's shoulder as he struck. The impact from his armored forearm knocked her ten feet and she landed on her back, halfway between us and Nazhivēr.

Crimson streaked up Nazhivēr's arms as his glowing eyes focused on Zylas. A spell building. A lethal attack.

I pressed my palm to the back of Zylas's hand, waiting for red magic to light up our skin. I waited to feel the searing heat of his power inside me.

Zylas!

Nazhivēr launched for us, wings snapping out to propel him forward with greater speed. Zylas's fingers twitched convulsively, and red power flashed over his hand—but not mine.

He began a cast, but his magic wasn't fast enough. We didn't have three or four seconds—we had two, and only a cantrip was that fast.

But his magic didn't touch me, didn't reach me.

Spear-like blades extended off Nazhivēr's fist as he closed the final few feet between us.

"*Impello!*"

On her knees, Zora had one hand thrust toward us, a round medallion squeezed in her grip. The simple hex hit me and Zylas, throwing us backward, and Nazhivēr's piercing blades flashed above us as we fell.

We hit the ground yet again. Nazhivēr landed almost on top of me, but he didn't swing those lethal blades down into me or Zylas. Instead, he pivoted on one foot.

Changing direction. Switching targets.

Zora was halfway to her feet as the unstoppable demon turned on her. Three lightning-fasts steps. The glowing blades adorning his fists, an attack meant for Zylas—meant to shred his unbreakable armor and snap his inhumanly strong bones—blazed with power.

My terrified scream rang through the night as the demon slammed those blades into Zora's body. Driving her down. Smashing her into the ground, the spears of power piercing concrete as easily as they'd passed through her flesh.

Her limbs thudded into the ground, unmoving. She hadn't even had time to cry out.

Nazhivēr lifted his fist, his spell shimmering away. He turned back to us, ready to continue now that he'd dealt with the human pest who'd dared to interfere.

Zora! Zora! I was shrieking her name in my head, but my voice had disappeared.

Zylas shoved off the ground and braced his feet. Magic sparked over his hands—dim, weak. Frost sparkled across the ground as he drew in the faint warmth from the air, seeking every vestige of power he could get.

Nazhivēr's glowing eyes shifted, focusing on something behind us.

He gave Zylas a slashing look, then whirled away. He strode past Zora to the crumpled albino sorcerer, still out cold from Zylas's strike to his gut. The demon grabbed the mythic, spread his wings, and leaped into the air. His dark silhouette blended with the night.

A crackle in my ear.

"*A team is coming your way,*" Amalia warned me, her voice hushed and shaking. "*They saw the light from Zora's spell.*"

Noise behind us. Thumping footsteps. A low call—one mythic signaling to another.

"Zylas," I croaked, pushing onto my knees. "Heal … heal Zora. Please."

He turned. Dark eyes, gleaming with the faintest hint of scarlet, gazed at me without emotion. His magic was too depleted. He didn't have the strength to heal such terrible wounds—and had too many terrible wounds himself.

The approaching footfalls grew louder.

Red light flared across his extremities. He dissolved into power that streaked into the infernus. The pendant buzzed against my chest, then went still. I stared at Zora, blood shining on the concrete around her, as my vision blurred with tears.

The combat team arrived, their ruckus surrounding me. Someone yelled Zora's name. Mythics surrounded her.

"She's alive!" someone shouted.

My head came up.

"Sin, dose her, quickly! Bryce, get the nearest healer over here!"

I blinked my vision clear. A woman with a kit of potions was pouring liquid over Zora's wounds, colored steam rising as it touched her. Another was holding her wrist to count her pulse while a third elevated her legs. More mythics rushed around. Dark shapes. Blurred shapes.

"Robin? Robin?"

The voice penetrated my daze, and I realized a woman was crouched beside me, squeezing my shoulder. She seemed familiar. They were all familiar, but I couldn't remember a single name.

"Robin," the woman asked, "are you hurt?"

Hurt? No, I was fine. Bruised and aching and totally *fine*. I wasn't the one lying in a pool of blood, my life slipping away while a crowd of my friends desperately tried to keep me alive.

Tears spilled down my face, and I crumpled forward, shaking with sobs.

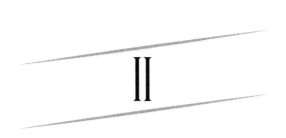

SITTING ON MY BED with my knees pulled up, I watched Zylas. Spirals of magic patterned the floor all around him, and he stiffened with pain as crimson power pooled in the gouge in his shoulder. He'd been healing his injuries for ten minutes now, the dark slashes disappearing one by one.

Before beginning, he'd spent over an hour in the shower, soaking up the heat so he'd have enough magic. I'd fed him three bowls of steaming soup while he'd been in there, one after another. It probably hadn't helped compared to the steady warmth from the shower, but I hadn't been able to do anything else.

The crimson glow faded and Zylas sat up. His naked torso, uninterrupted by his armor, was pristine again, showing no sign of the slices that had crisscrossed his body. Standing, he trudged to the bed and slumped onto his stomach beside me.

As he pillowed his head on his folded arms, I rubbed at the tears building in my eyes.

How were we supposed to defeat Claude, get the stolen grimoire pages back, and avenge my parents if we couldn't defeat Nazhivēr?

"You cannot kill all enemies." Zylas's voice was a husky murmur. "How much you hate them does not make you stronger or them weaker."

The leaden weight in my chest pressed on my lungs. "You don't think we can defeat Nazhivēr?"

"Not without *dh'ērrenith*."

A hopeless silence fell between us. Zylas stretched out his legs, sighing as he tried to get comfortable. I stared absently at his bare torso, then uncurled from my miserable ball. Shifting to his side, I pressed my hands to his back.

He twitched in surprise, then settled again. I ran my hands up to his shoulders, found the tightest muscles, and began to knead them.

"What about that sorcerer?" I asked. "He knew Nazhivēr, so he must know Claude too." I thought back to the old photo in Tori's folder as I dug my thumbs into a knot below his shoulder blade. "Is that man even human?"

"He smells like a *hh'ainun*."

"Why hasn't he aged, then? And his sorcery is ... I've never seen anything like that. It was so fast." I shifted to Zylas's other shoulder, firmly tracing his tight muscles. "I'll see if I can find that case Tori was referencing. Someone took his photo, so maybe the MagiPol database has information on him or why he was under investigation twenty years ago."

"*Hnn.*"

I leaned sideways to see his face. His eyes were closed, his breathing slow. A faint smile touched my lips. The last—and only—time I'd massaged his stiff muscles after a healing, he'd snarled and complained and tried to shove me off. We'd come a long way.

But some things hadn't changed—like him suffering terrible injuries while protecting me.

"Zylas?" My voice trembled on his name. "You almost died, didn't you?"

He cracked an eye open. "Nazhivēr was not trying to kill me."

"He wasn't?"

"If he wanted to kill me, I would be dead."

My hand was on the back of his neck, but I didn't remember putting it there. My fingers sank into his tangled hair, gripping tight. "I couldn't hear you. We couldn't combine our magic when it might've stopped Nazhivēr. Please, Zylas, tell me how to hear your mind."

He turned his head, one softly glowing eye gazing at me.

"You ask for everything like it is nothing."

As confusion buzzed through me, a thud sounded from the main room—the front door closing. Amalia was home.

I scooched off the bed. "I'll be right back. Just—just hold that thought, okay?"

His forehead wrinkled at the idiom. Leaving him to puzzle over it, I hurried into the main room.

Amalia was unzipping her tall boots, her blond hair hanging limply around her shoulders. As I rushed into sight, she shrugged off her coat and tossed it onto the shelf in the front closet.

"Zora is alive," she said.

A painful knot in my chest eased. "She's going to be okay?"

"Too soon to tell." Passing me, Amalia dropped heavily onto the sofa. "The healers stabilized her, but she's still in critical condition."

"Zylas can't heal her." I pressed a hand against my stomach to quell my anxiety. "Even if we could get him over there to do it without anyone noticing, how would we explain how her injuries vanished?"

Amalia shook her head. "I'm not sure his fancy demon healing could make those injuries disappear. She has internal ruptures and … stuff where it isn't supposed to be. I don't think any magic can prevent sepsis."

My knees went weak and I sat on the coffee table before they buckled.

"The healers' place was a zoo. That didn't go wrong for just you guys. Loads of guild members were injured, some pretty badly." She let her head fall back. "It would've been worse if the three of you hadn't taken out those golems."

"What about all the demon magic Zylas and Nazhivēr were throwing around? Did anyone notice?"

"I don't think so. There was so much magic flying and everyone was focused on their own shit." She pushed off the sofa and stretched. "On the plus side, our guild came out on top."

"But we never found out what Claude wanted from that Varvara woman," I pointed out with a sigh, "or whether he got it. And we aren't any closer to finding him. *And* we still don't know—"

She lightly whacked the top of my head. "Don't be so gloomy. We'll figure it out."

Surprised, I smiled faintly. "Thanks, Amalia."

"Sure. Is Zylas done with the shower?"

"It's all yours."

As Amalia got a towel and locked herself in the bathroom, I trudged back to my bedroom. Zylas had his face pillowed on his arms, his eyes closed. When I crawled onto the bed, his eyelids fluttered.

"*Vayanin?*" he mumbled drowsily.

I sat beside him. "Why can't you use my name?"

He grumbled something.

"What were you saying before? Zylas?"

His shoulders rose and fell with slow breaths. I leaned forward to peer at him. He was either asleep or very close to it.

I tugged my spare blanket, folded at the foot of the bed, out from under his legs and flipped it over him. He stirred, then relaxed again. I returned to my spot and debated pulling out my laptop to search the MPD archives for that photo of the mysterious sorcerer, but I was exhausted too.

My hand crept toward Zylas's warmth of its own accord. I combed my fingers through his dark hair, then traced one of his horns to its point.

My fingers were still tangled in his hair when I fell asleep.

IN MY DREAM, I was crouched on a rocky outcropping. Dawn tinged the horizon deep blue, and my long shadow stretched away toward the edge of the rock.

Below me was a sheltered bowl, the only break I could see in the vista of jagged rocks, waves of sand, and sparse, dark plant life. Dome-like structures, almost like igloos but made of roughly chiseled rock, dotted the dips and curves of the terrain, and around them, half a dozen large bonfires burned.

A persistent noise penetrated my dream, rumbling emphatically.

The sun breached the horizon behind me and warm golden light washed across the landscape, illuminating the burnt-red rocks and sand. My dream self stood and walked to the outcropping's edge.

The noise grew louder, tugging at my consciousness. So strange how I knew I was dreaming, and that something was waking me up.

I stared down at the crude settlement, then hopped off the rock and onto loose sand. I walked toward those odd structures. Time sped up, and in seconds, I was striding between rock domes with arched entrances, curtains covering the doorways.

Rustling sounds and quiet voices competed with the loud rumbling, but I didn't look for the source of the noises. I stopped in front of the largest dome, watching the curtain. It fluttered, then a delicate hand with reddish skin and dark claws appeared. The hand curled over the drape, pulling it open in invitation.

I stepped into the dark interior, and the curtain fell shut behind me. Everything went black.

My forehead scrunched, and I squinted my eyes open. Gray morning light leaked through my bedroom drapes, and enthusiastic purring filled my ears.

Zylas was stretched out on the bed beside me, Socks lying across his chest. As she purred like an overworked motor, he lazily rubbed her ears with both hands. She tilted her head side to side, her paws making small kneading motions.

I watched him, not breathing. For reasons I couldn't explain, I was unable to tear my gaze off his hands and the gentle way he caressed the small, fragile kitten. His eyes were half closed, drowsiness clinging to him, and in his sleepy state, an unexpected openness touched his features, a vulnerability I rarely glimpsed.

Socks purred, unaware that her source of pets and caresses was a demon that could kill without regret or mercy, a creature of another world superior to humans in strength, power, and brutality. She lifted her chin for neck scratches, which the savage demon obligingly provided.

My gaze followed the hard lines of his forearm to the heavy muscles that bound his upper arm, flexing with the movement of his wrist.

His head turned. "You are awake."

I snapped out of my daze. Heat rushed into my face and I rolled off the bed so fast I almost landed on the floor. Catching myself, I straightened my wrinkled sweater. "Um. Good morning."

"Why are you changing color, *vayanin*?"

I abandoned my bedroom and the scantily clad demon in my bed.

Brushing my teeth in the bathroom a few minutes later, I tried to remember more about that strange dream. A desert landscape … a rudimentary community of stone houses … that red-skinned hand, small and feminine, drawing the door-like curtain open.

The more I tried to analyze the details, the more they jumbled together until I wasn't sure *what* I'd dreamed. Putting it out of my mind, I focused on my tasks for the day.

An hour and a half later, Amalia trudged out of her room, her hair tied into a messy ponytail. When she saw me in front of the coffee table, she broke off her yawn.

"Do I want to know what you're doing?" she asked dryly.

I shrugged, playing it cool even though I was proud of my efforts. Spread across the table was a web of flashcards and colorful sticky notes.

"Okay, so." I pointed to the card in the center. "Claude. He's in the middle of everything, so that's where I put him. Here, the vampires. Here, Varvara and the golems. Over here, the albino sorcerer. I added Ezra too, since we don't know if he's connected to Claude."

Amalia wandered closer. "You've got my family on there, I see. And yours. And the grimoire."

I nodded. "Without knowing Claude's goal, it's difficult to guess what the connection is between all these people. The only clear link is Demonica, even if it's just demon blood."

She sat cross-legged beside me, studying my work. "We know Claude wants all twelve demon Houses. He told you he was the first summoner since the Athanas family to have all twelve names, but he doesn't know how to summon the Vh'alyir House."

"If that's all he wants, why steal those grimoire pages? They were spells, not names." I chewed on the back of my pen. "That makes two things he wants that we don't understand—the spells in the grimoire, and an alliance with Varvara."

"If we figure out one, we could probably figure out the other, but we just don't have enough information." She pointed at a flashcard. "I think the creepy sorcerer is our best lead. He knows Nazhivēr, and he was taking one of the golems. I'd bet he knows the deal Claude made with Varvara."

"I'm going to find Tori's case about him."

"You do that." She pushed to her feet again. "I have some errands to run, and we're low on groceries. Want me to stop at the store?"

"Yes, please. Can you pick out something for Zora while you're there? Flowers or a get-well card or something …"

Amalia's expression softened. "How is she?"

"I called the healer this morning. No change."

After Amalia left, I checked on Zylas—catnapping in the middle of my bed with Socks sprawled across his legs—then set up with my laptop. I started searching for demon mage cases, since they were what Tori had asked Naim Ashraf about, but when that turned up nothing, I tried a bunch of keyword combinations. Morning crept into afternoon as I clicked through case after Demonica case.

As the afternoon waned, I set aside my laptop with a frustrated sigh. My head ached from too much time staring at a screen. I needed to do something else.

When I pulled the grimoire's metal case from under my bed, Zylas woke up enough to give me a sleepy stare, but he didn't shift from his lazy sprawl. I promised him something to eat later, then carried the grimoire out to the breakfast bar.

Opening the ancient book to Myrrine's first entry, I studied the short passage, then flipped ahead. I found her name only six pages later, squashed in the bottom corner of a page detailing incantations for one of Anthea's experimental arrays. This entry was longer and took a while to translate. By the time I set my pencil down, my headache had increased significantly.

My eyes linger, sister, on a marvel unlike any other.

As I write these words, a son of Vh'alyir watches me. He is not beastly as I expected, and I confess I am surprised to find his form and visage pleasing to look upon.

Do you laugh at my foolishness? At times, I question my own wisdom, that I would trust this creature. You certainly doubt, Melitta, though his promises are sound and thus far, he has held our safety above all else.

I have not told you my promise to him. You are too young yet to understand, but an elder sister must walk harsh roads to protect her family.

I have two years still to tell you...two years before my soul is his.

To think I have set the final moment of my life makes my heart tremble, but if this astonishing, bold, regal Vh'alyir lord ensures your escape from the nightmare that has descended upon us...in that event, my dearest sister, I will go happily into the ether by his hand.

   – Myrrine Athanas

My pulse beat hard in my throat. Myrrine had successfully summoned a Twelfth House demon—and she'd promised him her soul. She'd chosen to end her life to protect her younger sister and keep the Athanas legacy alive.

She had been far braver than I could ever hope to be.

Though Myrrine had survived summoning a Vh'alyir, and even made a contract with him, she hadn't mentioned the grimoire's dire warning about the Twelfth House. Had she learned anything from the ancient *Dīnen*? Was the warning wrong, or had she not yet discovered why her predecessors had so feared the demons of Vh'alyir?

Turning on my stool, I studied the link chart on the coffee table with Claude in the center. Why did every new thing I learned create more questions?

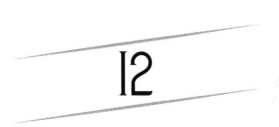

12

"I GIVE UP," I groaned, my cheek resting on my laptop keyboard. "It's not here. Someone deleted it."

"Don't be so dramatic." Amalia leaned a hip on the counter as she scooped a spoonful of yogurt into her mouth. "If Tori found the case, you can find it too."

"I've looked at every single case about demons, summoners, and demon mages from the last thirty years. I'm seeing case files in my sleep."

She scraped the last of the yogurt out of her bowl. "Or, like I suggested yesterday morning, you could just *ask* Tori."

I flopped back against the sofa cushions. "If I ask Tori, I might as well tell her friends too. Aaron and Kai think I'm a rogue traitor. You haven't seen the way they look at me—like I might sic Zylas on the whole guild any second."

She threw up her hands. "What do you want me to say? Either you ask Tori, you spend the next three months sifting through every single case in the archives, or we move to the Bahamas and forget Claude exists. Those are our options."

"Claude killed my parents," I said quietly. "I can't forget he exists."

"Then take a chance." She smoothed her hair. "How do I look?"

I glanced over her black skirt and mauve blouse. "Very professional. Where are you going?"

"Um … out. I'll tell you about it later." She grabbed her jacket and hoisted a tote bag over her shoulder. "See you in a few hours."

"Sure …" I muttered dubiously as she breezed out the apartment door and locked it behind her. She'd been going out for "errands" a lot lately, and I figured it had something to do with the obsessive amount of sewing she'd been doing when she was home. She'd fill me in when she was ready.

Yawning widely, I looked again at my laptop. The MPD's archive search tool stared back at me, mocking my lack of new ideas on how to find the case.

"Fine," I growled under my breath. Picking up my phone, I opened my contacts. I'd looked up Tori's number before our Odin's Eye meeting, but I'd never used it. Gulping, I hit the call button.

It rang in my ear, over and over. Just as I was about to hang up, the line clicked—and sound blared in my ear.

As I jerked the phone away from my face, a voice shouted furiously, "Twiggy, turn the TV down before I throw your green ass out the window!"

The background noise dropped. A clatter echoed across the line, then a puff of air into the mic. "Hello?"

"Tori?" I queried hesitantly.

"Who's this?"

"Robin."

"Oh. How are—*Don't you dare turn that up again!*" she suddenly shouted. "Wait until I'm off the phone. Geez! Sorry, Robin. Roommates, I tell ya."

She had a roommate named Twiggy? I shook my head. "I just have a quick question, if that's okay."

"Sure. What's up?"

"When we were meeting with Naim at Odin's Eye, you, um … you had some MPD cases in your folder. I noticed a photo in one, and I was wondering … could I get the case file?"

"Oh?" A rustle as though Tori were getting more comfortable. "Sure."

I relaxed. That'd been easier than—

"On one condition."

I tensed up all over again. "What condition?"

"You tell me what's special about that photo."

I scrambled for an explanation that wouldn't contradict the case details. "One of the men in the photo looked like the mythic who summoned my demon."

A pause. "It doesn't have anything to do with that ancient amulet thingy?"

"No."

"Hm. All right, give me a moment."

More rustling, followed by a thud and a muttered curse. "Sorry, I'm in the middle of packing and my place is a mess. I think I buried the folder."

"Are you moving?" I asked curiously.

"Huh? Oh, no, not that kind of packing. I'm going on a trip."

"Where to?"

A pause. "South."

That was specific.

"We're leaving soon, so I need to—" A louder thump as though something heavy had landed on the floor. "Shit. What was I ... right, the folder."

I hesitated, then asked, "Are you going with your friends? The mages?"

"Yeah," she replied distractedly. "Aha! Got it. Let's see ... it was a photo of two dudes, right?" Papers shuffled. "Here it is. Case 97-5923."

I scribbled that down on a sticky note. "Thank you."

"No problem. So, you think your demon's summoner is skeevy?"

"I *know* he's skeevy. Just not sure how much."

"Hope that case has some juicy details for you, then. Let me know if you need any help. I owe you one for taking me to see Naim."

"He wasn't any use."

"Yeah, but you still shared your lead with me." She was quiet for a moment. "Robin, can I ask you something?"

I straightened, surprised by the change in her tone from light to somber and intense. "Okay."

"That amulet. Do you know what it does?"

"No ... I'm trying to learn more about it."

"If you find out anything, will you tell me?"

"Have you seen it, Tori?" I pressed my phone into my ear. "Do you know where the amulet is?"

A long pause. "I have to go. I'll talk to you when I get back, okay?"

The line clicked as she ended the call. Lowering my cell, I looked up.

Zylas stood in my bedroom doorway, watching me with faintly glowing eyes. He wasn't wearing his armor, but he'd left the dark underlayers on—sleeves that partially covered his arms and matching pieces that ran from the arches of his feet up over his knees.

"Could you hear her?" I asked.

He nodded.

"Was she lying?"

"I cannot tell lies through the … *phone*."

I'd been afraid of that. Setting my cell aside, I typed "97-5923" into the MPD search bar and hit enter. The case popped up on the laptop screen, and as I read, Zylas sat on the sofa beside me. He withdrew a large book from under the coffee table and opened it at random.

Finishing my read of the case description, I scrolled down to the photos: the one showing Claude and the albino man talking; another shot of the albino man walking out of a Blockbuster; and a blurry photo of a black Ford pickup with an American license plate.

Zylas turned a page in his book. "Is it useful?"

"I have no idea, but at least I know why this case didn't come up in any of my searches. I was looking for something local, but this is a murder case from Oregon. That's—it's a place far away."

He pointed at his book. "It is a place in here?"

Yesterday, after visiting Zora at the healer's house—she hadn't regained consciousness yet, but Amalia and I had sat with her for an hour—I'd stopped at the bookstore on a mission to find a particular sort of book.

I couldn't remember much of my dream on Sunday morning, but the vague impression of an alien landscape had stuck with me. My world was an alien landscape for Zylas, yet he'd seen so little of it. He was curious about everything, but I couldn't jaunt off on vacation to show him more varied scenery.

Instead, I'd bought a copy of *The Big Book of Beautiful Landscapes*, which was exactly what it sounded like—the biggest, most gorgeous collection of full-spread landscape photography from around the world I could find.

"It might be." Scooting closer, I reached across him to flip the book to its index. "Let's see … United States – Oregon, page seventy-seven."

I turned to the indicated page, and we leaned over a stunning photo of a craggy mountain cradled by a winding river, the warm rocks and coniferous trees bathed in the pale orange light of a sunrise.

"That's Oregon," I informed him.

He tilted the book up, his weight shifting the cushions. I slipped into the depression, my hip bumping his.

"This is a good place," he decided.

Distracted over whether I should put space between us, I asked, "How do you know?"

"It has no *hh'ainun*." He canted his head, appraising it. "I like the shapes of the ground. Good cover. High and low places." He grinned and tapped the rugged mountain. "I would like to climb this."

"You can," I blurted without thinking the words through. "Well, maybe not that particular mountain, but if we have time while I'm figuring out how to send you home, I'll take you mountain climbing."

He weighed me with his gaze, as though testing my sincerity, then flipped through the book until he reached a dog-eared page—a habit he had *not* learned from me.

"What about here? Can we go here?"

My eyes widened at the exotic waterfall plunging down dark rocks, surrounded by lush greenery. I read the description in the corner. "The Amazon rainforest? That's *really* far away … but yes." I laughed, a little giddy. "Why not? We'll go there too."

A slow smile curved his lips. Realizing how close our faces were, I swallowed against the flush rising in my cheeks. Hastily looking down, I flipped to the next page to find a white-sand beach with palm trees and an aquamarine ocean.

"Fiji," I read.

He leaned in. "Is that water, *vayanin?* The blue?"

"Yes." Without intending it, I'd ended up squashed against his side, the book half resting on my lap, his warm arm pressed against mine. "It's the ocean, the same one as here."

"The color is different. I would like to see this too." He shifted toward me and I slid into him, catching myself on his chest. "Can we go to all these places?"

My hand was pressed to his warm skin, hard muscle beneath my palm. "I—it—that would take a lifetime," I stammered. "I thought you wanted to go home."

He looked down at the tropical vista, his smile gone. He snapped the book shut. "What did you learn about the *murder case from Oregon?*"

"Uh." Hastily pushing off him, I settled back on my cushion and tried to remember what I'd been doing. I picked up my laptop and squinted at the screen. "It happened twenty-two years ago. A nineteen-year-old girl, an apprentice sorceress, went missing. This is her."

I pointed to an ID-style photo of a young woman with a generous sprinkling of freckles over her nose and dark hair lightened with chunky blond streaks.

"The albino man was seen on security footage lurking around her workplace for a couple of weeks before she disappeared. He was named a suspect, but he disappeared before he could be identified or questioned.

"For this photo with Claude, the report says he was the last person the suspect spoke to before he vanished, but no one knew who he was either. There's only one other piece of evidence: three days before she disappeared, the girl reported to her GM that a demon with wings had followed her from her guild."

"A demon with wings?"

I nodded. "Seeing as a photo of Claude was taken shortly afterward, we can assume that demon was Nazhivēr." I skimmed the case details again. "The girl's guild had just begun to investigate the demon sighting when she went missing. None of the local contractors' demons had wings, and the guilds' only suspect dropped off the map the day after those photos were taken. They had no other leads."

Unable to link the demon sighting with the suspect, the case had been flagged with "Demonica – Contractor" and "Demonica – Summoner," which must have been why it'd ended up in Tori's collection of files.

As I scrolled back up the webpage, my gaze caught on a note at the bottom of the case description. "'Possible link to 97-5881 and 97-5770.'"

I opened two new tabs and pulled up those cases. "Two other missing women, a few months apart in the Portland area," I muttered as I skimmed the details. "No suspects or demon sightings for these ones, but the circumstances were similar. The girls vanished on their way home from work, and they were Arcana mythics."

The back of my neck prickled as I studied the women's photos. Both so young, twenty and twenty-two, one with black hair in a pixie cut and one with brown hair styled into crimped curls. Neither ever seen again.

"No information on the albino man," I said, an inexplicable bout of nerves tightening my gut. "Who knows if these are related to the first case?"

"Maybe yes, maybe no." Zylas stretched his legs out. "If the pale *hh'ainun* is *īnkavis*, he will kill over and over, many times."

"If he's what?"

"A killer who likes to give death."

A serial killer, or the demon equivalent. If the albino sorcerer had killed three young women twenty-two years ago, was he still at it now?

I opened a new archive tab and searched for unsolved missing women cases in the Vancouver area within the last six months. Only a few hits appeared and they didn't seem related. The women were neither young nor Arcana mythics.

"I'll have to do more research, I guess," I said gloomily, the prospect of reading up on murdered women holding little appeal. "But at least we know Claude and this sorcerer were up to no good twenty-two years ago. They must be up to something now too."

Abandoning my laptop, I rose to my feet, stretched, and headed over to the kitchen, craving a sweet snack. Unfortunately, Zylas had eaten all the cookies 'n' cream brownies I'd made yesterday—which was a shame, because they'd been delicious.

I investigated the fridge but found nothing appealing. As I closed it, I spotted a box tucked in the corner—chocolates Amalia had picked out for Zora. We'd decided to leave her flowers and a card instead, seeing as she might not be eating solid foods for a while, so the chocolates were fair game.

Feeling vaguely guilty, I ripped the plastic off.

"What is that?"

I jumped. Zylas stood behind me, looking over my shoulder.

"Chocolates," I told him. "I'm having a snack."

"Smells good."

I rolled my eyes. "I haven't even opened the box yet."

Squeezing past him—and out of the corner where I couldn't escape his hickory scent—I set the box on the breakfast bar and slid the lid off. Zylas hovered close as I lifted a card off the top, revealing the small delicacies underneath.

"*Hnn.*" He leaned over the counter. "So many?"

"They're all different." I referenced the card, which had a legend of flavors printed on the back, and selected an oval chocolate with a swirl on top. "This one has strawberry cream filling."

He took it, eyes gleaming at the prospect of trying new food.

"You have to chew it," I warned him. "All the flavor is in the middle."

He popped it in his mouth and bit down. He gave it several chews before swallowing.

I arched my eyebrows. "Good?"

"Sweet. Good. These are *all* different?"

Giggling at his wondering tone, I checked the legend again. Hmm. Did I dare?

I *did* dare. Picking out a square one, I offered it to him. "Licorice caramel. Try it."

He took the chocolate, peered at me suspiciously, then put it in his mouth. He chewed once, chewed again—

"*Guh!* Why did you give me this?"

I fought back a laugh. "Some people like licorice."

"Disgusting." His jaw worked. "It's in my teeth! What is this *zh'últis* food?"

As he swallowed with a grimace, my laughter broke free. He scowled, waiting while I regained my composure.

"Give me a good one, *vayanin*. More like the first."

"Okay, okay," I panted, wiping a tear from my eye. "How about … orange cream? That's like the first one."

I passed it to him. With another suspicious glare, he bit it in half. When it wasn't offensive, he tossed the second half in his mouth and chewed it up.

"Better."

"Now it's my turn." I perused my options, then chose a large oval chocolate. "Vanilla caramel! This will be good."

As I raised it to my lips, Zylas leaned in, his chest brushing against my shoulder. "But *vayanin*, you said each one is different."

"Yes."

"I want to try it."

"There's only one."

His scowl returned. "You can eat these again sometime, *na*? There is nothing like this in my world."

"Are you guilt-tripping me?"

"I do not know that word."

I tried to frown but just laughed again. The big bad demon, pouting that he wouldn't get to try *every* flavor of chocolate. More giggles built up in my throat.

"Okay, I'll have half, and you can have the other half." Snickering at his immediate nod of agreement, I bit into the chocolate.

Liquid caramel spilled over my fingers.

"Mm!" I exclaimed, trying to catch the escaping filling. "Here!"

As caramel ran everywhere, I stuffed the chocolate in his mouth. My fingertips pressed against his lips—and I realized what I'd done. I snatched my hand back, my cheeks burning with instant heat.

Zylas stared at me, eyes wide and shocked as though he couldn't believe what I'd done. His throat moved in a slow flex as he swallowed the messy chocolate.

His tongue slid across his lower lip, running over a smear of caramel. "*Vayanin?*"

Was his voice huskier than usual? No, I was imagining it.

"Um. I … uh …" I wrenched my gaze off him and looked at my sticky fingertips. "That wasn't … I mean …"

With no idea what I intended to say, I gave up and faced the sink.

He caught my wrist. His other hand closed over my elbow, and he drew my hand up. His warm breath brushed over my skin, and my heart stalled, the air locking in my lungs.

He held my fingers close to his lips, his eyes on me, watching, weighing … deciding. A long moment passed where he didn't move, where I didn't breathe—then he closed his mouth over my fingertips.

My heart restarted with a frantic leap directly into my ribcage.

He licked, or sucked, or … something … the caramel off my fingers, and all thought vanished as sensations bombarded my brain. His hot tongue against my skin. The brush of sharp, predatory teeth. The dizzying swoop deep in my center.

His eyes gleamed—different, darker. His pupils were dilated, pronounced against the glowing crimson. Pulling my fingers from his mouth, he turned my wrist and ran his tongue up my thumb, licking away a final drip of caramel. His pointed canines pressed against the pad of my thumb, pinching gently as his stare pierced me, searching, seeking ...

I stared back at him, heart trembling at the base of my throat.

Hand tightening on my elbow, he pulled me closer—closer to his heat, to those eyes holding me hostage. My socked feet slid across the linoleum, the sudden movement jarring my brain back into gear—and I jerked away.

My hand tore from his grasp. A wild breath rushed through my lungs, my stunned gaze flashing across his face. The room was spinning.

I was going to faint. No—*no*. I wouldn't faint. I just needed to breathe.

Or better yet, run.

I bolted out of the kitchen and slammed through my bedroom door. It hit the wall as I ran to my bed and stopped, breathing hard. My heart careened through my chest as I stared at my hand.

His tongue sliding across my fingertips.

Sucking in air, I faced the doorway, half expecting him to burst in and yell at me for being a stupid *hh'ainun*. A minute dragged past. He didn't appear.

I crept to the open door. Holding my breath, I peeked out.

He stood at the counter, staring down at the box of chocolates, the fluorescent lights casting harsh shadows over his face. After a long moment, he lifted a hand and touched the edge of the box.

His tail slashed sideways—and he shoved the chocolates off the counter. They crashed to the floor, the small delicacies scattering over the linoleum.

13

A BELL JINGLED CHEERFULLY as I opened the pub door. A dozen guild members were scattered around the tables—more than I'd expected for a Wednesday afternoon. The mood was relaxed, but with a worried undertone. Though the threat to the guild had passed, not everyone was out of danger. No one would rest easy until all injured members, including Zora, had recovered.

As I unzipped my leather coat, I scanned the bar. A man in his twenties with greasy, chin-length hair was half-heartedly scrubbing the counter. Tori usually worked weeknights, and since she wasn't here, I assumed she'd left on her "trip" with the three mages.

Nibbling my lower lip, I traipsed to the second level. The guild's large workroom occupied the same footprint as the pub downstairs. Long worktables filled most of the space, with computer kiosks on one side, cupboards on the opposite side, and bookshelves along the back.

A large screen displayed a scrolling list of MPD notices and new bounties as I headed for the back corner. Only a few people were in the room, all focused on their work. I recognized a young woman, surrounded by textbooks, as the guild's apprentice healer, Sanjana.

Slinging my jacket over the back of a chair, I pulled my laptop out of my bag. It took me almost ten minutes to connect to the printer in the corner, but finally, the machine whirred to life. Pages pumped out one after another—cases for all the missing mythic women from Portland and Vancouver over the last twenty years.

It was probably stupid, but I was hoping that looking at physical pages rather than a screen would help me figure something out. The change of scenery didn't hurt either—especially since, here, Zylas had to stay in the infernus.

Not that avoiding my demon had *anything* to do with my new desire to work outside the apartment.

I sent three more files to the printer—the case Tori had given me and the two linked ones. Crossing to the corner, I gathered my stack of papers off the printer tray and waited for the final pages to spit out.

With a grinding sound, the printer jammed.

"No," I groaned under my breath. I leaned from side to side, examining the machine, then looked helplessly toward the other end of the room where the others were working.

"Need help?"

At the smooth, unfamiliar male voice, I smiled in relief. "Yes, please. I have no idea how to …"

My mouth sagged open, words forgotten as I stared up at the man beside me. Six feet tall, messy brown curls, bronze skin, and a white scar running from his temple down to the hollow of his left cheek. His right eye was chocolate brown, but his left, the scarred one, was pale white with a distinct limbal ring defining the colorless iris. The asymmetry was disconcerting.

"Ezra," I gasped.

He smiled. "Hi."

I inched backward, trying to think of a good excuse to flee. He stepped into the spot I'd vacated and opened the printer's side panel. He stuck his hand into the machine's innards, prodding different bits and bobs.

He tugged, and with a rasping sound, the page came free. He smoothed it out. "You might need to print it again."

I nervously took the paper—the photo of young Claude and the albino sorcerer. A bit crumpled, but good enough.

"This is fine. Thank you." Clutching my printouts, I ducked away from him and hurried back to my chair. As I set the papers on the tabletop, a shadow cut across the light.

Ezra pulled a chair over and sat beside me.

Steadying my breathing, I flattened the crumpled page on top of the pile. "Um … is Tori around?"

The fiery bartender was rarely far from her friends, and if I could steer Ezra back to her, I could sneak out and go back home. What had I been thinking, coming here to work?

"Tori's out of town." He propped his chin on his hand. "Zora sent me an email on Saturday night."

Oh, right. The email. I considered prodding him about where Tori was and why he wasn't with her, but instead, I asked, "What did Zora's email say?"

"That you had information for me. Something about a rogue summoner?"

My blood rushed in my ears, nervous indecision pulling my thoughts in every direction. Though I had no real evidence, the fact that Claude had printed out Ezra's profile suggested the aeromage was the source of the demon scent Zylas kept detecting. I didn't want to involve him in anything I was doing.

But he was here, he was asking, and he might know something about Claude.

"I'm investigating the summoner behind the escaped demon on Halloween," I told him, tweaking the truth. "While searching his house, I found a copy of your MPD profile near his desk."

"My profile?" His face gave nothing away, as unreadable as Zylas's when he locked down his thoughts. "Hm."

"Does the name Claude Mercier mean anything to you?"

"No. Do you have a photo of him?"

I smoothed the crumpled page. "This man. The photo is from 1997."

He squinted at the page, the dark ink marred by white crinkles. "I don't think I know him, but it isn't a good photo." He waved at the stack. "What's all this?"

I blew my bangs off my face, wishing Zylas was out of the infernus to play lie detector for me. "I think Claude made a deal with Varvara. On Saturday night, I encountered this man"—I pointed to the albino sorcerer—"with one of Varvara's golems, and he seems to be Claude's minion."

Ezra listened attentively as I explained the case of the murdered girl who'd been stalked by a demon, as well as the other two missing girls who may have been targeted by the same killer.

"So," I concluded, "I'm looking for similar cases of missing girls, either here in Vancouver or in Portland, that could be linked to this sorcerer in the hopes they'll lead me to him, and that he'll lead me to Claude.."

"In Portland ..." Ezra mused. He turned the photo of Claude and the albino man toward me. "Varvara Nikolaev, a rogue summoner, and a possible serial killer is a dangerous combination. I think you're right that the albino sorcerer is the one to focus on first."

I nodded uncertainly.

"Do you want some help?"

"H-help?"

"Aaron, Kai, and I earn our paychecks with bounty work. We've conducted more investigations like this than I can count."

I blinked. This guy had some sort of terrible Demonica secret, didn't he? Why would he want to work with me? What was he after?

Pulling the original missing women cases closer, he reviewed them carefully, then arranged the pages in a row. He gestured to the photos of the three missing girls. "Notice anything?"

I looked from one to the other. "They're all Arcana. They're also young and pretty."

"With dark hair," he pointed out. "And petite. The tallest one is five-foot-two."

"Oh ... you're right."

"Know who else is a young, pretty, petite girl with dark hair?"

"Who?"

"You."

Ice plunged through my gut. "He said ... the sorcerer told me ... 'You have the look.'"

"You're his type." He split the stack of cases in half. "Let's see if any of these women are also his type."

It took us two hours to sort through all the cases, but we only found a handful where the missing women matched the sorcerer's preferences, and they were of no use. They'd all been solved—the women found or their killers caught.

"Nothing," I sighed.

Ezra leaned back in his chair and rubbed the scruff darkening his jaw. "The suspect disappeared two decades ago when guilds started investigating. Maybe he learned his lesson and changed his MO."

"Based on what he said to me, I don't think he's changed his … tastes."

"No, but maybe he doesn't require a specific mythic class … or even a mythic." He pushed his chair back. "Come on."

I followed him out of the workroom and up the stairs to the large office with the guild officers' desks. He tapped on the open door as he walked in.

Felix, the third officer, looked up from his monitor. Dark circles smudged the skin under his eyes, his goatee was muddled from several days without maintenance, and his blond hair was tangled.

My gut clenched with guilt. Felix was Zora's husband. He probably hadn't slept properly since she'd been injured.

"Felix," Ezra said with a frown. "You're working tonight?"

"Darius offered to take my shifts, but I—I needed a distraction." He took a long drink from his coffee mug. "What can I help you with?"

"How is Zora?" I asked softly.

A faint smile lightened the exhaustion on his face. "Better. She's awake on and off now. She asked about you. She was worried."

"Oh, I'm so glad!" I rushed to his desk. "Can I see her? Can I bring her anything? What can I—"

"She needs a lot of sleep. I'll let you know when she's up for visitors." He sat back. "What do you need?"

Biting my lip, I glanced at Ezra.

"Can you run a Vancouver PD search for us? Missing women under thirty, five and a half feet or shorter, with dark hair."

Felix jotted that down. "Date range?"

"Last six months."

"Sure. Give me a few minutes."

As he typed rapidly on his keyboard, I shifted closer to Ezra and whispered, "You think the sorcerer could be targeting human women?"

"The mythic community is tiny. We don't sit around when someone goes missing, and a dozen guilds combing the city for a killer makes it really hard to get away with anything. He might've switched to easier victims."

As we waited, I surreptitiously peered from the aeromage to the guild officer and back. I hadn't noticed it until seeing Felix's weariness, but Ezra also had an air of exhaustion clinging to him. Though his warm complexion disguised the dark circles under his eyes, he had the look of someone who needed a lot more sleep.

Felix typed for a minute more, then the printer beside his desk whirred to life. A dozen pages spat onto the tray.

"There you go. Let me know if you need anything else."

"Will do." Ezra collected the pages. "Get some rest, Felix."

We returned to our worktable and spread the pages out. Six women. Three had gone missing last year, and the police had clear suspects—a boyfriend, a mother-in-law, and a pimp. The other three …

"Reported missing January third," I read off the first one. "Reported missing January eleventh. Reported missing January eighteenth."

"Last Friday," Ezra murmured.

"No bodies. No suspects. Disappeared on their way home." I looked up at him. "It must be the sorcerer. He's killed *three times* just this month?"

"I suspect that means he only arrived in town this month. If we check the Portland police database, we'll probably find more cases like this."

I shuddered. "He needs to be stopped."

Ezra slid the most recent disappearance in front of me. "This one is our best shot."

"Our best shot at what?"

"At finding the sorcerer. Are you busy tomorrow?"

"No …"

"Meet me here at nine a.m. and we'll get started." He tapped the page. "Her workplace first. We know what this guy looks like, which gives us an advantage the police don't have. Someone must've seen the sorcerer scoping out the girl."

"Right. Okay." My brows pinched together. "What about Claude and his printout about you?"

He got to his feet. "Find one and we might find the other. See you tomorrow."

"Sure."

Crossing the room, he angled toward the stairs. Just before stepping out of sight, he glanced back. Our gazes met, and I shivered. His eyes were eerily expressionless, hiding his thoughts, but their intensity reminded me of a viper staring down its prey right before it struck.

He disappeared down the stairs, and I let out an explosive breath. Ezra Rowe, the Crow and Hammer mythic I most wanted to avoid, was now helping me find the albino sorcerer. On the plus side, he knew way more about investigating killers than I did.

On the downside, he was likely concealing a secret as dangerous as mine.

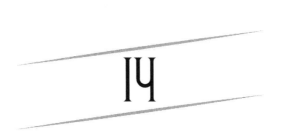

14

TALKING TO STRANGERS was exhausting. I'd never had a stronger desire to live in the middle of a forest a thousand miles from another human being.

Bundled in my jacket and a sunshine-yellow scarf, I followed Ezra down the sidewalk. We'd spent the morning impersonating private investigators at the café where Yana Deneva had worked before disappearing a week ago. We'd asked her coworkers, and almost every customer who came in, when they'd last seen her and if they'd noticed an albino man.

Results: nothing. No one had seen the albino man. He must've gotten better at scoping his victims—or he hadn't gone to her workplace.

I puffed out a breath and extended my stride to keep up with Ezra as we ascended the steps of an old four-story building with lots of windows. The lime-green sign above the entrance read, "Vancouver Community College."

"Tori is taking classes here," Ezra remarked as he opened the door. "Maybe it's a good thing she's away."

"She'd be safe, though." I patted the front of my jacket, absently checking for my infernus. "She isn't the sorcerer's type."

"No, but the moment she learned a mythic was kidnapping and murdering young women from her neighborhood, she wouldn't sleep until she personally kicked him face-first into the ground."

I could see that. "Have you talked to her since she left?"

"No." He looked away, speaking so quietly he couldn't have intended for me to hear his next words. "I don't want to talk to her."

A cluster of chatting college students traipsed past, carrying large portfolio bags over their shoulders. Ezra adjusted his black beanie, untidy curls sticking out from beneath its knitted edge, and checked our info sheet on the victim.

"Yana was a theater student." He looked around. "This way, I think."

A few minutes later, we found ourselves standing at the back of a black-box theater room with tiered seating for a hundred people. A handful of students sat in the front row, and an older woman with her hair in a messy blond bun—the instructor, I assumed—stood in front of the stage. A young man paced back and forth, speaking passionately in iambic pentameter to his female costar.

"*Romeo and Juliet*," I realized.

"They aren't in costume," Ezra noted, "but we should probably wait for their rehearsal to finish."

Relieved he didn't plan to burst in on the performance, I sidled into the nearest row and dropped onto the second seat.

Ezra took the one beside me. Sighing with relief to be off my feet, I stretched my legs out.

He watched the stage, his expression guarding his thoughts. Despite having spent the better part of a day in his company, I couldn't get a read on him. I had no idea what kind of person he was—but I'd gotten a few more glimpses of his viper stare, and each time it unnerved me more than the last.

I turned my focus to the performance. Yana should have been here with the other students. What had her role been? The ineffective Lady Capulet? The Nurse, Juliet's confidant? Fragile Lady Montague? Or had she played naïve, tragic Juliet?

"Do you think Yana is dead?" I asked softly.

"We don't know what the sorcerer does with his victims," Ezra said heavily, "but it's been almost a week. I don't think her chances are good."

My shoulders slumped.

"We'll find him," he promised. "If you and I don't manage it, we'll get the others to help once they're back."

"When are they returning?"

"I don't know."

Brow furrowing, I blurted without thinking, "Aren't you all best friends?"

He looked at me with that cold stare, saying nothing. My face flushed and I hastily focused on the stage—a mistake, for Romeo had just drawn Juliet close.

"Then move not," he breathed, "while my prayer's effect I take."

He lowered his head and their lips met in a kiss somehow chaste and burning with passion at the same time. He lifted his mouth, staring besotted into Juliet's face.

"Thus from my lips, by thine, my sin is purged."

Juliet leaned into him, her chin tilted up. "Then have my lips the sin that they have took."

"Sin from thy lips? O trespass sweetly urged!" Romeo exclaimed with a roguish smile. "Give me my sin again."

His lips met hers a second time, and their kiss deepened—fervor overtaking chaste reserve. A kiss between forbidden lovers. The sin of their passion, shared by both.

I dropped my gaze to my lap, my heart beating strangely fast and my body flushed with heat. What was wrong with me?

The instructor called a stop, and when I looked up, the woman was ascending the stairs toward us. Ezra rose to his feet, and I followed him into the aisle.

"How can I help you?" the instructor asked.

"Ezra Rowe," he said in a professional tone. "And my partner, Robin Page. We're private investigators looking into Yana Deneva's disappearance. Would—"

"Disappearance?" The woman's jaw trembled. "Don't you mean murder?"

"I'm sorry?"

"Her murder! Her body was found this morning. What sort of investigators wouldn't know that already?"

Her body? I went cold all over.

"We are aware," Ezra lied smoothly. "However, we didn't want to be insensitive in case you didn't know."

"Oh." She sniffed wetly. "The faculty knows—they told us so we wouldn't find out on the evening news tonight. Yana was such a personality—perfect for the stage. She …" Another sniff. "What do you need?"

I tugged the sorcerer's photo out of my pocket. "Have you ever seen this man?"

The instructor squinted at it. "Does he have albinism? There was a pale blond man at our last performance of *The Glass Menagerie*, the Wednesday before last. He sat in the front row."

"Is this the same man?"

She gave the photo another assessment. "It could be, but I thought he was older … I'm sorry. I can't be certain."

Ezra and I asked her a few more questions, but she had nothing else to share. Thanking her for her time, we left the theater room and hurried out of the school.

Back on the sidewalk, I stuffed my hands in my pockets to hide their slight tremble. "Yana is dead."

Ezra slid his phone out of his pocket. "I'll have Felix get the location where her body was found, but we won't be able to get near it today. We'll need to wait for the police to finish with the crime scene."

"Will you send me the location as soon as you have it?"

His gaze flicked to mine, his hesitation so slight I might've imagined it. "Sure. Until then …"

Until then, there was nothing we could do. We had no leads aside from the possibility that the sorcerer had attended a play.

"Keep me posted," I said.

"I will." With a wave, he walked away.

I watched him go, my skin prickling with inexplicable dread.

"THREE," I SAID, "two, one. *Luce!*"

"*Luce*," Zylas said with me.

The cantrip, drawn in his glowing red magic, didn't react. Our palms were pressed together, our fingers linked, but at the simultaneous incantations, nothing happened.

I dropped my hand into my lap. The faint crimson glow veining his wrist faded, and the cantrip disappeared.

"Why won't it work?" I huffed. "We've shared magic twice before."

He shrugged. "Times of battle are different."

"But we couldn't do it a few days ago and that was in battle." I tucked my hair behind my ears. "We should try again."

"Why? We have tried many times." He gave me a hard look. "Or do you think my magic is not enough?"

"Your magic is extremely powerful and you know it. But combining our magic ... that could be *more* powerful. That's how we defeated Vasilii, and we can use it against Nazhivēr too."

He grunted.

I studied the demon sitting cross-legged on the opposite side of the coffee table. Socks was crouched beside the TV stand, watching the barbed end of his tail twitch with her ears perked.

Yesterday's incident with the chocolates lurked in the back of my thoughts, refusing to be forgotten. Feeding him had meant something—something more than merely *sharing* food—but I wasn't sure what. His reaction ...

I gulped. His reaction had been instant. The way he'd reached for me, the way he'd drawn my fingers to his mouth—my cheeks flushed at the memory—but he'd also been uncertain, seeking something from me. I couldn't imagine what. His thoughts, the mysterious workings of his mind, were like a siren call I couldn't resist. I needed to know, except—

Except I couldn't even *imagine* asking detailed questions, let alone bringing it up again. Especially since bringing it up might lead to ... could trigger ... he might think ...

My heart started to hammer again, just as it had when he'd first slipped my fingertips between his lips.

Shaking my head jerkily, I refocused. "Sharing our magic isn't working because I can't hear your thoughts. We need that connection for it to work, I'm sure of it."

He wrinkled his nose.

"Is letting me into your head that big of a deal? You can hear loads of my thoughts."

"But not everything. You hide more than you share."

I leaned across the table. "Don't you want to unlock this power? Using my cantrips with your magic could be the advantage we need to defeat Nazhivēr."

His grimace deepened.

"Will you try, Zylas? Please?"

Grumbling, he braced his elbows on the table. "I will try."

Excitement flashed through me, fueled by more than my desire to recapture the power of our shared magic. I wanted to taste his mysterious mind and hear his agile thoughts. One brief glimpse hadn't been enough. I wanted to get inside his brain and figure out what made him tick.

Wariness cooled his eyes as he extended his hand across the table. I eagerly grasped his warm palm, and his fingers curled around mine.

"What do I need to do?" I demanded.

His tail snapped against the floor. "Listen."

I scowled. "What do you think I've been trying to do for two weeks?"

"Try again."

Settling more comfortably on the floor, I gazed into his eyes, straining to hear his inner voice. The seconds stretched into a full minute.

"I can't hear anything."

"You are bad at listening."

"You aren't telling me what to do!" I growled. "I need better instructions. How do you hear me?"

"It is easy. Your thoughts are there, like you are speaking in my ear."

"Are you thinking things at me right now?"

His eyes narrowed. He stared at me silently.

I huffed. "What am I doing wrong? You said before that I could *always* hear your thoughts."

"That is what I thought, because you had not tried to listen."

"I'm listening now, but it isn't working."

Jaw tightening, he wrapped both hands around mine and again stared into my eyes. I could practically see him shouting thoughts at me, but I heard only silence.

My shoulders slumped. "Why won't it work? Why am I so bad at this?"

He dropped my hand and shoved to his feet. "Forget this, *vayanin*. My magic is good. I will find *dh'ērrenith*."

I drooped further at the frustrated snap in his voice. He was angry at me for failing. "I'm sorry."

He paced across the room with his tail lashing, and I curled inward, familiar feelings of inadequacy piling up inside me. We needed this to work, needed every advantage we could get, and I was screwing it up.

"I'll keep trying," I told the tabletop. "Is there anything else I can do to—"

Near-silent footsteps stalked in my direction. Zylas stopped and glowered down at me, as though I'd just insulted him, then dropped to his knees and took hold of my head.

He pushed his face into the side of my neck.

I froze, my pulse drumming wildly. A tiny part of me panicked, wanting to tear free of his hold. The rest of me was too focused on the strength of his hands, his hot breath teasing my throat, and his hickory scent in my nose. *That* part of me didn't want to move at all—and didn't want him to move either.

"*Vayanin.*"

His voice was a whispering rumble. I could feel his lips moving against my skin, and my core swooped with heat.

"Why," he asked in that quiet tone, "does your skin change color?"

For a second, his question didn't compute.

"*What?*" I burst out, instantly angry. I tried to push away from him. "That *again?* Why do you keep—"

His grip on my head tightened, his face hidden against my neck. "Tell me."

"Why are you so obsessed with that? This is *important*, Zylas. We're beyond ill-equipped to fight a demon like Nazhivēr, and—"

"I need to know this, *vayanin.*"

"No, you don't. It has nothing to do with Nazhivēr or Claude or magic or *anything.*"

A long moment of silence, his breath warming the thudding pulse in my throat. "But it has something to do with me."

Tension stiffened my back. "It isn't important, Zylas."

Again, he was quiet for several slow exhalations. "That is not a lie, but it is not truth."

He opened his hands. Pushing away, he turned his back to me and sat on the floor, silent.

I struggled to pull myself and my thoughts together. "Zylas … is this related to me hearing your thoughts?"

"I hear what you want me to hear. I do not hear what you are afraid to show me."

A prickle ran over my skin as I stared at the back of his head, small horns poking through his tangled black hair. A tearing sound dragged my attention down. He'd sunk his claws into the carpet.

"That is why my thoughts are silent to you."

My brow furrowed. "I don't understand."

"I tried. I can't."

"Can't what?"

"Let you hear me."

It took me a moment to figure it out. A sharp, disbelieving inhale caught in my throat. "You ... I can't hear you because you won't *let* me?"

The back of his head moved in a nod.

My mouth hung open. At least it wasn't my fault, but ... "Zylas, we need this to work."

"I know," he snarled. "I tried."

"Well, try harder, then!"

"I did!" He whirled around, crouched on the balls of his feet, teeth bared. "I tried, but *need* does not make all things happen."

"If you tried and it didn't work, then why not?"

"Do you *decide* to hide thoughts from me?"

"No. I didn't realize I was doing it until you told me." I pushed my bangs away from my eyes, not understanding why his temper was so cutting. "Do you know *why* you're blocking me out?"

His upper lip curled. "Why does your face change color?"

"Zylas!" I yelled furiously. "This is serious!"

"I am serious."

"I *told* you, that isn't important—"

"You hide too much." He stood, towering above me. Cold red eyes stared down. "When you think of me, your mind is silent. When I ask, you refuse to speak. You say it is not important, but untruth creeps in your meaning. All deep, important thoughts about me are hidden in your mind."

My mouth opened, but I didn't know what to say.

"I trust you in many things." His voice dropped, huskier—and more dangerous. "I do not trust you with my everything. I do not trust you with my mind and thoughts and all things I feel and know and wonder. Not you who hides so much from me."

"But … but it's not …"

Not important. Except his preternatural ability to detect lies told him I was not being entirely honest.

"It worked before," I whispered. "You trusted me once."

He stared down at me, then turned away. "I will find a different way to defeat Nazhivēr."

No arguments sprung to mind as he disappeared into my bedroom. No simple solutions manifested as I sat alone on the living room floor, waiting for him to return.

He didn't trust me. He couldn't open his mind to me.

His persistent questions about my face changing color had seemed so frivolous—just another way to annoy and embarrass me. I'd never considered that it was important to him. That he needed to understand. That he was searching for an insight, however small and insignificant, into what I thought of him.

But I'd locked all those thoughts away, and as a demon conditioned by a lifetime of violence to mistrust everyone, he couldn't abide my secrets. He would only open up to me if I opened myself up to him first—all my secret, private thoughts bared to his scrutiny.

And that … that was *never* happening.

15

CHEWING ON THE END of my pencil, I studied the translation I'd just finished. My face was warm, my heart pulsing slow and hard against my ribs.

I'd pored over fifty pages to find Myrrine's third journal entry. Based on the amount of grimoire she'd recopied before this addition, I assumed weeks or even months had passed since her account of successfully summoning a Vh'alyir demon. Her new entry—so long she'd dedicated a full page to it—seemed to confirm that some time had passed.

But that wasn't the part that had triggered the flush heating my neck.

> I am losing myself, sister.
> Some days, I think I have never been so whole, so alive. Never have I felt this safe. Never have I felt this protected. Never have I felt such freedom from fear.

My Vh'alyir is ruthless. He is power and cunning and strength, and he commits it all to our safety. But he is so much more.

The questions he asks me, sister! Curious as a child, he wants to know everything. The conversations we have, about our world and his, fuel my wit and grip my imagination, but sympathy wells in my bosom as well. The violence he has known, so great the terrors of my life seem mild to him, makes me ache.

Last night he told me of the ferocious battles between demon males. Rivals fight to the death, all for the honor of passing on their seed—of breeding and raising warrior sons to continue the battle.

I asked him, Does it not seem pointless?

He looked at me with sadness, with a resigned heart, and asked, What else is there?

And sister, this is where I wonder if my mind slips, for the urge to comfort him was so strong. I know he is powerful, yet he is no beast. His conformation is well matched with a human man, his countenance is fair, and his physique...here I sigh, for his physique is magnificent. Am I mad to long to touch him?

Am I mad to see beauty in this demon?

Am I mad to want more?

Perhaps where my madness truly lies is in this urge to put my unseemly yearnings to the page. Do not judge me harshly, sister, for I dare not share this confusion even with you. I can only pray that sense returns to me before I fall any deeper.

— Myrrine Athanas

My gaze roved across my careful printing, then to the grimoire. Myrrine hadn't written the words on its pages with her own hand, but I couldn't help imagining a reed pen in her slim fingers, the tip scratching across rough paper in fits and starts as she penned questions that would go unanswered in her lifetime—questions that had probably never been answered.

μαίνομαι ποθοῦσα αὐτοῦ θιγγάνειν
Am I mad to long to touch him?

μαίνομαι ὁρῶσα ἐν τούτῳ τῷ δαίμονι τὸ καλόν
Am I mad to see beauty in this demon?

μαίνομαι πλείω θέλουσα
Am I mad to want more?

I slid my fingers to her first line, her opening fear written boldly—*I am losing myself.* Myrrine would never know how much empathy I felt for her through those four words.

A heavy weight grew in my chest as I shuffled my mother's notes, her pages sitting beside my own. If fate had played out differently, Mom and I would have translated this together. I could imagine how we would have gasped and tittered after the initial translation, shocked that our ancestor thought she might be in love with a *demon*.

Once the surprise had passed, we would've discussed Myrrine's thoughts. Was her confused yearning for a deeper connection with the demon genuine, or was it misplaced gratitude for the safety he provided? Was she attracted to the demon or merely drawn to his strength? Had she been losing her mind, or was she simply a lonely girl carrying too many burdens and aching for affection?

We would've dissected each sentence for clues. I would've pointed out that Myrrine had known the direction of her thoughts was unhealthy—she'd questioned her sanity, called her feelings "unseemly yearnings," and prayed she'd return to her senses.

I could hear my mother's reply, her sunny outlook shining through no matter the scenario.

"*But look here, little bird,*" she would've murmured, pointing at the page. "*What about this? 'I have never been so whole, so alive.' And here, 'The conversations we have fuel my wit and grip my imagination.' Myrrine might've questioned her feelings, but that doesn't mean her feelings weren't real.*"

"*But a demon, Mom?*" I would've replied, exasperated. "*She was a bit infatuated, maybe, but a few moments of attraction don't mean anything. No one could fall in love with a demon, not for real.*"

I imagined how Mom would've laughed fondly and tweaked my hair. "*Maybe she couldn't help herself. It sounds like he was one hot demon.*"

Her imagined voice made my cheeks ache. How could a smile hurt so much? How could I smile through tears like this?

I banished the fantasy, angry with myself for letting my thoughts wander in such painful directions, and packed up the grimoire, my notebook, and my mother's notes into a neat pile on the breakfast bar. Returning them to their protective case was the next step, but the case was in my bedroom.

And in my bedroom was my demon.

He'd avoided me all evening, and I hadn't seen him since I'd gotten the grimoire out several hours ago. The trust between us was crumbling so fast, and I couldn't stop the breakdown. What was holding him back? Was he afraid of what I might be hiding?

Or was he afraid of what I might discover in *his* head?

I'd thought giving him the grimoire would show him that my intentions were pure, and I didn't know how much more I was willing to give. Letting him all the way in my head … letting him dig deep into every dumb thought and silly whimsy and … and … and *unseemly yearning* that'd ever crossed my mind …

No. No way. Trust didn't—shouldn't—require a complete sacrifice of personal privacy. I'd find a different way, a *better* way to rebuild our trust.

My phone chimed, startling me. I felt around my pockets, then checked under scrap papers and reference books until I found my phone. A text message waited, and the sender's name sent a chill down the back of my neck: Ezra Rowe.

I opened the message and frowned at the short compilation of words. *Vernon Dr under E 1st Ave overpass.*

An address? Sort of? Bullying my brain into focusing, I thought back to our last conversation—and realized what it must be.

"The crime scene!" I gasped, shoving my stool back from the counter. That address was the location where Yana Deneva's body had been found, which Ezra had promised to send me.

I scooped up the grimoire and my notes and turned toward my bedroom. Ezra had said we needed to wait until the police were done with the crime scene, but I had no intention of sitting around when there was a quick, easy way to determine whether the albino sorcerer had been there.

All I had to do was get Zylas close enough to use his nose.

VERNON STREET was not a good place for a woman to walk alone at night.

I kept one hand on my infernus as I hurried down the center of the road, eyes darting side to side. Most of the streetlamps were broken, and I navigated by the lights of the major thoroughfare that arched across Vernon Street. To my right was a dodgy repair shop with old vehicles parked three deep in the front, and on my left was a corrugated steel fence covered in graffiti and gang tags.

Not a safe place to walk at all.

Despite the late hour, traffic zoomed along the overpass, headlights flashing by. Reaching the steel and concrete bridge, I stopped to crane my neck back, grimacing at the roar of engines and tires echoing off the pavement. Beneath the overpass, it was even darker, and I squinted nervously.

On one side, the space under the bridge was fairly open, my line of sight interrupted only by the concrete supports. On the opposite side, a windowless three-story building and a copse of trees hemmed in the dark gap.

As the cold breeze tugged at my leather jacket, I spotted a fluttering strip of yellow in the darkness—police tape. I'd found the right spot.

A chain-link fence blocked my way, but I found a wide gate that allowed vehicles access to the neighboring building. No lock, so I pushed it open enough to squeeze through.

Someone was using the space beneath the raised road to store massive tractor tires, and I wound between stacks of rubber before halting at the line of police tape, my stomach aching and sick. Traffic roared overhead, the echoing clamor obliterating all noises of my approach—just as it would've muffled Yana's calls for help, if she'd cried out. It was so dark back here, the stacks of tires and heavy concrete supports cutting off the view from Vernon Street.

It was a dark, hidden hole. Easy to access, easy to escape, difficult to spot.

Lifting the police tape with a gloved hand, I stepped onto the crime scene.

Fifty yards from the road, the gap beneath the overpass ended in a concrete wall where Yana had died. Her body was gone, but it wasn't dark enough to hide the bloodstains.

Forcing my horrified stare away from the wall and Yana's dried blood, I glanced around one more time. Footprints and other tracks disturbed the dirt where a forensic team had gathered evidence, but otherwise, the spot was devoid of any signs of life.

The killer had chosen the location well. No one from the street or neighboring buildings—if anyone was even around this late—would see me, just as they hadn't seen a murder taking place yards from their workplaces.

Zylas, I whispered inside my head.

Red light flared over the infernus, then streaked toward the ground. My demon took form, fully armored and eyes already narrowed as his gaze swept his new location—analyzing everything from the terrain to escape routes to signs of danger.

"It is loud." His nose wrinkled. "And it stinks."

I twisted my hands together. "Can you smell the sorcerer?"

He canted his head, nostrils flaring, then sank into a crouch to sniff unenthusiastically at the ground. Grumbling complaints, he moved closer to the bloodstains and inhaled again.

"I smell …" His head snapped back, eyes blazing as he looked up into the steel crossbeams that supported the overpass.

His lips curled in a silent snarl. His claws unsheathed and power snaked up his hands and over his wrists.

A shadow moved: the shape of a man uncoiling from the darkest nook.

As crimson light washed over the steel beams, the man dropped to the ground. He landed with a near soundless thud, air swirling out from his feet, and straightened, his attention locked on Zylas.

I stared at the man, my body cold. "Ezra?"

His eyes, one dark and one pale, focused on me. He was dressed for combat, with a pair of long, fingerless gloves running from his hands to upper arms, the knuckles and elbows studded with shiny steel. "Robin."

"You …" I swallowed hard. "What are you doing here?"

"Waiting for you."

I'd been afraid of that. "Is this actually the crime scene?"

"Yes." He began to move—his steps slow, prowling, graceful. His attention returned to Zylas, unflinching despite the power crawling up the demon's arms. "Well? Is the sorcerer's scent here or not?"

"Smell for it yourself," Zylas growled as frost spread in a ring around his feet.

Pacing wide, Ezra circled me and my demon, forcing us to turn with him. "Human noses aren't sensitive enough for tracking."

"*Eshathē nul hh'ainun.*"

Ezra's smile was bitter ice. "You're right and wrong. I'm not quite human … and he's not quite demon."

Fear cut through me, colder than the chill tainting the air around Zylas.

Ezra stopped and faced us. Crimson light reflected off his pale eye—or … no …

His pale eye wasn't reflecting Zylas's demonic power. It was glowing with its own, the crimson gleam brightening. Ezra's breath puffed white as the temperature dropped. Ice formed on the ground around him, creeping outward in a frosty ring.

Red magic lit his fingertips, then shot up his arms in tangled lines. It snaked up over his shoulders, up his neck, and across his cheeks. As power bled from his glowing left eye, two pairs of phantom horns formed above his temples.

"*Kin adairilnus, Zylas et Vh'alyir?*" he rumbled.

Zylas's tail lashed to the side—and he lunged. Ezra caught his wrist, halting his slashing crimson claws before they made contact. It shouldn't have been possible. Ezra's human body and human muscles shouldn't have been capable of stopping a demon's strike.

Except Ezra had admitted it moments ago: *I'm not quite human.*

Zylas twisted free with a snarl. He and Ezra faced each other, then in unison, began to circle. Ezra's pale eye glowed like magma, those phantom horns rising from his head.

Since my and Tori's visit to Odin's Eye, the possibility had lurked in the back of my mind, but Amalia had agreed with me: despite the demon magic scent Zylas could detect, there was no way one of the three mages could be a *demon mage.*

We'd been so wrong.

Panting fearfully, I backed away. Trapped inside Ezra's body was a demon. A Second House demon, like Nazhivēr, who was far more powerful than Zylas.

"*Silisērathē?*" Zylas spat.

"I know you," the demon mage answered, switching back to English—but this time, his words carried a guttural accent Ezra didn't possess. "I remember very well. The *Naventis* ten years ago—my last before I was summoned. Your first. Do *you* remember, Zylas?"

Zylas continued to circle, the demon mage matching his steps.

"When the spell struck, obliterating the Kahh'rūa *Dīnen* with an attack I'd never seen, we thought a female in a rage had come to challenge us. Instead, *you* walked in. A third rank *Dīnen* at the *Naventis* when none had attended in centuries— and a Vh'alyir, no less, who hadn't dared show their faces for a thousand years."

As though a signal had passed between them, they stopped. Ezra's left eye glowed even brighter.

"You strutted to the remains of your enemy and claimed a horn as your prize—the largest piece of him that remained. Then you told us, *Dīnen* far above you, '*Raistilthē nā nulla, ait ah shālin, raistilnā thē.*'"

The demon mage turned his eerie gaze on me. "'You will never find me, but from the shadows, I will find you.' And that year, he killed all four *Dīnen* of the second rank."

I have taught them to fear Vh'alyir. Zylas's savage declaration when he'd first told me how the Twelfth House was relentlessly hunted.

"You are *Eterran et Dh'irath*," Zylas said abruptly.

The demon inside Ezra smiled viciously. "Well met, *Dīnen*."

"We are not *Dīnen* anymore."

"But we may yet become *Ivaknen*."

Ivaknen—a word Zylas had mentioned that meant "the Summoned."

I scanned the demon mage's face. We were talking to the demon, but what had happened to Ezra? Was he still there?

Zylas bared his teeth. "Tell me what you want or I will see how many holes I can rip in that soft *hh'ainun* body before you die."

Unfazed, he slid his gaze to me. "We want to trade."

Those words … they had no accent.

"'We'?" I whispered.

"Eterran and I want to trade with you and Zylas."

Ezra. This was Ezra speaking.

I swallowed hard. "You and your demon … you can … uh …"

"Cooperate?" His mouth thinned with something like disgust. "Obviously we can. We want to live, and neither of us will survive much longer sharing a body."

The red glow in his left eye flared. "Which is exactly why we are here," Eterran added in his harsh accent.

My head spun. From the little I knew about demon mages, I was pretty sure "cooperation" wasn't usually an option for the demon and its host.

"No demon would ask for a prize without offering an equal payment," Eterran continued, "but I have learned many things in my time here. Sometimes prize and payment don't align."

"Say your meaning," Zylas snapped.

"I want something from you, and I want it now."

"You have nothing to exchange."

"Not now." A cold smile. "But what if you want something from me later?"

Zylas's eyes narrowed.

The demon mage's gaze shifted to me. "Maybe Robin will need something," Ezra said, "that we can help with."

"Or maybe you will need help protecting her," Eterran added silkily, "against an enemy stronger than you."

Zylas hissed. "Or maybe you will take what you want from us and give nothing in return."

The demon mage shrugged. "Risk for reward, Zylas."

I minced to Zylas's side. "What do you want from us?"

He considered me as though weighing how to respond—and how much to reveal—then his attention darted away. Shadows flickered as headlights cut across the railings on the overpass above our heads, and traffic roared, the echo under the bridge setting my teeth on edge.

Zylas slid sideways—closer to me.

Like an extinguished candle, all the red power crawling over Ezra snuffed out. He stepped backward, deeper into the shadows, and canted his head toward the street in warning.

I turned as gravel crunched underfoot. Someone was approaching from the street.

Ezra had already crashed my and Zylas's reconnaissance mission, and now someone else was barging in. My fingers curled into fists as I debated the wisdom of calling Zylas back into the infernus.

A man stepped out from behind a thick concrete support. Lights from overhead flashed across him, gleaming across his pale hair, and my breath caught in my throat. We didn't need to worry about whether Zylas could find the scent of Yana's killer here. Not anymore.

The albino sorcerer had returned to the scene of the crime.

16

HE SMILED PLEASANTLY. "I wondered if I'd find you here, Robin."

First Ezra, now this guy.

"Why would you think that?" I demanded, proud that my voice had held steady.

"Just a hunch …" His smirk broadened, pulling at the half-healed scratches I'd left on his face a week ago. "I'm glad my tip to the police paid off."

My eyes widened.

He unzipped his jacket and shrugged it off, revealing the metal bands that circled his arms from wrists to shoulders. "Submitting a fake address to the MPD for your profile is illegal, you know. And you really should spend more time at your guild. That would've made finding you much easier."

Prickles ran over my skin.

The sorcerer dropped his jacket as his pale blue eyes raked across me. "I've been dreaming about you, *payashē*."

Zylas hissed, and on his other side, Ezra twitched his shoulders. The motion drew the sorcerer's attention.

"And you are?" he asked politely.

"I'll tell you my name if you tell me yours."

The sorcerer smirked. "Why would I do that? *Ori quinque.*"

A silvery ripple blasted out from him. It struck us so fast not even Zylas could dodge it. The shimmering magic threw him and Ezra backward. They crashed to the ground with painful crunches.

I didn't move, the spell a cool tickle across my body. I'd barely felt it.

Zylas skidded on his back, twisted, and sprang to his feet with his tail whipping out for balance. Magic shot up his arms as he whirled on the sorcerer, and Ezra was almost as fast, though he'd yet to call on his demonic magic. Crimson gleamed faintly in his left eye.

The sorcerer grinned, laughter in the creases around his mouth.

"*Ori septem.*"

Pale blue light flashed—but not from the sorcerer.

The spell whipped out of the darkness behind Zylas. A glowing ring of blue latched around his left wrist, and the crimson power veining across his skin and radiating through his armor dimmed, then vanished.

From the trees that bordered the overpass, the caster stepped into view. Metal bands circled his arms from wrist to shoulders, and his pale hair fluttered in the breeze.

My neck twinged as I looked between the two men. Identical. They were identical.

With a shocked glance at the newcomer, Zylas grabbed the ring around his wrist to tear it off. His fingers curled around it—and the power coating his skin faded. He snatched his hand away, and his magic reignited over that hand.

"*Ori septem*," the first sorcerer barked. A blue disc shot toward us like a bullet—and Ezra twisted aside with lightning reflexes, the spell just missing his arm.

"*Ori quattuor!*"

From the second sorcerer, a barrage of indigo spikes launched at us. Zylas grabbed my arm, yanking me clear off my feet, while Ezra leaped in the other direction, but neither was fast enough. Shards of magic bombarded me, blasting into my torso.

"*Ori septem!*"

The blue ring struck from the opposite side, locking around Ezra's right elbow. He lurched upright, spikes jutting from his shoulder, side, and thigh.

"*Vayanin!*" Zylas hissed in my ear.

Panting harshly, I looked down at myself. Not a single spike protruded from my body. They'd passed right through my torso like I was a phantom.

The second sorcerer strode closer, stopping just beneath the overpass. "Who's the other one?"

"A demon mage, apparently," the first one answered.

"Enright?"

"I don't know." The sorcerer turned a questioning look on Ezra. "Tell us who you are and we might spare you."

Ezra bared his teeth. Crimson blazed in his left eye and power streaked up his left arm. His right arm, with that blue ring locked around it, didn't ignite with power. Zylas, too, couldn't summon any magic from his spell-locked arm—but that didn't stop him from casting with his other hand.

Spell circles flashed across his wrist. Ezra faced the other sorcerer, his fingers spread as he summoned his own spell. The temperature plunged, ice forming over every surface. The heat rushed from my body, drawn into the demons' magic.

The sorcerers raised their hands.

Spells exploded from the demon and demon mage, a spiraling blast from Eterran and a spear-like attack from Zylas.

"*Ori tres!*" the sorcerers shouted in unison.

Glittering green light expanded in front of the sorcerers. The demonic magic struck the barriers and dissolved into nothing.

Zylas and Eterran glanced at each other—then lunged in opposite directions, attacking both sorcerers simultaneously.

"*Ori quattuor!*"

Another volley of indigo spikes launched at Zylas. He cut sideways, avoiding all except one, which pierced his ankle. As he stumbled, the original sorcerer swung his arm toward his twin.

"*Ori unum!*" the twin snapped.

Ezra's crimson-lit fist slammed into a blue barrier, a blast of wind erupting from the impact. The second sorcerer staggered back a step—but the first was shouting his incantation.

"*Ori septem!*"

The blue ring flashed across the distance and caught Ezra's left wrist. The demon magic veining his arm extinguished.

"*Ori duo!*"

Zylas flew backward, hurled away before his claws could touch the sorcerer.

"*Ori unum! Ori duo! Ori tres!*"

Breathing hard, the demon and demon mage backed away from their opponents, unable to break through the sorcerers' impregnable defenses. Standing in the gap between them, I clenched my hands, limbs shivering with cold and mind spinning.

Unum. It meant "one," and the spell was a shield that Zylas's fists couldn't break.

Duo. "Two." A rippling reflection that threw Zylas back with the same force he attacked with. A reflector spell.

Tres. "Three." Green magic that voided Zylas's power. A negation spell.

Rare sorcery. Powerful. Difficult. And I finally knew what kind of magic it was: abjuration.

Shields and defenses. Undoing magic. Erasing magic. But abjuration wasn't as simple as making a shield that could block everything. It was complicated, I'd read. The most complicated branch of Arcana, more intricate even than healing.

Zylas! I mentally shouted. *Let me in your head! We can beat them together!*

His gaze jerked to me, eyes wide, but the dark, fierce touch of his mind didn't reach me. He couldn't do it. His mistrust was stronger than his drive to win.

I yanked my infernus off my neck. *Then distract him!*

As I launched into a sprint, Zylas slashed at the sorcerer's knees.

"*Ori unum!*" the man barked.

As Zylas's strike bounced off the shield, I sprang straight for the sorcerer. He whirled toward me, spitting an incantation.

"*Ori duo!*"

"*Ori eruptum impello!*"

A silver dome burst out from my artifact as the reflector spell formed in front of the sorcerer. My spell met his—and kept going right through the rippling barrier. It struck him full force. He hurtled backward as though he'd been shot out of a cannon and hit a stack of tires. The pile toppled and the sorcerer crumpled to the ground.

Zylas leaped after him. He landed on the man's chest, hand clamping over his mouth to prevent further incantations. I whirled around, searching for Ezra and the second sorcerer.

A man flew out of the darkness.

The twin sorcerer slammed down with a breathless grunt. Ezra stalked out of the shadows after him. His left eye glowed crimson, but no other sign of demonic magic touched him, those blue rings glowing on his arms. Wind swirled around his feet, carrying dust and debris.

He extended a hand and his fingers formed a fist. The sorcerer writhed in the dirt, clutching his throat, his eyes bulging. My mouth hung open in confusion as the man's face turned purple.

Ezra glanced at me, one eyebrow arched. "His spells don't work on aero magic."

Cold plunged through my gut. "You can … pull the air … from a person's lungs?"

Ezra opened his fist and the sorcerer gasped wildly, his chest heaving. The aeromage let him breathe for a few seconds, then curled his fingers again. The sorcerer went silent, clawing helplessly at his neck.

"A few minutes of this," Ezra said quietly, "and he'll tell us everything."

I nodded numbly. "Should we—"

The roar of traffic on the bridge. The cold breeze tugging at my hair. A shiver of warning down my spine.

"*Ori novem.*"

Purple light blazed. The winter wind flashed hot with magic, the gust flinging grit into my eyes. With the light came dull thuds. Sickening crunches. The sound of bodies hitting the earth.

My heart had taken up residence in my skull, beating so loudly I couldn't hear anything else. I jerked around.

Thrown ten feet from the half-suffocated sorcerer, Ezra was sprawled on his back, limbs convulsing. Sticking from his lower chest, glowing with violet light, was a harpoon. Its thick shaft pinned the aeromage to the ground.

On my other side, Zylas was no longer crouched over the twin sorcerer. He was ten feet away too, facedown as his claws tore furrows in the ground. An identical harpoon stuck out of his lower back. He shuddered against it, tail lashing and elbows digging into the earth as he tried to push himself up.

"*Zylas!*"

His name burst from me in a scream. I sprinted to his side and dropped to my knees. My shaking hands passed right through the glowing shaft. I couldn't touch it.

Abjuration. A spell made to harm demons. To me, it was nothing more than light.

Zylas turned his head, cheek grinding against the dirt as his wide eyes sought mine. "*Vayanin!*"

I sensed it more than heard it—someone approaching from behind. I started to turn.

The blow struck the side of my head. Pain cleaved my skull, stars bursting across my vision. I crumpled beside Zylas as the world dissolved.

"JUST WAIT. I think she's coming around."

The smooth voice trickled into my ears, prodding me toward consciousness. The muscles in my face twitched as I tried to remember how to open my eyes.

"*Robin.*"

That husky growl was far more familiar than the first voice, but I wasn't used to hearing my name in his tones.

I cracked my eyes open. Zylas leaned over me, red eyes glowing. My head and shoulders were in his lap, his hands gripping my upper arms. The roar of traffic hadn't changed—we were still beneath the overpass—but the air had warmed slightly.

Beside him, Ezra sat on his heels, watching me with concern. Only the faintest red gleam touched his pale left eye.

I drew in a shaky breath. "What happened?"

"A third sorcerer, I think," Ezra said, rubbing his scruffy jaw. "He hit Zylas and me with the same spell, then knocked you out. He dragged the other two sorcerers off. I heard a car drive away."

"He left?" I looked between him and Zylas. "But they had us beat. Why didn't they … do anything to us?"

"I was almost free," Zylas growled. "I got the *vīsh* out but he had left."

Ezra nodded. "I couldn't get that harpoon out of me, but it disappeared a couple minutes later." He raised his hands. "Those blue rings wore off too. I think he knew he was about to lose his advantage."

I gingerly sat up and touched the side of my head.

"I healed you," Zylas said. "You are not hurt."

"What about you? That harpoon …"

"It did not make a wound."

I squinted at his midriff, seeing no sign of a gory hole.

"The smaller spikes didn't break the skin either," Ezra revealed. "That wasn't their purpose."

"What did they do, then?"

Zylas curled his upper lip. "It was like poison. It made my body cold and numb and weak."

I shivered. "More abjuration."

"Abjuration?" Ezra's forehead creased. "I see."

Zylas scowled. "I do not know this word, *abjuration.*"

"It's a type of sorcery," I explained. "I didn't recognize it until I realized their magic had no effect on me. Abjuration is used to block, reflect, or erase other magic. I don't know much about it, but I've read how abjuration spells are all really specific—they block or negate one thing only."

"Then that's why they couldn't stop my aero magic," Ezra guessed. "They developed their spells for demon magic."

"It looks like it." I leaned tiredly against Zylas's shoulder. "They've created the ultimate demon-fighting toolkit. Their incantations are numbers, and that harpoon was number nine. I'm guessing a higher number means a more powerful spell."

"How do they fight so fast?" Zylas asked. "You said sorcery needs time to get strong again once the spell is used."

"I was wondering that too." Ezra straightened his long glove, realigning the steel studs with his knuckles. "No spell can recharge in a matter of seconds."

I hugged my knees. "I don't think the spells are recharging. I think they're carrying dozens of each one."

"Those armbands?" Ezra realized.

"Armbands," Zylas muttered. He twisted, looking behind him, then reached back. A scuffing sound, then he straightened and raised his hand. "This?"

I blinked at the broken band of steel he held. "Where did you get that?"

"I tore it off the *hh'ainun* when I had him down."

Taking it, I turned the band over in my hands. Spell arrays were etched into the metal, minuscule and dizzying. My lips moved as I counted. "Five. If each band holds five spells, and they're wearing around fifteen bands on each arm ..."

"One hundred and fifty," Ezra mathed. "There goes the plan I was hatching to waste all their spells before attacking in earnest."

"Before we figure out how to beat them, we need to figure out how to find them." My shoulders drooped. "We're no closer to that now than we were yesterday."

"On the contrary." The corner of Ezra's mouth lifted in a smile. "We have a trail now."

Zylas scowled. "I cannot track scents from *vehicles*."

"You won't be doing the tracking." The demon mage pushed to his feet. "Meet me here tomorrow evening. Eight o'clock should be late enough to avoid traffic and witnesses."

My lips quirked downward. "But ..."

He tapped the artifact I held. "Bring that with you. We'll need it."

My frown deepened as he walked away. "Ezra!"

He glanced over his shoulder.

"You didn't tell us," I reminded him. "What you and Eterran want to trade for."

Red flared in his left eye. "We will show the *Dīnen et Vh'alyir* first that debt and payment can take many forms in this world." Eterran's lips curved in a smile very different from Ezra's. "Especially since he will not defeat this enemy without help."

Zylas snarled under his breath. The demon mage strode to the sidewalk, and a moment later, he disappeared from sight.

I slumped against Zylas's shoulder, exhausted to the bone. "All we were supposed to do was snoop around a crime scene, and look what happened."

Zylas grunted. "You did not tell me a *crime scene* is a place for ambushes."

Closing my eyes, I rocked my head back and forth in disbelief. "I didn't know it was."

17

STANDING OVER THE COFFEE TABLE, I squinted at my spread of notes. Claude and Nazhivēr. Varvara Nikolaev and the demon-blood-enhanced golems. Uncle Jack and Amalia. Me, my parents, and the Athanas Grimoire. Zylas and the mysterious Twelfth House. The Vh'alyir Amulet that was "the key to everything."

I picked up my copy of the photo with young Claude. The printer had crinkled the paper when it had jammed, faint white lines webbing the two men's faces.

Studying the albino man, I searched for differences between him and the twins. Had someone cloned these super-demon-hunter sorcerers? Had they invented an anti-aging potion? Were they immortal? I wouldn't be surprised if it had taken twenty years to perfect their demon-battling technique.

I'd done more reading on abjuration because I couldn't understand why I'd never heard of demon-magic abjuration before. As I'd discovered last Halloween, when most of the mythic community had been hunting Tahēsh, mythics were unprepared to battle a demon in control of his magic.

My brief research had uncovered a famous abjuration sorcerer from the fifties who'd developed the best reflector spells in modern history, but aside from his work, no one had ever invented a spell to combat demon magic—for a very simple reason. Developing counter magic required detailed study of the origin magic. And no one could study demon magic because what demon would allow his magic to be studied?

But the twin sorcerers had studied demon magic, and I had a good theory on how: Nazhivēr. Twenty-two years ago, one of the sorcerers' victims had seen a winged demon, which suggested Claude had already formed his contract with Nazhivēr. He could have loaned his demon to the sorcerers to study over two decades ago.

And the result? A perfect arsenal of spells that could stop a demon in his tracks.

Massaging my temples, I abandoned the coffee table and headed for my bedroom. I pushed through the door—and came to an abrupt stop.

Zylas sat on my bed, a towel over his head as he scrubbed his hair dry. He wore only his dark shorts, devoid of even his belt. And that left *a lot* of smooth, reddish-toffee skin on display, dotted with water droplets from the shower.

I cleared my throat, wishing in vain that my face wouldn't flush—but heat was already gathering in my cheeks.

He pulled the towel off his head, his hair sticking in every direction, and blinked lazily. "*Na?*"

"We need to talk."

"*Hnn.*" He tossed the towel on the floor. "Now?"

"Yes, now." I picked up his discarded towel—trying very hard not to glance across the thick muscles of his thighs. "Get dressed and we'll talk."

"I am dressed."

"You're practically naked."

He shrugged, and I huffed. What I'd give to be that unselfconscious.

I'd asked him early on if he needed supplies to wash his clothes and maintain his armor, and he'd smugly informed me that he had *vīsh* for that. I hadn't believed him until he'd run a crimson spell across his clothes and I'd watched the dust and dirt sift down to the floor. The scuffs and tears had mended beneath another spell. A third had smoothed the scratches in his armor.

Talk about convenient.

"I've been thinking," I began, twisting his towel nervously. "Those sorcerers use Arcana designed specifically to stop your magic. But if you and I combine magic, it becomes something new. Their abjuration shouldn't work on it."

"I tried, *vayanin.*"

"I know." I ignored a slash of hurt at his reminder of our weak trust. "I understand that you don't want me to know every single thing in your head. But maybe we can get to a point where you can share *some* thoughts with me, the way I do with you."

He was silent as I strangled the towel. Realizing what I was doing, I set it on the foot of the bed.

"I was thinking ..." I said again, my words slowed by hesitation. "We spend so much time together, but I don't know very much about you. And you don't know much about me either. Maybe if we talk more ... about ourselves ... we can know each other better and trust each other more."

He gazed up at me, dark brows drawn in thought. My hand rose toward his face, then stuttered. I shyly brushed a damp lock of his hair out of his eyes, half expecting him to bat my hand away.

He merely watched me, and I knew exactly what he'd meant when he'd talked about "thoughts in your eyes."

"What do you think?" I asked.

"*Hnn.*"

Rolling my eyes at his unhelpful murmur, I straightened another piece of his tangled hair. He didn't seem to mind, and his messy mop had been making me itch to grab a hairbrush for months. As I tugged another lock in a more natural direction, my fingers brushed against one of his small horns.

Curious, I pressed the pad of my thumb to the dull point.

"Our horns show our age."

I froze. He looked up at me.

"Child demons have no horns." His voice was low, vibrations sliding under my skin. "The oldest demons have the biggest horns."

Remembering Tahēsh and the huge horns sprouting from his hairless skull, I again traced the dark, bone-like protrusions poking through his hair, estimating their length—or lack thereof.

"You're young," I whispered. I'd suspected, but now I knew for sure. He was an adult, but only just. Same as me.

His eyes glowed faintly. "Eterran has lived my years many times."

"How long do demons live?"

He shrugged. "We live until we die."

Not a helpful answer, though if their society was as violent as it sounded, old age might be a rare occurrence.

The shadows in his eyes mesmerized me—the hidden knowledge, the cunning and savagery, the experience and survival instincts honed from years of struggle and danger. My fingers slid down, brushing across his temple, his cheekbone.

"What is the *Naventis* that Eterran talked about?" I asked.

His gaze trailed across my face, then down. He tugged at a decorative button on the bottom of my knitted sweater. "It is a gathering of *Dīnen*. The stories say that once, all *Dīnen* came to talk, and the *payapis* would come too."

"*Payapis?*"

"The oldest female demons who will have no more young. They are very powerful."

"Are they queens?"

"They punish females who are too much trouble, but they give wisdom, not commands." He canted his head, his cheek pressing into my hand. "There are stories that they killed foolish *Dīnen* who ruled too long, but that was the before time."

The before time ... before the onset of summoning, after which humans stole *Dīnen* away long before a demon matriarch might need to eliminate unruly leaders.

"What is the *Naventis* like now?" I asked, almost afraid of the answer. My fingertips drifted to the corner of his jaw, and I shifted closer, standing between his knees.

"*Dīnen* of the first rank gather to eat and talk and say compliments to themselves. Sometimes *Dīnen* of the second rank will come, but they are lucky to last a season before they disappear to the *hh'ainun* world."

"And the third rank?"

"The Ninth, Tenth, and Eleventh Houses do not have *Dīnen* anymore. They are summoned every day, every night. Gone, gone, gone. No one knows who holds the *Dīnen* power. They disappear too fast."

I swallowed hard. "And the Twelfth House?"

"We do not go to the *Naventis* because the Lūsh'vēr and Dh'irath will kill us."

"But you did."

He grinned, flashing his pointed canines. "My plan was good. After I warned them, I disappeared and they could not find me. They searched and searched, and I laughed."

His amusement was contagious and I grinned back. Without realizing what I was doing, I leaned closer—leaned into him, my weight settling against his chest. My fingers had curled around the back of his neck.

His hand fisted around the hem of my sweater, and he pulled my hips into his stomach.

I jolted, my trance breaking. My breath halted in my lungs, my heart surging. Rigid with sudden inner turmoil, I forced myself to inhale—and got a nose full of his hickory scent. His warmth was soaking into me, his body hard and strong as I leaned into him, and I didn't want to move my hand from the nape of his neck.

Steeling myself, I withdrew my hands and stepped away. My sweater slid easily from his grasp, and he made no attempt to pull me back—though he watched me with strangely somber eyes.

Surprised he hadn't taken the opportunity to hold on and make me squirm—his favorite pastime—I sidled over and sat on the bed beside him, enough space for a third person between us.

"I want to tell you something about me," I declared, forcing my brain back on track. "But I don't know what. What do you want to know?"

"Why does your—"

I shot him a glare. "Not that."

He snorted in annoyance, then tipped his head back, squinting thoughtfully at the ceiling. "Tell me about your mother."

"My mother? You don't want to know about me?"

"Our mothers create us. Knowing her is knowing you."

An odd flutter rippled through my center. Such a simple concept, yet from the lips of a demon, astonishingly profound. I wondered what he'd make of a philosophy class.

"My mother …" I fought a wave of grief as I was swamped with memories. "She was more optimistic than me. Always cheerful and smiling. Her job was restoring old books and grimoires, and she loved it. She said people put their souls in their books, and she was repairing their souls as much as the pages and bindings and covers."

His brow furrowed in confusion.

"It's just a thing she liked to say," I clarified before he ripped any books apart in search of hidden souls. "She meant that books could be very precious to people."

"A book is not useful. Why is it valuable?"

"Some books are useful, like grimoires." My eyes hooded as memories of her face swam across my vision. "She would've told you that objects can be part of you and losing them feels like losing a limb."

He frowned dubiously and I laughed.

"She would've liked you, Zylas. I know she would've. She'd want to know what you thought of everything, from books with souls to our cities to every silly thing humans do."

"Do you?"

"Do I what?"

"Want to know what I think?"

I opened my mouth, then closed it, exhaling silently. "I do. I'd ask you questions all day and night if I could, but you always complain and tell me I'm too noisy." I rubbed the heel of my hand over my cheek. "My mom would've pestered you until you told her everything, no matter how grumpy you got. She was braver than me."

A light touch under my eye. I flinched as he wiped away a tear I'd missed.

"Does it hurt, *vayanin*?" he asked. Soft. Unsure.

My throat closed, tight and painful. "I miss her. I wish every day that she was still alive. I miss my dad too, but Mom ... she was always there for me. So much has happened, and I wish ... I just wish I could talk to her one more time so she could tell me what to do. I've been so—so lost since she died."

A sob shook my chest, and I twisted away from Zylas. Scrubbing at my face, I gathered my composure as best I could. When I turned back, he was watching me, his expression a mystery but a small, almost invisible wrinkle between his dark eyebrows.

"What about you?" I sniffed, wishing I had a tissue. "Your mother? Did you know her?"

"I knew her."

That surprised me. My impression of female demons so far wasn't one of maternal love. "What was she like?"

"Young and *zh'ūltis*."

I blinked.

He leaned back, bracing himself with one arm. "No female will choose Vh'alyir if she can raise the young of Dh'irath or

Ash'amadē or Gh'ēlēis. Females want children who will be strong, not weak and small." He sneered to himself, then shook his head. "My mother was young and knew little, but she knew how to be smart prey and she taught me better than other demons learned. She is the reason I am alive."

Hands folded in my lap, I silently thanked his mother for teaching him those lessons so well. "What about your father?"

"Sires come for their young when their magic calls out. They take them to the lands of males to teach them how to fight."

"The lands of males?" I interrupted. "You mean males and females live separately?"

He nodded. "Females live in groups. Males do not go near those places or the females will kill them."

"How then do …" My cheeks flushed. "How does, uh, mating happen?"

"A male will approach the place of females with gifts. Usually food, *na*? It is a dangerous thing. He will bring gifts until a female chooses him or tries to kill him."

That sounded terrifying. "So, did your father come to take you away?"

"*Var*. I went with him, and we traveled into places of sand, far from other demons, where he could teach me everything he knew—how to fight, how to win. It would take many years. I knew only the easiest *vīsh* and how to scratch with my claws and how to hide in the *Ahlēvīsh*."

Before I could ask what that was, he continued.

"He taught me one thing—*dh'ērrenith*—then he made a *zh'ūltis* mistake and died."

"He died? How?"

"A beast of my world ... an animal." He huffed angrily. "Not even a death in battle. *Imadnul.*"

I pressed my hands into my knees. "If you were so young and didn't know how to fight ... did you go back to your mother?"

"I could not go back. Females do not allow male young who have grown from child to not-child."

"What did you do?"

He stared across the room, gaze distant, then pushed off the bed. Arching his back, he stretched his arms above his head. Muscles rippled across his bare torso, and his biceps and triceps bunched with strength.

I dragged my stare up, focusing on his face. "Zylas, after your father died, what did you do?"

Lowering his arms, he looked at me with eyes that had seen and lived nightmares.

"I survived."

18

HUMMING QUIETLY, I cradled the piping bag as I squeezed sweet vanilla buttercream onto the last pale gold cookie. Perfect.

I set aside the bag and surveyed my work. One tray of butter cookie tops with a layer of buttercream, and one tray of butter cookie bottoms with a thin layer of raspberry jam. Smiling in anticipation, I picked up a top and bottom, gently squished them together, and set the finished "buttercream whirl" on a plate.

Working quickly, I assembled the remaining cookies, then dusted the tops with icing sugar, the powder clinging to the delicate whorl top, the edges baked to the perfect shade of golden brown.

I picked up the plate, carried it into the living room, and set it on the coffee table with a flourish.

Zylas looked over the top of his landscape book—and another head appeared from behind it. Socks' furry black ears swiveled as she sniffed the air.

"Buttercream whirls," I told him. "Try one."

He sat forward, and Socks braced against his legs so she wouldn't fall off his lap. Plucking a cookie off the plate, he examined the delicate shape, sniffed it, then popped the whole thing in his mouth. His jaw moved with a few chews before he swallowed.

"Well?" I demanded.

He flicked me an unreadable look, then moved the plate to the sofa arm for easier access. Socks stretched her nose toward the cookies and he waved her away before taking another icing-filled whirl.

Snorting—but secretly pleased—I returned to the kitchen to clean up. A few minutes later, I settled on the sofa beside him, the grimoire and my notebook balanced on my lap. Earlier today, I'd found Myrrine's next entry and I had a few hours to translate it before meeting Ezra at the crime scene.

The thought of that appointment triggered a wave of anxiety—the prospect of interacting with the unnerving and dangerous demon mage was as intimidating as a potential conflict with the sorcerers. I huffed out a breath, fighting back my apprehension.

As Zylas ate his way through the plate of cookies, I focused on Myrrine's ancient words. Bit by bit, the translation came together, and with each phrase and sentence I completed, new unease gathered in my chest. As the sunlight outside the window dimmed and disappeared, I set the grimoire aside and gripped my notebook with both hands, my translation filling the page.

My heart hurts.

This day was the worst kind, sister. Where the sky was dark, where the wind blew cold and cruel, and where our enemies came for us.

This day they found us, and my Vh'alyir fought them. We live, and they are dead.

I should rejoice, but sister, my chest aches. I saw him bleed. I saw him fall. They died, but my Vh'alyir... I feared he would die too. I feared he would perish in this unfamiliar world of mine, his strength consumed, his eyes black as night, his fire spirit gone cold.

And I would be without him.

The madness in me has not abated, and now a new insanity grows. I no longer question why I want to touch him. I question whether he will let me.

He reveals so little. He does not stare like a besotted boy, nor does he pant or paw or grope like a human man. Does he feel the burn of desire as a man would? Does he crave my womanly shape or am I too human to arouse him?

These questions! I debate if I should strike them from the page.

The yearning in my bosom strains to reach him. Can I bear it alone? Do I guard my heart or tempt the Fates?

Pride or passion, sister, and I know what I must choose.

— Myrrine Athanas

I gulped. Was Myrrine saying what I thought she was saying? She was thinking of *revealing her feelings* to her *demon*?

My hair swished against my cheeks as I shook my head. That couldn't possibly be her intent. After all, she had no idea how her demon felt about her—or about human women in general. She'd said herself he showed no signs of attraction toward her. For all she knew, he thought women were ugly compared to females of his own kind.

I must be misunderstanding her meaning. Or I'd translated wrong. Myrrine wouldn't be so foolish as to lay her heart, not to mention her dignity, on the line by telling a demon she was in love with him. I still wasn't sure if Zylas understood empathy; no way would a demon understand *love*.

Even if Myrrine's demon *could* comprehend the concept of love and attraction, what did she think might come from sharing that with him? What result was she hoping for? Did she simply hope her demon could return her feelings in some way, or did she want ... more?

Did she want her demon to reciprocate her attraction? Did she want to ... with *a demon*?

My throat moved with a harsh swallow, my throat inexplicably dry.

"*Vayanin?*"

I jumped half a foot off the sofa. Zylas peered at me, the last cookie in his hand and crumbs scattered across the plate.

"I'm fine," I chirped, voice too high. Snapping my notebook shut, I gathered up the grimoire. "I need to put all this away. We're leaving soon."

He glanced at the window, where darkness had just fallen. It was only six. We had two hours yet before our meeting with Ezra.

Deciding not to mention that, I scooped up the books and rushed into my room. What was wrong with me? Why was my heart pounding like this? Maybe I was anxious for Myrrine, who was poised on the brink of humiliation and heartbreak.

My breath hitched as I realized I was thinking of her as though her story hadn't concluded centuries ago.

I ran my fingers across the grimoire's worn cover. Whatever Myrrine had decided, it was done. Somewhere among the ancient pages was the next part of her tale, and I was desperate to find it—but aside from curiosity, I had no reason to. I'd been searching out her journal entries for answers about the Vh'alyir Amulet, but Myrrine had yet to mention it.

I considered pulling out the grimoire and searching for the next page with Myrrine's name, but I wouldn't have enough time to complete the translation.

Besides, I reminded myself, it wasn't important—no matter the anxious anticipation gripping my chest. No matter the powerful need to know what she had decided.

Shoving the feeling away, I locked the grimoire and my notes in their metal case, slid the heavy box under my bed, then turned to my dresser. The twisted armband Zylas had ripped off the sorcerer glinted in the overhead light. I picked it up and traced one of the tiny, powerful spells etched into it.

I had better things to worry about than Myrrine's love life—like my upcoming rendezvous with a demon mage and, if we were lucky, a pair of demon-hunting sorcerers.

EZRA WAS WAITING on the sidewalk beneath the overpass when I arrived. The gap under the bridge seemed darker, the echoing clamor of traffic louder. It hammered into my skull.

I managed a weak smile as I joined him. "I brought it."

When I held up the armband, he nodded. "We'll begin as soon as Blair arrives."

"Blair?"

"One of the Crow and Hammer's telethesians." He arched his eyebrows amusedly. "You didn't think *I* would track the sorcerers, did you?"

I didn't admit I'd assumed he would use some sort of fancy demon magic to do it. A telethesian was a much better plan, and I was embarrassed I hadn't thought of it myself. I'd even met one of the guild's telethesians, Taye.

"While we wait," he said, "we should discuss our plan. Let's go over here."

He led me past the chain-link fence and into the stacks of tires. I went as far as necessary to lose sight of the street, but when I glimpsed the concrete wall where the overpass joined the hillside, I stopped.

"This is far enough." I turned my back on the dried gore where Yana had died. "I don't need to stare at old blood while we talk."

"Those aren't bloodstains."

"What?"

"It's ... paint."

My brow furrowed. "How can you tell?"

"I got a copy of the Vancouver PD's preliminary findings and the autopsy report." He pressed his lips together. "Those sorcerers are sick bastards."

Crimson light flared through my jacket. Power pooled on the ground, and Zylas took form beside me.

"*Īnkavis* are always broken in their minds, *na?*" he remarked casually, using the demonic word for a serial killer.

Ezra's left eye gleamed scarlet. "These ones are even more twisted."

"How so?" I asked.

"You're better off not knowing."

I almost dropped it, but I remembered Yana's smile from her photo, and the *Romeo and Juliet* performance she'd never get to be part of. I straightened. "I can handle it."

His expression suggested he disagreed. "The stains back there are red body paint. Yana was found covered in it."

"You mean they *painted* her? Why?"

"To make her look like a *payashē*." The gleam in his eye intensified. "A female demon."

Zylas hissed.

All the hair on my body stood on end, revulsion closing my throat. I struggled to swallow.

"They stripped her, tied her up, and painted her red." Ezra's voice was flat, but his eyes—both his and Eterran's—burned fiercely. "Then they raped her."

I started to shake. *You have the look*, the first sorcerer had told me.

Zylas huffed. "I do not know that word."

"It means ..." Red flared brighter in Ezra's pale eye and his voice deepened into Eterran's tones. "*Dh'keteh hh'ainunith amavren cun payilasith.*"

Zylas's eyes widened. "*Dh'keteh?*"

Eterran's upper lip curled with scathing disgust. "Some human males *enjoy* this act. Human females fear males for that reason."

"But ..." Zylas stepped back as though distancing himself from the conversation. "But *forcing* ..."

Arms wrapped around myself, I frowned at him, confused by his stunned reaction, as though the very concept were alien to him.

"Rape does not exist in the world of demons," Eterran told me. "To be chosen by a *payashē* is an honor. To *force* her would be—"

"*Gh'akis!*" Zylas spat. "Better to die with no sons than do *that. Eshais hh'ainun dahganul.*"

"I agree."

Eterran and Zylas could and would slaughter anyone without hesitation, but the idea of a sexual predator repulsed them? I couldn't wrap my head around it. In a world as violent as demonkind's, how could rape not exist?

Realizing they'd fallen silent, I looked up. Zylas was scrutinizing me, his eyebrows low over critical red eyes.

"Um." I blinked. "Zylas?"

He turned to the demon mage. "*Naileranis et na. Eshailla kir?*"

"Probably."

Jaw tightening, Zylas returned his stare to me, his expression intent as though he were rearranging his understanding of my incomprehensible human brain. I looked away, unsure what conclusions he was drawing—not just about me, but about a world in which females were at the bottom of the power spectrum instead of the top.

"Time's up," Ezra said, the glow of Eterran's magic in his eye dying. "Someone is coming."

I waved at the infernus hidden under my jacket. "Zylas, quickly!"

He growled low in his throat, then power swept over him, dissolving his form before streaking toward my chest. Just as the light faded, a sharp whistle rang out.

"Here!" Ezra called.

Footsteps clomped across the ground, and a tall, thin woman strode into view. Long, straight hair the color of ice swept down her back, a shade only alchemic dye could achieve. Her skin was almost as pale, its porcelain tone accentuated by dark-lined eyes and blood-red lipstick. Her entire outfit was leather, but not the combat type—too many studs, chains, and ornate crosses decorated it.

"Hi Blair," Ezra said. "Thanks for helping us with this. Do you know Robin?"

Blair's eyes—bright violet, which couldn't be natural—slid to me and she nodded. I forced a smile, desperately trying to remember if I'd seen her before. I vaguely recalled a tall woman with long, straight *black* hair from the last monthly meeting. Could that have been Blair?

"Hi," I said awkwardly.

She nodded again.

Ezra pulled the broken armband from my hand and held it out. "This belongs to the sorcerer. He has a twin brother, so you'll probably detect two similar trails. They were here last night and left with a third sorcerer. We need to know where they went."

A third nod. She took the armband, pinching it gingerly between two fingers. Her smoky eyelids lowered as she focused on it.

I'd never had the chance to see a telethesian at work. Blair held the armband, presumably to get a psychic feel for its owner, then turned in a slow circle and walked back the way she'd come.

Falling into step beside Ezra, I followed Blair into the middle of the road. There she stopped, looked one way, then the other. Ezra and I hung back, waiting.

I chewed my lower lip. "She ... um ... she seems ..."

"Confused?" Ezra guessed, keeping his voice low. "She isn't. Blair is an extremely gifted telethesian, but she doesn't do jobs often because her ability is so sensitive. She can sense too much."

"Is she better than Taye?" I asked curiously as Blair turned in another slow circle.

"We call in Blair when Taye can't find a trail. She never fails to find someone, even if it takes her weeks."

"Wow," I whispered, reassessing the Goth woman.

"Taye thinks she has a touch of clairvoyance, but she's never—"

He broke off as Blair picked a direction and began to walk. We hurried after her, but Ezra slowed while we were still ten feet back.

"We don't want to distract her," he murmured.

"Didn't the sorcerers escape in a car?" I peered down the street. "Will that be a problem?"

"Not for a telethesian. The only way to obscure a psychic trail is to cross moving water or take to the air. We might have a long walk ahead of us, though, depending on how far they drove."

We traipsed along for a block, passing graffitied fences and concrete walls, before I spoke again.

"Why are the sorcerers kidnapping women and making them look like female demons before killing them?"

"Because they're insane." His shoulders tautened and a chill grew in the air around him. "Demon worship isn't a new concept. It exists in the mythic community too, and in any fringe group, you'll find obsessed, delusional fetishists."

I tucked my cold, shaky fingers in my pockets. "That's messed up."

"Extremely."

"We need a plan for beating these guys."

He shrugged. "I think we'll have to wing it. But Robin"—his stare took on that viper-like intensity again, but this time, I could see concern behind it—"you need to be careful. The one sorcerer was already calling you *payashē*."

A shudder quaked through my limbs.

Blair led us off the back streets and into the middle of Clark Drive. The six-lane thoroughfare delineated Strathcona's commercial district and the residential neighborhoods that stretched east until they merged with Vancouver's suburbs. Even this late, a steady stream of traffic whizzed by.

Ezra caught Blair's arm and pulled her onto the sidewalk. We waited for a red light to create a break in traffic, then accompanied Blair into the middle of the road. She turned in several circles before we pulled her back to the safety of the sidewalk.

We retraced our steps three times before Blair chose a direction, but we couldn't let her walk in the middle of the road. We headed up the sidewalk, and whenever there was a lull in traffic, she returned to the pavement to check for the sorcerers' trail.

It was slow going. We passed dingy businesses and a disreputable grocery mart before Blair led us into an alley. It sloped steeply up the side of a hill, and I puffed as we followed the pale psychic. She trekked along the cracked pavement, then slowed. Clutching the broken armband, she rotated on the spot and came to a halt, facing a building.

The small structure, shingles peeling off its roof, had once been a detached single-car garage. Someone had converted it, replacing the overhead door with a flimsy steel wall and a door. The back of the grocery store and neighboring trees shadowed the garage on both sides.

Blair minced to the door and touched her fingers to it. Shivering, she stepped back and gestured to Ezra.

He took her place, listened for a moment, then tried the handle. When it didn't turn, he shifted back and unleashed a powerful front kick. The jamb splintered and the door swung inward, revealing a dark interior.

Apprehension tightened my chest. Pulling out my phone, I activated flashlight mode and followed Ezra inside.

Tangled blankets covered a futon bed, and a flimsy cot had been set up beside it. A rickety table sat against the opposite wall, three folding chairs arranged around it, and a black trash can, the kind seen on every curb on garbage day, overflowed with fast-food bags. A plastic curtain with yellow and white stripes hid the remaining corner.

Ezra pulled the curtain aside, revealing a toilet and a showerhead, the cracked concrete floor around the drain stained white. There wasn't even a sink.

Blair waited in the doorway as Ezra and I scoured the dingy apartment, but though the sorcerers might be sleeping here, the only personal belonging we found was a duffle bag stuffed with t-shirts, jeans, and boxer shorts. Ezra dumped it onto the futon bed and we sorted through each garment.

"Nothing," I muttered. "How could there be *nothing*?"

Ezra threw a pair of jeans on the mattress, the pockets turned out. "They've been kidnapping and murdering women for years. They know how to operate."

I glanced at the garbage can, less than eager to look through their trash, then whispered to the mage, "Maybe a better sense of smell could find something."

His gaze flicked to Blair. "You and I can come back later."

"Or you can take Blair around the neighborhood to see if the sorcerers have a second hideout nearby, and I'll catch up to you."

"I don't want to leave you alone."

"There's no one here," I insisted, "and I don't want to waste time. They could already be scoping out their next victim."

"I doubt that." He pinned me with a hard stare. "They've already chosen their next victim."

Gooseflesh ran over my skin.

"Blair." He turned to her. "Were the sorcerers here last night?"

She nodded and held up three fingers.

"Three of them? And they left together?"

Another nod.

"Can you follow their most recent trail?"

She pointed confidently toward the alley.

He leaned toward me. "I'll take Blair and follow their trail. You give this place one more pass, then take a cab back to the guild. I'll meet you there when Blair is done. *Don't* hang around here. Got it?"

"Got it. And *you* don't try to take those three on by yourself," I warned.

A faint smile. "Wouldn't dream of it. Be careful."

"You too."

He joined Blair at the door, asking her in a gentle tone if she was doing okay. She patted his arm reassuringly as they exited the small garage, and only as Ezra's voice trailed away outside did I realize Blair hadn't spoken a single word.

I waited two full minutes before placing a hand on my chest. *Okay, Zylas.*

With a flare of crimson, he appeared beside me. His nose wrinkled, upper lip curling in a disgusted sneer.

"This place reeks of the *hh'ainun*."

"We can't find anything but their clothes."

He prowled deeper into the room. His gaze passed over the garments, the futon and cot, and the table and overflowing garbage. He took a few steps toward the shower corner, then reeled back, his disgust intensifying. Gliding steps carried him in a circle around the room, and he came to a stop beside the trash.

I cringed. "We don't need to dig through that, do we?"

He crouched, head tilted, then pushed on the trash can. It slid sideways with a gritty rasp, a drink cup and crumpled brown napkin toppling to the floor. He ran his fingers across the cracked concrete, then dug his claws into a short, fat crack.

An oblong chip of concrete popped free, revealing a metal handle embedded into the floor. Zylas grabbed it and pulled. A rough circle lifted—a trapdoor, disguised to look like part of the floor, its seams lost in the cracks.

He dragged the door off the opening, and we peered into the dark hole. The light from my phone illuminated a flimsy aluminum ladder propped against the wall.

Grasping the edge, Zylas stuck his head and shoulders into the hole. He leaned farther in, then straightened, repositioned, and dropped into the gap feet-first. I heard the faint thump of his landing.

"*Vayanin.*"

Holding my phone with my teeth, I sat on the edge and slid my feet into the gap. His hands curled over my thighs, and I pushed off. He caught my weight and lowered me onto the floor. My shoes settled against hard-packed dirt. Taking my phone from my mouth, I shone the light across the space.

It was a roughly dug basement, gray cinderblocks supporting the walls and the floor left as unfinished dirt, except for a circular pad in the center, twelve feet across. A familiar shape had been etched into the concrete: a thick ring ten feet in diameter, with lines and runes swirling in and around it.

A summoning circle.

No demon waited inside it, but the sight still chilled me. I moved my light across the walls. Boxes and crates were stacked on one side, and on the other was a wooden table constructed of two-by-fours, the surface covered in papers, notebooks, leather-bound texts, and an assortment of pens, rulers, and calculators.

I crossed to the table, and Zylas followed, both of us walking around the summoning circle. Embossed titles in Latin and Greek glimmered on the tomes' spines, but the notebooks and binders had blank covers. A stack of steel armbands waited beside a grimoire-shaped book, and I flipped the cover open to find a complex array and list of ingredients.

A quick perusal confirmed that replacing any damaged armbands would be a real chore for the sorcerers, requiring complex spellwork and days for the spells to charge.

Plus, I noticed with an unpleasant twist of my gut, each spell listed demon blood as an ingredient.

Closing the book, I handed it to Zylas to carry, then sidled along the table. Diagrams covered most of it—large sheets of brown paper filled with notes and corrections. The scrawled sketches and hasty annotations reminded me of Anthea's spell experiments in the grimoire.

I peered more closely at a scribbled array, where the sorcerer had circled a central element and drawn an angry question mark, then turned to the black binder lying in the middle of the mess.

Nervous prickles chased each other along my nerves. I flipped the binder's cover open.

"Zylas!" I gasped.

He pressed closer, leaning over the binder beside me, and together we stared down at the page, nestled in a clear plastic sheath. A grimoire page.

A page from *my* grimoire.

19

DISBELIEVING ELATION swept through me. I turned to the next page protector in the binder. It held another page stolen from the Athanas Grimoire, its edge roughly torn.

I flipped through each one. Twelve pages in all, carefully protected in the binder.

"We found them!" I grabbed Zylas's hand, squeezing hard. "We found the stolen pages!"

"Take it and we will go."

"Right." I scooped the binder up, then tucked the sorcerers' abjuration grimoire behind the sturdy cover. "Let's get out of here."

He grabbed the edge of the trapdoor and pulled himself up, and I hastily climbed the ladder after him. Twitchy apprehension wound into my muscles. We'd found more than a clue about the sorcerers—we'd found *the* prize. The stolen pages I'd feared we'd never recover. How had the sorcerers gotten them from Claude? Or had Claude never had them?

Either way, I now needed to escape with them.

I pocketed my phone and crept to the door, Zylas behind me. Cracking it open, I peered into the dark alley. Zylas leaned into my back as he too peered outside, his vision better suited to spotting enemies.

"Go toward the busy, noisy place," he whispered. "Quickly."

As I sucked in a deep breath, he dissolved into light and returned to the infernus. I flung the door open and rushed into the alley. With not a soul in sight, a notch of my tension released. I quickened my pace, making a beeline for the busy street at the bottom of the hill.

A man appeared on the sidewalk and turned into the alley. Fear skittered through me, but I could tell he wasn't one of the sorcerer twins. A white beard covered his lower face, and he had the thick middle of an older man who'd once been fit.

Exhaling unsteadily, I continued down the alley as the old man headed uphill, a hat pulled low to protect his ears from the chilly wind. We drew closer to each other, and I resisted the urge to veer toward the edge of the pavement, holding my course in the alley's center.

We drew level with each other. One more step and I'd be past him.

His hand swung up and pressed against the binder clutched to my chest, the unexpected push bringing me to a stumbling halt. His chin rose, bearded face turning toward me.

"That binder," he said in a gravelly voice as our gazes met, "doesn't belong to you."

I stared into his eyes—unnaturally pale blue and framed by white lashes. My heart hammered in my chest.

"Actually," I whispered, my petrified throat scarcely able to make a sound, "it does."

Twisting away from his hand, I leaped sideways, stumbled, then bolted downhill. If he was an abjuration sorcerer like the twins, then all his artifacts were built for demon combat. He wouldn't have anything that could stop a human. All I had to do was reach the busy street and—

I didn't see where the new man had come from until his arm had snapped into my path. His forearm struck my upper chest. I slammed into the pavement on my back, the impact seizing my lungs.

My assailant leaned over me—a familiar, pale face with no expression. As I struggled to breathe, footsteps thumped closer. Another face appeared, identical to the first except for his eager grin and the half-healed scratches on his cheek.

The old man joined them, his cold eyes assessing, and staring up at all three men, I finally understood. Not immortal sorcerers who hadn't aged since the twenty-two-year-old photo with Claude. The twins were the children of the albino man in the photo.

The father and his adult sons contemplated me like hunters appreciating their catch, then the grinning twin reached down, aiming for my throat.

Crimson blazed from my chest. Zylas appeared, a foot on either side of me and claws slashing.

"*Ori unum!*"

The incantation rang out from all three men, and Zylas's claws scraped across a trio of blue shields. He dropped and swung his leg into the shins of a twin. Rolling, he slammed into the ankles of the second twin, and both fell. His claws ripped into the calf of the nearer sorcerer.

"*Ori quinque!*"

The father's spell hurled Zylas backward—opening a gap so the sorcerers could unleash their arsenal without fear of Zylas's claws.

"*Ori eruptum impello!*" I yelled.

A silver dome expanded from my artifact and blasted all three sorcerers away from me. They crashed down on the pavement, and Zylas lunged for the nearest one.

"*Ori unum!*" he shouted.

Zylas pivoted, ducked, and slashed for his unprotected knee.

"*Ori quattuor!*"

Indigo spikes exploded from the other twin. Zylas leaped back, the barrage pelting the ground in front of me. They passed through the fallen sorcerer, harmless to anyone but a demon.

"*Ori quinque!*"

Another silvery blast flung Zylas off his feet. He landed in a skid, claws dragging across the ground and teeth bared. I shoved to my feet, panic choking off my air.

"*Ori duo!*"

"*Ori quattuor!*"

"*Ori quinque!*"

The spells, shouted almost in unison, struck too fast for Zylas to recover. He pitched over, glowing spikes peppering his limbs.

With a wild look around, I bolted away from the fight—racing for the busy street. If I could get to safety, I could call Zylas to me in an instant. The sorcerers wouldn't attack me on a busy street. Clutching the precious binder, I ran as hard as I could.

"*Ori impello potissime!*"

An invisible force struck me in the back. I fell for a second time, hitting so hard the elbows of my leather jacket tore. Pain burst through my limbs and my vision blurred.

Thudding footsteps, then rough hands grabbed me and hauled me up. An arm clamped around my throat, my back against my captor's chest. He squeezed, cutting off my air.

"We do carry a *few* extra spells," he whispered mockingly in my ear.

My mouth gaped, sparks flashing in my vision. I yanked on his arm, my fingers biting into the metal bands under his jacket sleeve. My lungs screamed. Where was Zylas?

Daimon, hesychaze! I cried silently.

Red light blazed in my blurred vision. The formless power streaked for my chest and hit the infernus, making the silver disc vibrate and glow.

And that's when I realized the sorcerer was holding my infernus.

In the instant before Zylas could bounce back out and take physical form, that one instant where his power was contained inside the pendant, the man spat his incantation.

"*Ori octo!*"

Sparkling green light appeared, forming a perfect cube around the infernus. Demonic power filled it, making the whole thing glow with hideous brown streaks, but Zylas didn't reappear. Not a single spark of his crimson magic could break through the green cube.

Zylas was trapped in the infernus, and it was my fault.

BLINDFOLDED AND GAGGED. Hands tied behind me, the hard back of a chair digging into my elbows.

My frenzied heart palpitated in my chest, my terror so consuming the organ was on the verge of complete collapse. My breath whistled through my nose, too fast, but I couldn't slow my lungs.

I couldn't stop seeing the red stains under the bridge. Couldn't stop hearing Ezra's disgusted description of Yana's death. Couldn't stop picturing the faces of the other girls who'd looked so much like me: young, petite, dark hair.

"Scared, *payashē?*" a man whispered in my ear.

I jerked away so violently I almost toppled my chair.

A hand grabbed my shoulder and pulled me straight. His breath washed over my cheek as he chuckled.

"Try to be brave. I like it better when they fight."

My stomach jumped, threatening to expel its contents.

Fingers brushed across my forehead, combing my hair back. "You're perfect, Robin. You look so close." Another quiet laugh. "You think I'm delusional, don't you? You're thinking, how could he know what a *payashē* even looks like? I'll admit, I've never seen one … who has? But I'm *very* familiar with their descriptions."

He caressed my jaw. "Compared to demon males, they're tiny—five feet, maybe a bit taller. Slim. Big, beautiful red eyes." He ran a fingertip up my temple and into my hair. "They have horns just like the males, but more delicate. More curvy."

I cringed from his touch, panting through the gag. The stale air, reeking of dirt, didn't have enough oxygen. My head spun.

"They don't have wings or scales. But they do have …" He forced his hand behind my back and slid it down, pressing his fingers into my lower spine. "… tails."

He dragged his hand back up and took a fistful of my hair. Damp lips pressed into my ear. "When I paint you red, *payashē*, you'll be too beautiful for words."

A violent, terrified sob shook my body. He *tsked* in disappointment.

Something thudded against the ceiling, then the clack of boots on the ladder as someone descended into the hidden basement.

"Get off her, Jaden. Fun's over."

"What?" Jaden snapped. "The fun is just getting started."

"She's too valuable."

"I wasn't going to kill her."

"Accidents happen when you get carried away," the newcomer sneered as the ladder creaked again. "Besides, I'm not the one saying no."

"If Dad thinks he can deny me the most perfect—"

"It isn't your father's decision," a different voice interrupted. "It's mine."

My entire body went numb with fresh panic. No. No, it couldn't be.

Not now. Not here.

Heavy steps drew closer, and the blindfold slid up my face. I squinted in the dim light of a lamp in the basement's corner, terrified of what I would see. My gaze stuttered across broad shoulders in a dark jacket, darted up to a clean-shaven jaw, and halted on an ugly scar that ran from the man's chin up to his distorted lower lip.

Claude's familiar dark eyes assessed me, cold and merciless. "We meet again, Robin."

A rough noise escaped my throat, muffled by my gag. I didn't know if it was a sound of fear or rage.

The twin sorcerers stood off to the side, one expressionless and the scratched one glowering like a put-out child—that must be Jaden. Their father stood on Claude's left, his coat removed to reveal the same armbands as his sons. He held the binder of grimoire pages in one hand, and in the other, the chain of my infernus. A green cube encased the dangling pendant. Crimson light flashed inside it, then died out.

Claude turned to the older man. "You have no idea the prize you've captured, Saul."

"Because you concealed her from us," Saul retorted, muted anger in his gravelly voice. "You didn't think we'd like to know that the Twelfth House has finally been summoned?"

"Don't lose sight of our goal, my friend." Claude glanced at the twins. "Though, I suspect you already have. You couldn't restrain yourselves for a few weeks?"

"You asked for my help. I came to help. What else we do while here is beside the point."

"Your obsession is the reason we parted ways twenty years ago, Saul. I warned you again and again that butchering women was—"

"Parted ways?" Jaden interrupted. "He's so tactful, isn't he, Braden?"

The expressionless twin sneered. "You ostracized us. You and that ludicrous—"

Claude sliced a hand through the air. "We've been through this enough times, Saul. I cautioned you. You didn't listen, and I had no choice but to cut you off."

"I know. That's why when you called me for help with the array, I came." Saul's pale gaze moved to the table covered in papers and notes. "We found a way to fill in the missing piece. We'll be ready tomorrow night, as long as we get a clear sky."

"Excellent. Now let's deal with our young guest, shall we?"

My skin chilled as all four men turned to me.

"What's the plan?" Jaden asked, licking his lips. A bandage was wrapped tightly around his lower left leg, the white gauze stained with blood.

"First we will relieve her of her demon, then we'll relieve her of her grimoire."

"Who gets the demon?" Saul asked.

Jaden and Braden shifted forward, their eager stares fixing on my infernus.

Claude smiled at me. "The demon is mine."

As the twins slouched with disappointment, Saul scowled. "How many demons do you need?"

"All of them, my friend. All of them."

He pulled my infernus from Saul's grasp and tossed it into the summoning circle. It hit the concrete with a clang and the green cube burst apart.

Crimson light exploded from the infernus. Bolts of power leaped upward, hitting an invisible barrier, and Zylas took form in the center of the chaos.

He crouched over the infernus, red eyes glowing and teeth bared. Shadows dimmed the circle's interior. Ice coated the floor. Ripples of magic snaked off the demon, but nothing passed the array's edge—the unseen dome that sealed him within. For the second time in his life, Zylas was trapped in a summoning circle.

Those fierce, enraged eyes locked on mine. His claws dug into the concrete.

"Zylas, isn't it?" Claude strolled to the circle's edge, studying the demon. "We finally meet—properly."

The demon's attention shifted from me to the summoner—a lethal predator homing in on his prey. He didn't snarl insults or hiss threats. He just stared, and his stare promised death.

Claude folded his hands behind his back. "Zylas of the Twelfth House, you will accept a contract with me."

A tiny, despairing sound rasped in my throat. When Zylas didn't react to the summoner's command, Claude crossed to me. His fingers closed around my hair, forcing my head back.

"I don't know the extent of your contract's protection clause, but we can certainly find out," he told the demon. "Should we start by inflicting pain? Making her bleed? Or should I let the boys have her for a few hours? I trust you've been in the human world long enough to know what they plan to do."

I jerked my head against Claude's hold. *Don't listen to him, Zylas.*

His jaw flexed as his gaze snapped from me to the summoner and back. The layer of ice on the floor thickened and the darkness inside the dome swirled.

Zylas, don't—

"I agree."

The gag deadened my cry of protest. *No, Zylas!*

Claude hesitated, then chuckled. "That was easier than I expected. You have an excellent contract with your demon, Robin."

I gritted my teeth, knowing what was coming next. This scenario had already played out once before with Red Rum.

"Now, my dear, you will give your demon permission to enter into a contract with me."

Nostrils flaring as I breathed deep, I braced myself. Zylas couldn't refuse because our contract bound him to protect me, but nothing could force me to agree. Claude could dislocate my fingers like Red Rum had done. He could cut me open. He could give me to those sick brothers. I would never—

"Do what he says."

Every muscle in my body locked up. Those words … they couldn't have come from my demon's mouth. He wouldn't … Surely I'd imagined it.

Claude peered at Zylas in surprise. The twin sorcerers arched their eyebrows, glancing between me and my demon.

Zylas …

"Say yes."

I can't—

"Do it!" he snarled, his glower locked on me. "Agree, Robin!"

My limbs shook, my heart tearing. I couldn't. I couldn't betray him, not to Claude. Not to our enemy. Not to the man who'd killed my parents. I couldn't let him have Zylas, my partner, my ally, my—

Trust me.

It was the faintest whisper in my mind, so weak and distant I might have imagined it. Across the distance between us, across the invisible, impenetrable barrier that separated us, Zylas stared at me. Stared into me. His eyes scoured my soul, a promise hidden in their glowing depths.

Trust him.

Tears spilled down my cheeks. I convulsed with a sob, the bindings on my wrists scraping my skin raw. I had to suck in air, had to search for strength. It took everything I had to force my head to move.

I nodded my permission. My surrender.

Everything around me blurred as tears streamed from my eyes. I wept, unable to stop. Men bustled and voices murmured, but I didn't hear them. In my head, I listened for Zylas's voice, needing to hear him again.

Desperate to understand.

Desperate for him to explain.

Why? Why was he letting this happen?

But I heard only silence, only my internal screams, my howling denials that this couldn't happen, wouldn't happen. I couldn't lose him. I needed him. I needed him with me.

I would rather die than let Claude have him.

Why won't you let me save you, Zylas?

A voice chanted an incantation. Claude. He stood in front of the circle, a grimoire cradled in his open hand. The three sorcerers waited, watching, listening.

Zylas crouched in the circle's center, darkness rippling around him. His eyes were on me, boring deep. As if in a dream, I remembered him crouched in a different summoning circle. Remembered him pressing against the transparent barrier, straining to reach me. Remembered sliding my blood-slick hand across the hardwood floor, my fingers crossing the silver inlay.

My arms jerked against the bindings.

"Zylas of Vh'alyir, you hereby bind yourself to my will. You will obey my commands without question or deceit. You will take no action without my permission. You will not harm me in any way, physically or mentally, or allow harm to befall me. You will ..."

I lost track of the contract clauses. Couldn't hear Claude listing them, one after another after another. All I could hear were my own hoarse, muffled cries against the gag, as though if I made enough noise, I could drown out the summoner and stop this.

Zylas, please don't. Please!

"I accept."

My body went limp, limbs slack against the bindings.

A chain jingled. A new infernus with a blank face—awaiting a House sigil. Claude passed his grimoire to Saul, then arranged the infernus over his palm. He stepped closer to the circle.

This couldn't happen. It couldn't. It had to stop. *Someone stop this!*

Zylas shifted to the circle's edge and pressed his hand to the unseen barrier. Claude pushed the infernus against the demon's palm, holding it in place.

I remembered cold metal edges digging into my palm. Zylas's fingers squeezing mine, my blood all over both of us. His arm supporting me. His breath in my ear as he whispered the command that had sealed us together forever.

"*Enpedēra vīsh nā,*" Claude declared, the foreign words rough and awkward.

"*Enpedēra vīsh nā,*" Zylas whispered, the same sounds guttural but elegant in his husky voice.

Crimson magic blazed out of the infernus, and Claude stiffened. Burning pain was blasting down his arm and into his chest as the magic bound his very being. I remembered that feeling too.

The light died away. Claude staggered back, clutching the infernus, its chain swinging from his white-knuckled grip. Zylas slowly lowered his arm, his gaze downcast, his unmoving tail coiled across the floor.

A rushing sound filled my ears. It had happened. It was done. Zylas was bound to Claude. He wasn't my demon anymore.

He belonged to Claude now.

20

"CONGRATULATIONS, MY FRIEND," Saul murmured. "You've achieved your dream at last."

Claude smiled modestly. "It's taken a long time to get here."

Zylas didn't move, gazing blankly at the floor. The men continued talking, their words mush in my ears. I didn't care. It didn't matter.

"Robin."

I started, shocked to find Claude standing in front of me. I hadn't noticed him moving closer.

"Where is the grimoire, Robin?"

My apathy shattered. I shrieked against the gag, lunging forward. The chair wobbled, its legs scraping the dirt floor. Hatred scorched my soul and I wanted my hands around his throat. I wanted demonic claws so I could tear him apart, so I could gouge those callous eyes from his skull.

He'd taken my parents from me, and now he'd taken Zylas too. If I killed him, Zylas would be freed from the summoner's command.

Grabbing my throat, Claude shoved me and the chair back into the cinderblock wall. He studied me as I screamed against the gag.

"I'll keep this simple, my dear. There's no way to move a contract from one person to another."

My shrieks cut off. I sucked in air, teeth gritted.

"Regardless of the rumors to the contrary, a contract can't be transferred, but"—he smiled coldly—"a demon *can* be shared. We spent many years developing the ritual you just witnessed."

He leaned close, his face filling my vision. "I, however, don't like to share. Your contract with Zylas is about to end, and there's only one way that can happen." Releasing my throat, he stepped back. "So here is my offer, Robin. Tell me where the grimoire is and how to get it, and I'll kill you so quickly you won't feel a thing. Refuse, and I'll give you to my old friends, who'd very much like to spend a good long time with you before you die."

Across the room, Jaden grinned hungrily.

I trembled against the chair.

Claude studied my face, then sighed. "Well, her stubbornness is good news for your boys, Saul."

The old sorcerer made a quiet noise. "Unfortunate for you, though. Aren't you in a hurry?"

"I can't linger for long." Claude turned away from me. "Someone has been meddling in our affairs, and if they go so far as to trespass in the Court, I intend to be waiting for them."

"Could it be the sorceress' doing? Dealing with a woman like that—"

"Varvara served her purpose well, and she even did me the convenience of dying once I had what I needed." Claude rubbed his jaw, the stiff scar on his chin pulling at his lip. "But I may not need to wait for Robin to change her mind. Her former demon should know where to find the grimoire."

As he moved toward the circle, where Zylas was still crouched, he waved at the impatiently waiting twins. "She's all yours. Just don't kill her yet."

Grinning, Jaden strode around the perimeter of the room, Braden following a step behind. Their gazes raked over me, anticipation burning in their faces and madness burning in their twisted souls.

"I hope you appreciate the lenient contract I gave you, Zylas," Claude murmured, stopping at the circle's edge. "I didn't bind your voice or magic. If you cooperate, you won't find service to me terrible."

Zylas slowly lifted his head, his glowing stare flat.

Holding the dangling infernus, Claude thrust his hand into the circle. "*Daimon, hesychaze.*"

Zylas dissolved into crimson power. The light leaped into the infernus.

As Claude pulled his infernus out of the circle and settled the chain around his neck, Jaden and Braden crouched on either side of my chair. I flinched, but I had no escape—no way to avoid their hands as they reached for me. Touching my arms. Squeezing my thighs. Jaden stroking my cheek as he whispered his sick fantasies in my ear.

Red light flashed. Zylas took shape again, standing obediently beside Claude.

The summoner tapped his chin thoughtfully. "Well, Zylas? Tell me where Robin hid the grim—"

A flash of claws, swift and deadly.

Blood sprayed from Claude's chest. He fell backward, shock blanking his face, mouth gaping.

Zylas sprang like a panther, canines bared. Jaden and Braden slammed into the walls on either side of me. The chair beneath me shattered. Then Zylas was sweeping me against him. Crimson power blazed over his arm as he stretched it toward the ceiling, palm turned up, fingers spread. A huge spell formed above his palm.

"*Ori quinque!*"

Saul's spell hurled Zylas into the wall, the cinderblock shattering from the impact—but the demon's cast didn't falter.

Magic detonated like a bomb.

The blast tore the ceiling off the basement—tore right through the garage above. Debris tumbled down, and Zylas smashed a beam aside as he leaped upward.

Saul was shouting Claude's name. He was shouting at his sons for help.

Zylas caught the broken edge of the floor and sprang again, soaring over the wreckage of the garage. Wind rushed past, streetlights gleaming brightly. He landed in the alley and whirled so fast my head snapped sideways.

Crimson flashed, Zylas leaped, and a blow like a speeding car hit us.

Everything spun, and we crashed to the ground. My arms wrenched painfully, still tied behind my back. Zylas rolled over and lurched up, standing over me in a protective crouch. Dust roiled through the air, a swath of pavement disintegrated from the attack.

Wings spread, Nazhivēr dropped through the haze and landed on the road. He bared his teeth in a vicious grin as he extended his clawed fingers toward us for another strike. Spells flashed up his arm, pulsing with power.

Somewhere behind us, an engine roared.

Zylas thrust out both hands, magic blazing up his wrists, but he'd never defeated Nazhivēr in combat. Had never even come close.

The roaring grew louder—and Nazhivēr unleashed his attack. An incomprehensible beam of pure destructive power rocketed toward us, and Zylas's counterspell wasn't ready, runes still forming, a second too slow.

Crimson lines flashed across the ground beneath me—magic that hadn't come from Zylas.

A wall of red light appeared inches from my face. Nazhivēr's blast struck it and deflected upward, the screaming power surging into the sky. The shield shattered, and a shockwave of power thudded into me. Zylas staggered, then slashed his hands down.

Red blades whipped at Nazhivēr. The unprepared demon shielded his head with his arms, the cutting attack scoring his armor and slicing his flesh. His blood splattered the asphalt.

The roaring sound grew louder, then tires squealed. The stench of burning rubber hit my nose—and someone grabbed my jacket.

"Come on!"

I was unceremoniously thrown across the front of a motorcycle, the air punched from my stomach.

"Zylas!"

A hand roughly grabbed mine, and a cold metal disc was shoved against my palm. My fingers closed over it, instinctive, reflexive, my grip so tight it hurt. Light blazed and the infernus vibrated as Zylas's spirit filled it.

234 ◆ ANNETTE MARIE

Tires screaming against the pavement, the motorcycle took off. I twisted, squinting past my rescuer. A gritty dust cloud hung over the street, and Nazhivēr was no more than a shadow with dark wings and crimson claws glowing through the haze.

"ROBIN? Robin, talk to me."

I blinked slowly. A face came into focus—bronze skin, a white scar, a pale eye that burned scarlet deep in its center.

"Ezra?" I mumbled.

"Are you hurt?"

Struggling to focus, I mentally catalogued my aches and pains. Nothing seemed too terrible. The worst pain came from my fingers, where I was clutching my infernus so tightly my skin had rubbed raw. My wrists were no longer bound, but I didn't remember who'd freed me or when.

I glanced around. I was sitting on the back of an idling motorcycle in an unfamiliar downtown alley, and I didn't remember getting here either.

Ezra stood beside me, frowning worriedly. He squeezed my shoulder. "I'll take you to a healer and—"

"Home," I croaked.

His frown deepened. "We should at least go to the guild so—"

"Home. Please."

"Where do you live? The address in the guild database is wrong."

Later, I would be annoyed that he'd tried to stalk me at my home. I told him my real address, too exhausted and shaky to worry about whether that was a good idea. He swung onto the bike in front of me and instructed me to hold on to him.

As I looped the infernus chain over my neck, I muttered, "I didn't know you drove a motorcycle."

"It's not mine. I borrowed it." He glanced over his shoulder. "And it's not my favorite mode of transportation, so you really should hold on."

That was reassuring. I gripped his jacket tightly.

The ride to my apartment was cold and terrifying, partly because neither Ezra nor I had helmets, and partly because he didn't take a direct route. He cut through alleys, zigzagged along the downtown streets, and circled several blocks. I understood why but I didn't enjoy it.

Finally, he pulled up at my dingy building and cut the engine. I fumbled through my jacket pockets to find my keys and unlocked the barred security doors. He followed me to the third floor and waited as I unlocked my apartment and stepped inside.

"Stay here," he said. "I'll make sure we weren't followed, then come check on you."

I nodded.

Searching my face, he gave my shoulder another brief squeeze. "You're okay, Robin."

"Y-yeah."

I shut and bolted the door behind him, then stumbled into the living room. Curled up on the sofa, Socks lifted her head to peer at me. Amalia's door was shut, no light shining under it. She wasn't home.

I kicked my shoes off and walked unsteadily into my room. My jacket fell to the floor in the doorway as I pushed it off my arms. Stopping a few feet from my bed, I stared blankly. My fingers ached and I realized I was clutching the infernus again.

Zylas?

The pendant vibrated under my hand. With a crimson flare, he appeared in front of me.

My gaze snapped to his face, and his to mine. For a moment, neither of us moved—then he was reaching for me. His hands passed over my cheeks and shoulders, cold sparks of his magic prickling my skin as he probed for unseen damage to my fragile human innards.

My hands were on him, running over his arms, searching for injuries. Other than the scuffs on his armor from being thrown into the pavement too many times, he seemed fine.

Except he wasn't. He couldn't be. He'd been bound into a contract with our enemy. Even if the magic had somehow failed, he'd lived one of his nightmares today.

My hands shook and I gripped his arms. The urge to collapse against him was almost too strong, but I pushed back. Stumbling to the bed, I sank onto the edge of the mattress before my legs gave out. My hand crept to the infernus again. I didn't know when or how Zylas had gotten it out of the summoning circle.

I crushed the disc in my fingers. Claude had said a contract couldn't be transferred, but what if …

I squeezed my eyes shut. *Daimon, hesychaze.*

Light flashed and the pendant vibrated. My eyes popped open as Zylas burst back out of the infernus, appearing almost on top of me with his eyes blazing.

"*Vayanin!*"

"I had to make sure," I whispered. "What if our contract was broken? What if …"

What if the only thing that connected us had been severed?

His anger faded, but his jaw didn't loosen. A muscle jumped in his cheek as he stared down at me. Then he dropped to his knees, pushing between my legs. His arms went around my waist, pulling me into him, and he buried his face against my side.

Frozen in place, I sat on the bed with my demon holding me. *Hugging* me. Arms encircling me, holding tight. Face pressed into the soft spot just above my hip.

My brain fizzed uselessly. Never before had Zylas hugged me. Caught me when I was falling, carried me, picked me up, hauled me around … but not an embrace. He'd touched me gently, fiercely, angrily, protectively, curiously … but never like this.

Never like he needed to be close to me.

My arms clamped around his head and shoulders, and I curled over him, my nose in his hair, my knees squeezing his sides. I hugged him with my whole body as emotion filled my chest to bursting—relief, despair, lingering terror, and a hot, swooping feeling I couldn't name and didn't want to think about.

In a way I'd never felt before, his strength surrounded me—his arms banded around my waist, his muscular shoulders under my hands, the hardness of his torso between my legs. But at the same time, I could feel vulnerability in him like I never had before. And that made my arms tighten, made me pull him closer.

We held each other like that, and I had no idea how much time had passed before his grip on my sweater finally relaxed. I untangled my fingers from his hair and lifted my cheek from his head.

"I thought they would kill you."

I stilled at his husky whisper.

He pushed his face into my side. "I thought they would hurt you and kill you and I would be trapped in the circle. I would not be able to protect you. I would have to watch you die."

He raised his head. His eyes burned, but I couldn't begin to decipher the emotion in them.

I brushed a tangled lock of hair off his forehead. "You saved me. You ... you *slashed Claude open.*" Shock rippled through me at the realization. "Is he—do you think he's dead?"

"It was not a killing wound. I cut deep to make him bleed but not die, so the others would stay to help him."

"But how did you do it? How could you attack him after he bound you in a contract?"

His gaze flicked between my eyes. His hands, resting on my hips, tightened until his fingers dug in, then relaxed again.

"It did not work," he said abruptly. "The *vīsh* did not bind me."

"But Claude's infernus worked on you. Doesn't that mean the contract was a success?"

He said nothing, and a strange shiver danced down my spine. "Zylas? Why didn't it work?"

He stared at me, an intent observation I now recognized as his attempt to hear more thoughts than what I was sharing.

"I bound myself to you. Only you, *vayanin.*"

I couldn't quite breathe. Still kneeling in front of me, he looked away from my confused stare. His hands slid from my hips to my legs, powerful fingers spanning the tops of my thighs.

Swallowing against the tightness in my throat, I slowly pushed off the bed and knelt on the floor with him. My hands went to his shoulders, then I pulled myself against his chest and wrapped my arms around his neck, my face buried against his throat.

I'd fallen into him. Leaned on him. Clung to him. But I'd never hugged him before either.

At first, he didn't move. Then his arms slid around me and closed tight, powerful muscles pressing into my sides and back, so strong I could never break free. And I pressed even closer because, for maybe the first time, no tiny voice in my head bleated in fear that a scary demon had me trapped.

No part of me, no baser instinct or cowardly gut reaction, was the slightest bit afraid of his strength. Because I knew, deep in the darkest and most doubtful corner of my skeptical soul, that he would never hurt me.

A loud clatter sounded from the front room.

I jumped in fright, and Zylas shot to his feet, hauling me up with him.

"Yeah, right," a loud voice exclaimed sarcastically. "You just happened to drive Robin home? Suuuure."

A quieter male voice answered as the door banged open.

"Well, you can just screw right off." Amalia's aggressive tones flooded the living room. "Or do you want me to tell the guild officers how you're lurking around our apartment? Or maybe I'll tell them some *other* interesting facts—"

Pulling away from Zylas, I rushed out of the bedroom. "Amalia!"

She jerked away from Ezra, who stood in the doorway. A plastic bag swung from her elbow as she pointed at the mage.

"He says you told him to—"

"I did," I said breathlessly as Zylas drifted out of the bedroom after me. "He just saved me and Zylas."

Huffing, she smacked her bag down on the counter. A corner of black fabric spilled out. "Fine. But don't think you're fooling us. Robin told me all about your little *secret*." Her eyes narrowed to slits. "Nice, law-abiding people don't end up demon mages by accident."

"I'm aware." Ezra stepped inside and shut the door behind him. "How are you, Robin?"

"I'm okay."

"And Zylas?"

I glanced at the demon, who was hovering behind me. "He's fine."

Folding her arms, Amalia leaned against the counter and glared at Ezra. "What happened?"

Sinking onto the sofa, I managed to keep my voice steady as I summed up my and Zylas's capture and escape. Ezra and Amalia listened intently, the latter's bad temper fading as I spoke.

"Well, shit," she muttered, her flinty stare on the mage. "Your timing was awfully convenient."

"It was lucky. When Robin didn't show up at the guild or answer her phone, I figured I'd better look for her."

"I'm glad you did," I mumbled.

Amalia twisted her mouth. "So Claude has a contract with Zylas now? Or did it fail?"

I gave the demon a brief look. He stood by the balcony doors as Socks wound between his ankles. Ezra frowned at the half-grown kitten as though worried for her safety.

"Well, Zylas?" Amalia demanded. "Are you in another contract?"

The demon shrugged.

"We have more urgent worries," I pointed out, not wanting to dwell on the possibility that the summoner had power over Zylas. "Claude is still alive, and he's got the abjuration sorcerers helping him with a spell from the grimoire pages."

"That must be why he called them to Vancouver," Amalia mused. "We think they've been here three or four weeks. That's when women started disappearing, right?"

"That lines up with when Claude stole the pages."

"But what's he after? What spells are even in the grimoire, aside from summoning rituals?" Amalia bounced her leg nervously. "Have you found any?"

"The grimoire is full of experimental arrays, but I haven't translated them," I admitted guiltily. I'd been too busy finding and translating Myrrine's story to pay attention to Anthea's spells.

"What grimoire are you talking about?"

I started. I'd forgotten Ezra was there.

"It's, um …" I cleared my throat. "It's my family's grimoire. Claude wants it because it has the name of the Twelfth House, as well as some ancient spells."

I doubted Ezra could preternaturally detect lies, but that didn't mean Eterran couldn't. Better to offer a partial truth than a lie.

Focusing properly on the mage, I sat forward, subconsciously gripping the cushions to brace myself. "Ezra, you saved our lives and I'm grateful, but I haven't forgotten that you want something from us. You still haven't told us what."

Leaning against the wall beside the door, he weighed me, then turned his focus to Zylas and performed the same assessment. A deep magma glow ignited in his left eye.

"We want the Amulet of Vh'alyir."

Silence pressed down on the apartment, then Amalia pointed at the demon mage and half shrieked, "What the actual f—"

"The *imailatē* belongs to my House," Zylas growled. "Not Dh'irath."

"We do not want to *keep* it." Eterran's accent bled into Ezra's voice. "We want to *use* it."

"What we need," Ezra clarified, "is information on how it works and how to use its power. Then we just need to … borrow it."

"You have knowledge of it," Eterran added. "You can tell us what we need to know."

My fingers bit into the cushion. In light of Tori's terse questions about the amulet, I wasn't entirely surprised, but it wasn't what I'd expected.

"We don't have the amulet," I told the demon mage. "We're hoping to find it, but …"

"But you lost it after Tahēsh's death."

"How do you know about that?" Amalia asked suspiciously.

"Tahēsh tried to give it to me." Eterran's power blazed in Ezra's left eye. "Our Houses have always been allied. He tried to free me. Together, we would have been unstoppable. We would have found a way to return to our world—or we would have spent our years in this world punishing all *hh'ainun* who have ever dared to enslave a demon."

His vicious smile morphed into a disgusted grimace. "But I didn't let him take the amulet," Ezra said. "Though I didn't know it's power then."

"Back up a hot minute," Amalia interrupted. "What *power?*"

Ezra was silent for a moment. If he and Eterran had been separate beings, they would've been exchanging a long look—an unhappy one.

"You do not know? Vh'alyir's *imailatē* grants its holder immunity to contracts. It is why *hh'ainun* do not summon the Twelfth House. They believe the *Dīnen et Vh'alyir* still possess it and would slaughter any summoner."

My mouth hung open. Zylas looked just as shocked.

"How do you know that?" I asked unsteadily.

"It is known by the Lūsh'vēr and Dh'irath *Dīnen*. I thought it was a mere story until Tahēsh offered it to me." He looked at Zylas. "You did not know this?"

The demon's lips pulled back. "Who would teach me the stories of my House, Dh'irath? You and Lūsh'vēr have killed all who know them."

"Then you do not know how the amulet works."

Anger buzzed across my nerves at Eterran's cool reply—his complete lack of remorse for his House's slaughter of Zylas's. How many Vh'alyir demons had Eterran killed before being summoned here?

"It sounds like you already know everything you need to know," I said frostily. "If you possess the amulet, you become immune to your contract and you can split with Ezra. All you have to do is find it."

"And good luck with that," Amalia muttered.

"We need to know more," Eterran growled. "The amulet—"

He broke off, a snarl twisting his lips. He slapped his hand over his left eye, shoulders hunching, tendons standing out sharply in his neck. The temperature dropped, a bone-deep chill permeating the air.

The tension slid from the mage. He straightened and lowered his hand—revealing a pale eye with no hint of crimson. "The part Eterran skipped over is that I won't let him—or rather, us—anywhere near that amulet until I understand

244 ♠ ANNETTE MARIE

exactly what will happen. The best-case scenario is it breaks our
contract and Eterran can leave my body. I'll be free of him."

"Does he even have a body anymore?" Amalia asked. "How
long can a demon possess someone before their body just …
stops existing?"

"He should be unchanged." Zylas's tail snapped against the
floor. "Demons have disappeared into *Ahlēvīsh* for years and
returned no different."

"What's an *Ah*—" I began.

"What is the bad case?" Zylas asked before I could get the
question out.

"That the amulet will break the contract but not break
whatever magic binds Eterran inside my body, and he'll take
full control." Pushing off the wall, Ezra crossed to the sofa and
sat on the opposite end. "Or its magic won't be compatible with
a demon mage, and we'll both be driven mad."

"But that'll happen anyway," Amalia pointed out. "All
demon mages go mad eventually."

Ezra nodded. Folding his hands together, he pressed his chin
against them. "I promised myself a long time ago that as soon
as I knew my mind was failing, I'd end it. But now that the
moment's come … it's not as easy as I thought to die."

I drew in a silent, sympathetic breath. I couldn't imagine
what circumstances had driven him to become a demon mage,
but he didn't seem like a bad person. And Tori definitely didn't
think he was rogue scum.

His eyes slid closed. "It would've been easier months ago,
before …"

"Do you really think the amulet can save you?" I asked
softly.

"I don't know, but I want to try. It's stupid … I gave up a long time ago, so why am I suddenly fighting now?"

A pair of hazel eyes, sharp with despair and determination, filled my mind's eye. He wasn't the only one fighting, and maybe that's why he couldn't passively accept his fate anymore.

"So you want to know *exactly* how the amulet works," I summarized. "You want the details of the spell's function and how it voids contracts."

He nodded.

"I don't know that … yet." I hesitated, considering what else to add, but while I was pretty sure Ezra had a conscience, I had my doubts about Eterran. "I think I can find the answers you need, but we'll need your help with Claude and the sorcerers first."

"Yes, of course. I need to have a chat with this Claude person about why he had my profile. I'm assuming that winged demon was his."

"And in a very illegal contract." I rubbed my hands together anxiously. "Whatever they're planning, it can't be good."

Ezra rose to his feet. "We can't solve everything tonight. Get some rest, and we'll talk tomorrow. I'll also …" His face lost expression, all emotion hidden. "I should give Tori a call and find out where she is."

"You don't know where she went on her trip?"

"I know where she *went*, not where she *is*," he answered flatly. "I should go."

As he headed for the door, I hastily stood. "Hold up. I'll walk you downstairs."

Ezra opened his mouth to protest, then changed his mind. I shoved my feet in my shoes, gave Zylas and Amalia a quick wave, then hurried after the mage.

In silence, we walked down the rickety stairs that always smelled like cigarette smoke. At the building's main doors, we found it pouring rain, the black motorcycle on the curb drenched and shining.

Ezra sighed at the sight.

"I don't want to pry," I began, wondering why on earth I was attempting this conversation, "but even though she didn't say it, I think Tori is worried about you."

His expression didn't change, remaining blank and unreadable—but Zylas did that too, and I'd learned to find hints of his feelings. A tick in the jaw. A flex of muscle. The slight contraction of his pupils.

I could see all that and more in Ezra's tight face, so I said nothing, waiting. Either he would walk out the door, or …

He exhaled harshly through his nose. "Has someone you cherished ever lied to you, Robin?"

"What kind of lie?"

"The kind of lie where the truth would have changed everything."

Rain poured down, droplets streaking the glass door.

"Yes." I folded my hands, fingernails digging in. "My parents. My mother. They hid something from me … they hid our family's past and my whole future. I can't even guess how many lies they told me to keep it a secret."

I could feel his stare on the top of my head, and I wondered if that was the response he'd expected.

"What did you do when you found out?"

"Nothing. My parents were already dead. Claude killed them."

A sharp inhalation, the sound almost lost in the pattering rain.

Tears pooled in the corners of my eyes as familiar grief swamped my lungs. "But if I could see her one more time, I would tell my mother that I understand ... and I would say thank you."

"Thank you?" he whispered.

"She was protecting me. Maybe she was wrong ... she thought so herself by the end ... but all she wanted was for me to be happy. Lying to me every day must have been so hard for her. I think it might've hurt her more than it ever hurt me."

Ezra was silent, and I wiped my eyes, embarrassed that I hadn't completely stifled the tears.

"Thank you," he murmured. "For sharing that."

I nodded, concern welling in me because his blank façade was cracking, and I knew what Zylas would've said if he'd been here. He would've told me the mage smelled of pain. Great pain.

"I'll text you tomorrow to set up a time to meet."

"Okay," I said softly, knowing there was nothing else I, a virtual stranger, could do for him.

He pushed the door open, and a cold, wet wind blew raindrops across the threshold. He stepped into the downpour, and as he walked to the motorcycle, I hoped he would make that call to Tori.

And I hoped Tori, wherever she'd gone, was ready for it.

21

I ignored Amalia's question as I slipped through the door and into the apartment, my gaze sweeping the room for Zylas.

"He just went for the shower. Any second—"

With a muffled *thunk* of the tap and a splash, the shower started up.

Oddly relieved, I toed off my untied shoes and slouched into the kitchen. I opened the fridge, my stomach aching with hunger but my mouth dry and taste buds completely disinterested in food.

"Ezra and Eterran want to know all about the amulet," I muttered crankily. "Just one more thing on our plate. The only bright side is that they'll probably help us find it."

"And if we're lucky, they won't steal it," Amalia added, bracing her elbows on the breakfast bar.

"They'd better not. Myrrine wouldn't have called the amulet the 'key to everything' if all it did was break contracts.

It must have a bigger purpose, but I wasn't going to mention that to them." I swung the fridge shut and crouched to open the freezer. "Or that we have no clue about the amulet's magic."

"Well, *you* don't have a clue, maybe."

One hand gripping the freezer drawer, I frowned up at her. "Meaning what?"

She held her neutral expression for a moment before her grin broke free. "While you were off chasing murderers," she declared triumphantly, "I was off finding answers."

"Wait, what?" I plucked a small tub of vanilla ice cream from the freezer and stood. "I thought you were working on your secret sewing project."

"I've been doing that too, but only when I couldn't do anything else." She tugged a wad of newly purchased black fabric from her shopping bag, then slid a book from its folds. "You're already translating the grimoire, hunting down those murdering sickos, and fencing with a demon mage. I figured I could handle one job."

"But … why didn't you say anything?"

"So you wouldn't try to help and end up shouldering all the work like you always do." She flipped the book open, revealing a paper stuck inside—my careful drawing of the amulet and its array. "Check this out."

She pointed at the array, where unusual shapes and runes filled a pentagram, then gestured at the diagram on the book's facing page. An almost identical pentagram spanned the shiny paper.

"No way!" I exclaimed. "What kind of Arcana is it?"

She snapped the book shut and angled the cover toward me, revealing the title: *Abjuration Theory in the Astral Sphere.*

I slapped my palm against my forehead. "Abjuration! Of course!"

"Those sorcerers made me think of it, and it still took *forever* to find any abjuration arrays that matched the amulet one. But if the amulet is a fancy contract-breaker, then it makes sense, right? Abjuration is *the* magic for interrupting other magic."

"It makes *perfect* sense." I slid the drawing out and frowned at it. "How much abjuration will we need to learn to figure out this array?"

"Too much, since it'd take years to learn. Luckily, I've got us covered there too." She tapped the ice cream container. "Are we going to eat that, or just let it melt?"

I pulled two bowls out of the cupboard. No point in getting one for Zylas. In his opinion, which he hadn't been shy about sharing, ice cream was no better than sweet poison. His prejudice against any food served below room temperature was unreasonable. A little cold wouldn't kill him—unless he was half dead already, but I'd never make that mistake again.

She pried the lid off the container while I got out the scoop.

"So?" I prompted, handing the utensil to her. "How have you got us covered?"

"I paid a visit to Arcana Historia and asked for recommendations on an abjuration expert. The librarian instantly started gushing about this abjuration prodigy who uses their library. She was practically fangirling."

She plopped an oversized scoop of ice cream into my bowl. "So, long story short, we have a meeting tomorrow at seven with an abjuration sorceress. You and I don't need to learn a thing."

"Perfect." I stuck spoons in our bowls. "*And* we can ask if she's ever heard of these sorcerers, too."

"Good idea." Grinning, she lifted her bowl like it was a glass of wine. "Cheers, Robin."

Laughing, I clinked my bowl against hers, then spooned an icy glob into my mouth. "So, we've got a lead on the amulet's magic. It's something, at least."

"I mean, we still don't have the amulet," Amalia mused. "Plus, Claude's got psycho sorcerers helping him now."

"Don't forget whatever mysterious thing he got from Varvara." I sighed. "And we're back to square one on finding them, since Zylas blew their lair to smithereens."

She sighed too.

"But hey." I waved my spoon. "We have a scary demon mage on our side now."

"Do you think Zylas is happy to have more power in our corner, or would he rather not share the spotlight?"

I snorted and ate another bite of ice cream. "I don't think he knows how to feel about Eterran. They're enemies, but maybe that doesn't matter outside the demon world."

"Which reminds me." Amalia propped a hip against the counter. "Are you going to tell Ezra and Eterran that you're trying to send Zylas home?"

"I don't know."

"If the amulet works and they separate, you realize what that means, right?"

It meant an unbound Second House demon would be loose on Earth, with no contract binding him.

"Let's wait for now," I murmured. "I think ... I'd like to talk to Tori first."

Amalia nodded. We ate our ice cream, the muffled sound of the shower filling the quiet. I set my empty bowl in the sink and turned on the tap, watching the white porcelain fill with water. As the bowl overflowed, my eyes lost focus and a memory resurfaced.

"Tomorrow night," I whispered.

Amalia pulled her spoon out of her mouth. "Huh?"

"The old sorcerer said to Claude … he said the array would be ready tomorrow night." I looked up, my face cold. "How on earth are we going to find and stop them in one day?"

MY HEAD HURT.

The coffee table was covered in pages torn from my notebook, my scribbles covering each sheet. Rushed notes, half-finished translations, angry slashes through my mistakes. Reference books sat in a stack beside a bowl of fresh strawberries, but the texts hadn't been much help.

The words Anthea had used to describe her work didn't seem to exist anymore. At least not in the Ancient Greek dictionaries and lexicons I had.

Saul had said they'd proceed with their spell "as long as we get a clear sky," which meant they needed either starlight or moonlight. I'd been flipping from spell to spell all afternoon, searching for a mention of astral conditions in the grimoire. Anthea had been a dedicated experimenter. The grimoire might contain earlier versions of the spells Claude had stolen.

But between my inability to translate most of Anthea's notes and my total lack of knowledge on what spells Claude had, I was fishing in the dark.

Huffing angrily, I slumped against the sofa, my legs sprawled under the coffee table. Useless. If only I could've stolen the grimoire pages back. Even if Claude had made copies, at least I would've known what he had.

I straightened with a sigh and plucked a strawberry from the bowl, the green tops removed and sugar dusted over them. Nibbling on the end, I stared toward my bedroom.

Zylas had spent the night prowling the neighborhood, ensuring Claude, Nazhivēr, and the sorcerers hadn't tracked us to the apartment. He'd returned just as dawn broke, his eyes dim with fatigue. I'd relinquished my bed to him—though I could've let him crawl onto the mattress with me. There was no reason I had to leave so he could lie down.

A slow blush warmed my cheeks.

As I popped the rest of the strawberry into my mouth, my gaze slid to the grimoire. Unable to resist, I started turning its pages again. Past the spells. Past the House descriptions. Past Myrrine's heartsore account of how she'd feared she'd lost her Vh'alyir, and her indecision over whether to share her feelings.

I kept turning the pages, searching for the next glimpse of her name.

Finally, I found it. Tearing a fresh sheet from my notebook, I began the translation, my heart in my throat as I worked. The words came fast, Myrrine's ancient sentences spilling out of my pencil as though she were whispering in my ear.

Sister, you cannot imagine how these past months have tormented me. How I questioned my heart, my mind, the fate of my soul. How I wondered what madness had overtaken me.

I have stood before a demon of another world and wondered that which no woman should ever wonder. I have yearned for that which no woman should ever claim. I have laid my hands upon that which no woman should ever touch.

I offered a demon my soul, and then I offered him my heart.

Madness, perhaps, but if this is madness, I will keep it. Love in a cruel world is a cruelty itself. Love is pain and it is hope. Love is peril and it is beauty.

Melitta, my sweet sister, if I have learned anything it is this: do not let fear hold you in darkness. Reach for more than this small, cold world says you may have.

Dare as I dared.

Elsewise, this life is but a shadow to the sun it could be.

— Myrrine Athanas

I gripped my notebook page, my knuckles white. Myrrine's words were like a surf beating against me, loud in my ears, but they weren't enough. She hadn't revealed what had happened when she'd offered her demon her heart. She didn't seem to have regretted it—but *what had happened?*

How had her demon reacted? Had he shared her feelings? Had he reciprocated? Or had he rejected her? Turned her away? Taken the precious gift of her heart and thrown it back at her?

I reread my translation, desperate for answers. Love was pain and hope? Love was peril and beauty? What did that even mean?

My fumbling fingers reached for the grimoire again. Myrrine must've explained herself in the next entry. She would tell me whether her demon had loved her—or whether she'd made a terrible mistake. She would say more than a flowery speech about being brave and following your heart.

Dare as I dared.

I gave my head a violent shake and flipped pages with feverish intensity, almost forgetting to be careful with the fragile paper. Pages and pages passed, and as the end of the grimoire approached, panic awoke. That couldn't be it. That couldn't be Myrrine's last entry.

Ten pages left. Five. Three. Heart sinking, I reached the final page before the torn ridges where the stolen spells of the book had been. I listlessly scanned the block of text, but Myrrine's name wasn't there.

No way. She *must* have written something else. I'd just missed it. Puffing for air as though I were running through time instead of turning pages, I started flipping backward, scanning each page carefully, searching, searching.

Page after page. The content here was different—more blocks of text, few spells or lists. Other names signed the passages, but not Myrrine's. I flipped past yet another dense section, almost passing it over, when my breath caught.

It wasn't Myrrine's name, but still a familiar one.

Μέλιττα Ἀθάνας

Melitta Athanas.
Myrrine's younger sister. She'd added to the grimoire as well?

An ominous chill whispered over me. Picking up my pencil, I got to work. The paragraphs came slowly, and with each word, the ache in my heart grew. When I finished, I had to sit for a long minute before I could bring myself to read it.

Honorable scribe,

Today, I finished what my sister began. The grimoire is complete, each word loyally recorded. In the final pages, I compiled Anthea's masterful work, as my predecessor did. I add nothing except this plea.

Honorable scribe, please do not erase my sister from these pages. I know her additions to this precious tome are arrogant and improper, yet I beg you to keep them. Her words are all that remain of her.

She died for Anthea's legacy, and for me.

The enemy killed her but a year after she began her transcription. Many times in that year I doubted her perplexing affection for a demon, but I will never forget that final night. I will never forget how I found them together.

He held her close, as though he could still protect her, even though she was already pale and still.

Do not take her soul, I thoughtlessly begged him.

He answered, Her soul was never mine. Her command never bound me, so her soul could never save me. I should have told her.

Those were his last words, for his wounds were terrible and the night was so cold. He perished where he lay, holding my sister to his heart.

I do not know if he loved her as she loved him, but I buried them together in the hope that wherever their souls go, they will go together.

Myrrine died for this book, and her legacy deserves preservation as much as Anthea's. If we must protect this hellish prize with our lives, let our lives be inscribed upon its pages. If Anthea would arm our enemies with the same terrible power we guard, let us arm each other with the conviction to carry on.

I, and those who follow me, will need that conviction desperately.

Without the lost amulet, without the secrets or the truth Anthea deemed too dangerous for the

written word, we will never know why she cursed us
so. But I ask you this, daughter of my daughter,
honorable scribe, survivor, sorceress:
   when will it end?

   — Myrrine Athanas

A tear slid down my cheek. Melitta's grief and despair clung to her words. How much time had passed between Myrrine's death and Melitta's plea to the future scribes of the grimoire?

Myrrine … I would never know what had happened between her and her demon. I'd never find out if, or how, she had confessed her love. I'd never learn what his response had been or if he'd shared her feelings—if a demon's heart could love as a human's could.

But he'd held her as she'd died. He'd held her even after she was gone and his own life was slipping away.

I slid my fingers across my hasty print until they rested just below the ancient Vh'alyir's final words. *Her command never bound me, so her soul could never save me.*

My skin prickled, every hair on my body standing on end.

Her command never bound me.

I could hear Claude listing clause after clause for his new contract with Zylas. I could hear Zylas's hissed acceptance. The ritual had tied him to the infernus. Claude's command had forced him into the pendant.

The vīsh did not bind me.

Zylas had wounded Claude, despite agreeing not to harm the summoner.

Their contract hadn't worked.

Never summon from the Twelfth House.

If Myrrine's contract with a Vh'alyir demon hadn't worked, and Claude's contract with a Vh'alyir demon hadn't worked, then *my* contract …

The notebook fell from my numb hands.

22

AS MY NOTEBOOK hit the tabletop with a smack, I shoved off the floor. My knee bumped the table, the bowl of strawberries rocking precariously. The room seemed to whirl around me as I rushed across it.

My bedroom door struck the wall with a bang, and Zylas, stretched out on my bed, jerked upright. With a frightened yip, Socks leaped off my pillow and dove under the bed.

Awake in an instant, Zylas twisted toward me, crouched in the middle of the mattress and ready to do battle as soon as I told him where the enemy was.

I strode to the bed and stopped, breathing hard. "Zylas, do we have a contract?"

His eyebrows drew down. "*Na? Vayanin—*"

"*Do we have a contract?*" I yelled.

His eyes widened. He shifted backward, tail lashing side to side. "*Vayanin—*"

"Answer me!"

"I am bound to the infernus."

Demons didn't lie. He was evading my question.

"That's all you're bound to, isn't it?" I stared at him as though I'd never seen him before. Maybe I hadn't. I'd been blind all along, trusting in magic that wasn't there. "You didn't obey the clauses of your contract with Claude."

"It did not work."

"You *knew* it wouldn't work. You knew the contract would be powerless, and that's why you told me to agree."

"It was the only way to escape the circle." He was still skirting the truth I wanted. "The only way to protect you."

My unsteady hands curled into fists. "You don't have to protect me. You've *never* had to protect me. That's why I couldn't figure out the terms of our contract—because we don't have one!"

"We do. I promised to protect you. You promised to bake food for me. I promised to act like an enslaved demon. You promised to search for a way I can go home."

A tremor ran through me. "How long have you known?"

His crimson stare searched mine, probing for answers to questions I couldn't fathom. "I guessed by the second day that the contract *vīsh* did not bind me. I do not know why."

"Because you're from the Twelfth House. Eterran was wrong. The amulet isn't the reason summoning Vh'alyir demons is forbidden. It's forbidden because *no* Vh'alyir can be bound into a contract."

"Why are we different?"

"I don't know." My jaw clenched. "Why didn't you tell me?"

He dropped backward, sitting on the mattress, and pressed his hands to the blankets. "Because you did not trust me and I did not trust you."

I tried to step closer and my shin hit the bed frame. "What about later? Why didn't you say anything yesterday after we got away from Claude?"

"I could not tell you." His voice dipped into huskier tones. "If you knew the contract *vīsh* did not sheath my claws, you would fear me. I did not want you to fear me more."

My throat closed. I stepped back. Stepped back again. My head was reeling, my brain stunned into incoherence.

"Why?" I whispered hoarsely. "All along, you could've done anything you wanted. Left me. Killed me. Let someone else kill me. Forced me to do whatever you wanted. Why did you protect me all this time?"

Shadows gathered in his eyes, dimming the crimson glow. Quiet sadness hid in their depths.

"Because I promised."

I stumbled out of the bedroom. Everything had a strange, disconnected feel as I sank onto the floor behind the coffee table, returning to the same spot for no reason other than I didn't know what else to do. Didn't know what to think. Didn't know what to feel.

Zylas wasn't bound by our contract. He'd *never* been bound.

My shock cracked, and fury welled up through the fissures. How dare he hide this from me! How dare he mislead me! How dare he let me think I was protected by the contract when all along the only thing protecting me had been …

Him.

I pressed my palms to the tabletop.

He had protected me, not our contract. He had protected me even when I was annoying. When I was weak. When I was stupid. When I almost got him killed by Tahēsh. When I abandoned the infernus and got myself kidnapped. When I yelled at him for trying to keep me safe in ways I didn't like. When I drove him so crazy he would snarl and slash at the furniture. When he thought I secretly wanted him dead. When I hid my thoughts and feelings so deeply he couldn't fully trust me.

He'd protected me because when I'd put my hand across that silver line, and when he'd pulled me into his icy prison, we'd bound ourselves in a different way. Both facing death, both finding a chance in each other.

I bound myself to you. Only you, vayanin.

My hands trembled.

A shadow fell across me. The soft scuff of feet against carpet, the whisper of his tail following behind him. I kept my gaze on the open grimoire on the coffee table, trying to steady my breathing.

Zylas sank into a crouch, not quite in the gap between the table and sofa where I sat, but right at the edge.

"*Vayanin?*"

I concentrated, breathing in and out.

"Robin?"

My head jerked up. My gaze snapped to him, then away. Inches in front of me was the page with Myrrine's last journal entry before her death.

I offered a demon my soul, and then I offered him my heart.

Part of me had hoped she was wrong. That her feelings had been misplaced infatuation. That her attraction had been imagined, not real. That her demon would never reciprocate her affection in the slightest.

It would have been better if she hadn't wanted him and he hadn't wanted her. Everything was so much simpler that way. No chance of rejection. No risk of hurt or heartbreak. No fear of whether it was right or wrong or a crime against nature.

Love is pain and it is hope.

The other part of me had wanted Myrrine to be right. I'd wanted her not to care what anyone thought, to forge her own path, to go where no woman had gone before. I'd desperately, fanatically wanted her to take the risk and try.

Dare as I dared.

I raised my eyes to the demon an arm's length away.

"It's called blushing." I'd meant to speak confidently, but it came out in a fluttering mumble. "When my face turns red."

His tail slid across the carpet. "Blushing?"

"I blush from embarrassment, and I'm usually embarrassed because of you."

"Why?"

My throat tried to close against the words. "Because you … you get so close to me. And you touch me. And I …"

I stole a peek at him, and his confused frown sent blood rushing into my cheeks.

"And you're … you …" Gritting my teeth, I scrunched my eyes and forced the words out. "And when you do those things, I think about you … and about things I shouldn't think."

He was quiet. Probably completely flummoxed. My explanation was a mess and I knew it.

"I do not know your thoughts about me," he finally said, his voice quiet.

I couldn't resist checking his reaction—frowning in a worried way, like he was wondering if he'd done something wrong—and at the sight, I had the wild urge to flee the room. But running away was what I'd been doing all along, and look where that had gotten us. I'd been undermining our trust from the beginning, all because I couldn't admit this one thing to him.

Buying myself a moment to think, I grabbed a strawberry from the bowl beside me and bit the bottom off.

He shifted his weight. "*Vayanin?* What are your thoughts about me that are bad?"

"Not *bad.* Just … I …" I looked at the half-eaten strawberry between my fingers, dusted with sugar. "I keep thinking things …"

Things like his amazing body of hard muscle—dips and planes and smooth skin that I wanted to touch. Things like the feel of those powerful arms around me, and how his strength both daunted and thrilled me. Things like the way his husky voice could caress me, and how I always lost my train of thought when he murmured in my ear.

But I couldn't speak those words. I couldn't make a sound.

I stared at the strawberry. *Dare as I dared.*

My gaze lifted. Darted across his face. Settled on his mouth. Raising my hand, I slowly stretched out my arm and pressed the bite of fruit to his lips.

His eyes widened.

"What does this mean?" I whispered.

Lips parting, he took the strawberry with his teeth. He swallowed, watching me with half-lidded eyes.

"If you were a *payashē*, it means you choose me for your bed." His hooded gaze gauged my reaction. "But you are not a *payashē.*"

A shiver started deep in my core and spread outward, trembling down my arms and curling my toes. My hand wasn't quite steady as I selected another strawberry and bit into it. A drop of sweet juice beaded at the corner of my mouth.

His gaze held mine, intense and questioning. A hint of predator lurked in those faintly glowing red eyes.

"I'm not a *payashē*," I agreed softly.

The tremble in my fingers grew more obvious as I extended my hand again, holding the strawberry in the space between us. An offer. Not choosing him, but inviting him.

He shifted forward. His fingers brushed my wrist, then curled around it, steadying my hand. His mouth closed over the strawberry—and my fingers. The fruit disappeared with a flex of his throat, then all I could feel was the heat of his mouth and the slide of his tongue.

My heart flitted weakly, my lungs empty of air.

"I thought," I mumbled breathlessly, "you didn't like the taste of humans."

He slid my fingertips from his mouth. "Your blood, *vayanin*. I do not like your blood. Your skin ..."

He pressed his mouth to my wrist and his tongue flicked across the slight bumps of tendons and veins. His fingers slid up my inner arm, over the soft skin he'd once marveled at and the scars from the day we'd joined in a contract of mutual survival.

Lightly gripping my elbow, he tugged me toward him. Gentle. An invitation instead of a demand.

I shuffled sideways, moving a little closer. Just a little.

His hand slid up to the sleeve of my t-shirt. Thumb brushing the fabric, he paused, then ran his fingers over my shoulder to the side of my neck. As he'd once carefully explored the fine details of my human hand, now his touch ran over my neck—tracing my collarbones, my throat, the soft underside of my chin.

"You are blushing," he murmured. "What are you thinking?"

Heat burned in my cheeks, but there was heat in my core too. I squeezed my eyes shut. "I'm thinking ..." The truth. I couldn't lie. Didn't want to. "I like it when you touch me."

"*Hnn.*"

His warm hands curled over the sides of my neck, his thumbs at the edges of my jaw—then his breath teased the base of my throat. I balked in surprise, the sofa against my back.

A brush of his lips in the spot between my collarbones.

I trembled, my heels digging into the floor, but I didn't move. Didn't panic. Didn't shove him away. Didn't open my eyes.

His hot mouth drifted across my skin, tracing my throat upward. The sudden touch of his sharp teeth sent tingles rushing down my spine, and I forgot to breathe.

"Do you like this?" His voice vibrated against my skin, his mouth pressed to my racing pulse.

"I ... I ..." An exhalation shuddered through me. I cracked my eyes open, but I saw only the ceiling, my head tipped too far back. "Yes, I like it."

His tongue slicked across my pulse, and I quaked.

His lips moved. Sucking, nipping. Another brush of his sharp teeth across my skin, and my head fell back even farther. He pushed his nose into the soft spot under my jaw, inhaling, then his mouth took its place. Teasing touches of teeth traced my jaw to my chin. My breath quivered in my lungs.

"What are you thinking, *vayanin*?"

"I ... I want ..."

Couldn't say it. Self-conscious shyness fell over me, silencing my voice. My blush reignited and I couldn't stop myself from pressing back into the sofa, retreating from him.

He leaned over me, head canted as he studied my reddening face. "Do you remember, *vayanin*, that you promised to tell me a secret thought?"

In the Arcana Atrium. He'd told me what "protect" meant to him, and I'd promised to share something in return.

I swallowed hard. "I ... I remember."

His face dipped down, his mouth finding my ear and his husky voice shivering through me. "Tell me what you want ... your secret want that you have hidden so long."

I stared wide-eyed at the ceiling. Heart pounding. Belly flipping. I gripped the sofa cushions, clinging on for dear life.

"I want ..." My head spun, too many thoughts at once, uncertainty and yearning and fear and desire. "I want you to ..."

"*Hnn*," he murmured.

My breath hitched, my eyes going even wider. His nose slid along my cheek, and my fingernails scraped across the cushion fabric. I reminded myself to breathe but my lungs ignored me.

The soft heat of his mouth brushed across the corner of mine.

I arched back against the sofa, my head thumping against the cushions. The motion was reflexive, driven by the part of me that kept running away from him.

His hands found my sides, then slid up my back until he was cradling the back of my head. Bracing me. Holding me steady. My hands unclamped from the sofa and latched onto his upper arms instead.

My fingers dug into hard muscle, strength and power, and my pulse leaped.

His lips found the corner of my mouth again. Air rushed through my nose. His hot tongue touched the spot, tasting the sweet residue of strawberry, then his mouth moved sideways, grazing my lower lip. I sucked in a breath and held it.

Another skim of his lips against mine—another test. My heart fluttered. My head spun. I stopped pushing back into his hands. Our noses touched, hesitation flitting between us.

His lips brushed across mine, careful and gentle—then his mouth covered mine.

Hot, soft, fierce. His lips moved hungrily, exploring, finding the shape of my mouth. His tongue traced my upper lip, then he pulled my lower lip between his. The press of his pointed canines surprised me and I gasped. My innards were molten, my breathing too fast.

A rumble vibrated his chest. He nipped my lower lip again, harder, the faint sting sending a fresh tide of heat rushing through me. My lips parted on another gasp, and when our mouths met, his tongue found mine. I tasted him for the first time.

Sweet and smoky. A hint of tartness.

As my hands slid over his arms to his shoulders, the last of my anxiety spiraled away. I melted into his arms, head tilted back, lips parted. My self-conscious fears had fled, and my core was liquid heat that danced with each press and pull of his mouth against mine.

In the place where fear had lived in my mind, suddenly there was dark fire.

A crimson presence with a core of sleek darkness. Ferocity and cunning and scorching passion. My eyes flew open, then slammed shut again as I wrapped my arms around his neck, my hands fisting in his hair.

Flashes of his essence collided with mine—thoughts, emotions, reactions, all tinged with the savagery that was his deepest essence. My mind was spinning just as much, a thousand thoughts careening in my brain at the same time I couldn't think at all.

A thought flickered from him to me—an awareness of our surroundings that I'd lost. A presence. An approach.

I jerked back with a gasp. "Amalia is coming?"

He looked toward the door. Footsteps. He could hear them even over my breathless panting. The door clattered—Amalia inserting her key.

Panic hit me, dousing the fire in my blood. Zylas still had me pinned against the sofa, his arms tight around me and one hand tangled in my hair. I might have faced some fears, but I wasn't ready to face my cousin.

The doorknob turned.

Daimon, hesychaze!

Zylas's body dissolved all around me, and I thumped to the floor as his power streaked into the infernus sitting on the coffee table beside the bowl of strawberries.

The door swung open and Amalia breezed in. "Sorry, meant to be back sooner! Are you ready for our meet—"

She broke off, staring at me.

"H-hi," I stammered weakly, hoping she couldn't tell how out of breath I was. Not to mention my flushed face. Rumpled clothes. Mussed hair.

Her eyes narrowed, then she shook her head violently. "I don't want to know. Are you ready to leave or what?"

"Leave?" I mumbled, dying of embarrassment.

"For our meeting!" She threw her hands up. "The abjuration expert?"

I shot to my feet, looking around wildly. Why didn't our apartment have a clock? A big one I could see from the sofa? "Right, sorry! Just give me a minute to put the grimoire away."

"Yeah, sure." She rolled her eyes. "Take your time."

I scooped up the grimoire, my notes, and the infernus and hauled them into my room. Catching my breath, I set it all on the mattress and stared at the infernus. My fingers crept to my lips and pressed against swollen, sensitive skin.

Less than three months ago, in an alley somewhere downtown, Zylas had licked blood off my wrist. And I distinctly remembered how, while lurching away from him in disgust, I'd declared that I *never* wanted to know what he tasted like.

So much for that.

23

THE LIBRARY was exactly what I needed to settle the jitters in my limbs—and my heart. Quiet, peaceful, the air tinged with the scent of paper and leather. Books, unlike a certain demon and my feelings for him, I understood perfectly.

Amalia surveyed the large room, glanced at the unmanned desk where the librarian normally worked, and huffed. "Are they late, or did they leave because *we're* late?"

I winced guiltily.

"I'll go look for the librarian. Wait here in case they walk in the moment I leave."

"Sure."

I managed to stand still for about thirty seconds, then headed for a nearby display labeled "Guild Favorites." Humming, I browsed the titles. I almost picked up *Mythics in Music*, which featured an intriguing photo of a violin in the center of an Arcana array, but instead lifted *The Visual Art of*

Luminamages off the shelf. Flipping it open, I read an introduction to the complexities of light magic.

With frequent glances toward the front desk and closed doors, I meandered farther into the library. Why were books so irresistible? I wanted to read them all. Taking mental note of several titles to check out after our meeting with the abjuration expert, I walked past a dim aisle and did a double take.

I wasn't alone in the library.

A young woman around my age stood with an open textbook in her hands, reading it intently. Her thick black hair was pulled into a neat ponytail, and dangling from the tie was an eclectic collection of baubles. A brown satchel hung off her shoulder, more charms clipped to the strap.

Glancing up at me, she turned just enough that I could glimpse the title of her book: *Advanced Abjuration for Combat and Defense.*

My gaze shot back to her face. No way. This girl couldn't be our abjuration expert … could she?

"Are you Lienna Shen?" I asked hesitantly.

"I am."

I squinted at her. Maybe she just *looked* young enough to get carded at every bar?

She arched an eyebrow. "Are you Amalia Harper?"

"Huh? No, I'm Robin. Amalia is my cousin. She arranged this meeting." I glanced around for said cousin. "She, um … she should be right back."

Lienna closed her book and slid it onto a shelf. I watched her, burning with curiosity. Abjuration took years to learn, so how could Lienna have mastered it already? I suddenly felt like an academic slouch.

"Well, uh … while we wait for Amalia …" I dug into my pocket and pulled out my drawing of the amulet. "This is the spell we're hoping for some help with."

Taking the paper, Lienna peered at it, her brown eyes darting across the tiny, detailed array on the amulet's reverse side.

"It's abjuration, right?" I asked, oddly nervous.

"Hmm. Yes and no."

My brow crinkled.

She pointed to the top of the array. "These elements are commonly used in high-level abjuration, but this here—are those demonic runes? What is this drawing depicting? An artifact of some kind?"

"It's a research project I'm working on. I'm trying to reconstruct what the artifact's purpose was. It may be a forerunner to the modern infernus."

"I'm not familiar with summoning arrays." She adjusted the strap of her satchel. "The first spell involves abjuration, but I couldn't begin to guess its purpose—not with demonic runes incorporated into the primary node."

"The *first* spell?"

"The second spell is trickier … certainly not abjuration. I think you'll need a Demonica expert for that." She tilted the paper. "This third spell …"

I stared at her. The amulet contained *three* spells?

"I can see why you thought it was abjuration, but it's actually a more obscure Arcana branch with heavy overlap. This is a very unusual composition, though. I've never seen anything like it."

"What is it?"

"Arcana Fenestram," she answered. "More commonly known as portal magic."

A strange sensation rushed through my body: the feeling that I was floating and falling at the same time. Lienna was still talking, but I couldn't hear her. My head was buzzing with one word: *portal*.

"Robin?"

I jolted. "Sorry?"

"I asked if I could have a copy of this."

"Oh ... I ... I'd rather ... not."

Her delicate eyebrows scrunched together. "Are you okay?"

I had no idea.

Footsteps scuffed on the tiles, and as Lienna's attention shifted past me, I pulled myself together. That must be Amalia returning. She could take over the conversation while I—

The newcomer stopped behind me, the solid, aggressive thud of boots too heavy to belong to Amalia.

"MPD," a male voice growled. "Put your hands in the air!"

Terror shot through me. Oh god. I was done. I was doomed. Someone had figured out I was an illegal contractor and now I was caught. Tears sprang into my eyes as I raised my shaking hands.

A moment of silence as I waited for the figurative gavel to fall.

"Oh," the voice remarked, surprise replacing his growl. "She actually did it."

Lienna rolled her eyes. "Kit, stop tormenting civilians."

With another scuffing footfall, a man stepped around me— my age or a little older, tall and fit, with brown hair and a stubbly jaw. He grinned, his baby-blue eyes laughing, and held up his empty hands.

"You do know MPD agents don't carry guns, right?" He ducked his head to get on my eye level, grin widening. "Seriously, I was only kidding. You aren't under arrest."

He poked my palm and I realized I still had my hands in the air. I dropped them so fast I hit my elbow on a shelf. My face burned with humiliation.

"Though …" He squinted at my face. "Wow, you're Robin Page, aren't you?"

Lienna's focus snapped to me. "Robin *Page*?"

Kit folded his arms. "Really, Lienna? We carried her photo around for, like, two weeks."

"My photo?" I stammered.

He gave an exaggerated shrug. "Well, you know, you showed up out of nowhere, joined the Grand Grimoire, went all John Wick on an unbound demon a few days later, then switched guilds and disappeared. You didn't think MagiPol might notice that, just a little bit?"

My panic rushed back. "Wait … you're actually an MPD agent?"

He plucked an ID with a shiny silver badge from his pocket and flashed it. "Kit Morris. Nice to finally meet you."

"*Agent* Morris," Lienna corrected with another eye roll. She slid a badge from her pocket. "I'm Agent Shen."

"You're an agent too?" I squeaked.

"You didn't know?"

I shook my head mutely. The librarian must not have mentioned that part while gushing about the abjuration prodigy.

Kit held a hand above my head as though measuring me. "You're shorter than I expected."

Lienna elbowed him. "What are you even doing in here? You were supposed to wait in the car."

"So you *want* me to lose both legs to a double amputation after my joints fuse from—"

"*Kit.*"

"The captain called," he said primly. "We've been summoned."

"Oh." Lienna handed the illustration to me. "Sorry, Robin. We need to leave."

"S-sure."

She marched past me, all business, and her partner strolled after her, flashing a grin on his way by.

"Don't worry," he called over his shoulder. "I'll arrest you next time."

"Kit!"

The door thudded, cutting off his laugh. I stared blankly. Was he serious? Was I on an MPD wanted list?

With a clatter, the door flew open again. Amalia strode in, scowling like a thundercloud. "The sorceress didn't show. Can you believe—"

"They were here." I stepped out of the aisle. "They just left."

"She left? Wait, you don't mean that couple I just passed—"

"MagiPol agents."

"Huh?"

I threw my hands up in her favorite gesture. "Lienna and her partner are MPD agents! You set up a meeting with *agents*!"

Her face went white. "But—no way. The librarian never said anything about—"

"I guarantee you they were agents. And they recognized me. They were carrying my picture around!"

"Oh shit," she whispered.

I looked down at the illustration of the amulet. "That's not the 'oh shit' part. Lienna said the amulet array isn't just abjuration."

"Then what is it?"

My fingers tightened convulsively. *The key to everything.* Myrrine had been right.

"I think the amulet can open a portal to hell."

"THIS IS MADNESS," Amalia whispered as the cab wound through the downtown streets. "The *amulet* can open a portal? To the demon realm? Why would Anthea put a spell like that in an amulet that could be stolen?"

"Maybe she thought it was too dangerous to put the spell in the grimoire."

"An amulet is just as easy to steal as a grimoire."

I sighed. "I don't know, Amalia. Melitta's letter"—I'd skipped a good chunk of Myrrine's story but had filled Amalia in on Melitta's final plea—"said that without the amulet, we'd never know what secrets Anthea left out of the grimoire."

Amalia swept a few loose hairs off her face. "Especially since the amulet ended up in the demon world for eons."

"Maybe that was on purpose." I bit my lip. "What if Anthea split up the most important magic? She kept the grimoire, and she gave the amulet—"

"To a Vh'alyir demon," Amalia guessed. "Which is why it's called *Vh'alyir's Amulet*. But why? It doesn't make sense."

"I haven't got a clue."

The cab pulled up to our apartment. Amalia climbed out while I hurriedly paid the driver, then followed her. As I hastened up the sidewalk, my steps faltered.

Ezra leaned against the wall beside the door, arms folded.

"What are you doing here?" Amalia demanded.

"Robin invited me over. This morning?" He angled his head, peering at me. "Did you forget to tell me about a change in plans?"

Not exactly. I'd just forgotten to mention those plans to Amalia. "No, it's fine. Come on up."

We hastened to the apartment, shed our shoes and jackets, and headed for the living room. In the corner, Socks was sprawled across my link chart, which I'd moved from the coffee table to the empty spot where Zylas usually did puzzles. The sticky notes crinkled as she rolled onto her back and peered at us upside down.

"Right." I nervously rubbed my hands together. "So, Claude and the sorcerers are planning to start one of the stolen spells tonight."

"And there's shit-all we can do about that," Amalia announced, flopping onto the sofa, "because we don't know where Claude or the sorcerers are."

"Or what the spell is," I admitted bleakly.

Ezra drifted toward my link chart. Socks stared at him with feline suspicion as he gazed down at it. "Should we assume the stolen spell is abjuration?"

"Why would we assume that?" I asked.

"Because the sorcerers are abjuration experts. What are the chances they're experts in *two* branches of sorcery?"

Amalia slapped her hand against her knee. "That makes sense. Abjuration is too intensive. It's probably all they've ever studied. That, or a closely related Arcana branch."

Closely related …

"We might be able to find similar spells in the grimoire," she added. "Robin hasn't had a chance to translate the whole thing yet."

Similar spells …

Ezra crouched to read a flashcard from my link chart. "Claude seems like a man with a plan, and that worries me. If he's gone to such lengths to get these spells, they must be valuable—or powerful. What kind of abjuration would—"

"Not abjuration," I whispered.

He and Amalia looked at me.

"Arcana Fenestram." The words rasped from my throat. "Abjuration and portal magic are related branches. Amalia, what if one of the stolen spells is a portal?"

Her eyes bugged out. "But I thought that was in the amulet—"

"Anthea created the spell. It would've been in the grimoire too—but not all of it. She left something out—the missing piece the sorcerers were talking about! It was her fail-safe!"

"Then Claude—"

"He wants the portal magic. That's what he wanted all along." I shoved to my feet, hands clenched. "Amalia, *that's* what's so valuable about the grimoire. Not the demon names but the spells. The portal."

Ezra looked between us with an arrested expression.

Amalia stood as well. "That's why your mom wouldn't give my dad a single demon name."

"And that's why our ancestors have been hunted for four thousand years. That's why so many Athanas women died protecting the book—to keep the portal spell out of the wrong hands."

"But Claude has it and—"

"—and he's going to cast the spell"—I pressed my hands to my cheeks, my body cold—"*tonight*. He's casting it tonight."

We stood in silence, staring at each other. I saw my own horror reflected in her wide gray eyes—and my guilt. We'd failed. Thousands of years, nearly a hundred generations, and we were the ones who'd failed to protect the grimoire spells.

Heat buzzed against my chest, then crimson flashed. Zylas materialized in the middle of the room, his tail lashing side to side.

"We will find him," the demon declared.

"But how?" I asked, defeated. "He could be anywhere—"

"Not if he plans to open a portal," Amalia cut in. "He isn't going to do that in his mom's basement, is he? And a spell of that magnitude can't be cast just anywhere. They said they needed clear skies, right? That means the spell has an astral element and needs to be performed outdoors."

"Plus the location will need to be private," Ezra added. "He won't want anyone seeing what he's doing."

I pressed a hand to my forehead. "That barely narrows it down. He—"

Zylas's red eyes fixed on me. "What do you know about the enemy?"

"He—I don't—" I took a deep breath, then crossed the room to join Ezra at the link chart. I stared down at it—at all the players and victims surrounding Claude. "He uses others. Even when he works with people, I don't think he trusts them. He has pawns, not allies."

Ezra nodded.

"Even when he wasn't in charge of something," Amalia said, joining us, "he always ended up making all the decisions. I saw that a lot with him and my dad."

"Everything Claude does has a purpose." I rubbed my temples. "Even if the purpose isn't obvious. And he's patient … He plans a lot of steps ahead."

We all analyzed the chart, trying to sift through the puzzle pieces.

"Golems," Zylas said abruptly, and I jumped. I hadn't realized he was right behind me. "They have no purpose, *na?*"

My brow furrowed. "Claude traded them to Varvara for something … and he got what he wanted. He said that last night."

"If he's been working toward this spell all along," Ezra murmured, "then whatever he got from Varvara could be related."

"Did he say anything else last night?" Amalia asked. "Did he mention anything related to a location?"

"He said someone had been meddling and he mentioned a … a court, but—"

"What? A court?"

I jolted, caught off guard by Ezra's change in tone.

"What did he say?" he demanded, the air chilling around him. "His exact words."

Before I could speak, Zylas answered for me.

"He said, '*I can't linger for long.*'" His imitation of Claude's tone and cadence was perfect. "'*Someone has been meddling in our affairs, and if they go so far as to trespass in the Court, I intend to be waiting for them.*'"

Right. Zylas had been there too, and his memory was far better than mine.

Ezra was silent—his face completely blank, his bronze skin bleached of color. For a long moment, he didn't move, staring at nothing. Reaching up slowly, he pressed his fingers to his chin, and his lips formed a soundless word.

"Ezra?" I whispered.

"Impossible," he rasped, not seeming to see the room.

Zylas jabbed him in the arm. He started, jerking away from the demon. His gaze flashed around the room, then he pulled out his phone and rapidly tapped on the screen. "I'm sorry. I just—give me a minute here."

I frowned.

Amalia shot him a "what the hell" look, then turned to Zylas. "Okay, Mr. Super Memory. Did Claude say anything else interesting?"

Zylas shrugged. "Maybe, maybe not. What is interesting?"

"Not helpful, demon boy." She paced away from the link chart. "If Claude has the grimoire page and the sorcerers figured out the missing piece, what else does he need? Ingredients, a location, clear skies—"

I raised a hand to stop her, my gaze locked on Varvara's card, where a list of guild names in my neat handwriting was topped with the title "Attack Locations."

"*Location*," I muttered. "Ezra, of the guild attacks Varvara initiated, which one makes the least sense?"

He looked up from his phone, his complexion still washed out. "Probably the SeaDevils. The Crow and Hammer does way more bounty work than them. It would've made sense to take out our guild first."

"The SeaDevils' headquarters was destroyed, wasn't it? The guild isn't there anymore?

"No, they moved into temporary HQ. It'll take months for the site to be cleared, and they might lease a new location instead of rebuilding."

"Where was their guild based? What's the location like?"

"It's on the south side of Vancouver Harbour, near Canada Place. The guild runs a shipping business, and aside from their office …" He squinted, picturing it. "Big parking lots. Train tracks across the street."

My hope crumbled. Nothing about that location sounded useful for setting up and casting a hugely complex array that would—

"Oh, and the floating helipad. You could land three copters on it at the same time. There's nothing else like it in Vancouver Harbour."

A tremor ran through my muscles. "That's it, then. It has to be."

He and Amalia peered at me questioningly.

"Water cleanses impurities. Building a difficult, sensitive array surrounded by flowing water is an ancient technique to ensure an untainted spell. I read about it in a book on Arcana myths."

"But if it's a myth—" Amalia began.

"No, the myth was about buried treasure on islands, when it was actually sorcerers using small islands for spell engineering."

"The helipad." Ezra raked his hand through his hair. "You think Claude provided Varvara with golems for her takeover, on the condition that she would drive the SeaDevils guild away from their helipad? That's …"

"Messed-up shit?" Amalia nodded. "Almost as messed up as befriending my dad for *years* so he could murder Robin's parents and steal our family grimoire."

"We should go," I said, looking between Zylas, Amalia, and Ezra. "Right away. If we get there in time, we can sabotage the array or prevent them from starting it. Ezra—"

"I can't come."

"What?" I asked sharply.

He shoved his phone in his pocket. "They're not answering. I might be wrong—I hope I'm wrong—but if I'm not—" He broke off with a sharp shake of his head. "I need to go."

"What are you going on about?" Amalia demanded. "We need you!"

He swept past us and grabbed his coat. "I know, and I'm sorry, but I have to do this."

"Ezra—"

He stopped at the door. "Be careful with those sorcerers. If I'm right, you won't have to worry about Claude. I'll deal with him." Red sparked in his left eye. "And his demon."

Zylas flicked his tail. "*Kah vh'renirathē izh?*"

The crimson glow intensified. "*Vh'renith vē thāit.*"

Zylas nodded, and the demon mage swept out the door, swinging it shut behind him. Quiet fell over the apartment.

"Well, shit," Amalia muttered. "I was counting on the creepy demon Two-Face helping us."

"He will fight Nazhivēr. I will fight the three *hh'ainun.*" Zylas arched his back, stretching. "We will go now?"

Putting aside the mystery of how or why Ezra thought he could intercept Claude and his demon, I checked that my infernus and lone artifact were hanging around my neck where they belonged. "Yes, we need to—"

"Hold up." Amalia straightened, her eyes flashing with sudden eagerness. "We shouldn't go into this completely unprepared if we don't have to."

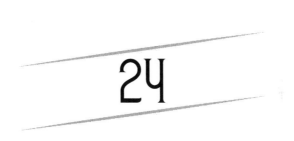

24

THE CAB DROPPED US OFF at the farthest edge of the parking lot, which spanned most of the SeaDevils' property. We stood on the curb, and as the vehicle's headlights receded, darkness fell over us. High above, stars peeked through a thin, streaky layer of cloud, the waning moon casting silvery light on the harbor's dark water. The salty ocean tang, underlaid by a tinge of rot, filled my nose.

"I don't see anyone," Amalia muttered as she adjusted the backpack on her shoulders.

"We're too far to see the helipad," I countered nervously, blinking against my contacts and wishing for my glasses instead.

"Not what I meant." She glanced around one more time. "Call Zylas out."

My infernus lit up. As the demon appeared beside me, she slung her backpack off her shoulder, unzipped it, and lifted out a swath of black fabric embroidered with runes—shield cantrips, just like the shirts she'd made for us. This one, however, wasn't sized for a woman.

Zylas's nose wrinkled, but he held still as Amalia and I pulled the garments over his limbs and buckled them on with small black clips.

The top resembled a vest that fell to his thighs, with large armholes for flexibility—and to leave room for his shoulder armor. Four fitted pieces protected his legs, leaving his knees unencumbered, and black sleeves slid over his armguard and ran up to his shoulders.

Amalia pulled the hood up and lifted an extra flap of fabric. It crossed the hood's front, loosely covering his lower face. He turned his head side to side, checking his visibility in the hood.

She stepped back, giving me a clear view of him, and I swallowed. There was something extra terrifying about dressing the lethal demon in black. He was a shadow with glowing magma eyes.

"Those clothes are full of arcane energy," Amalia told him. "It should interfere with the sorcerer's abjuration, though it won't stop it. And if you're in big trouble, the incantation is *indura*. Their magic won't be able to penetrate the fabric for thirty seconds."

"It will work if I say it?"

"Um, well … I think so? Anyone can trigger a cantrip. I don't see why it wouldn't work for a demon."

His eyebrows lowered, and I knew he was scowling at her.

"Let's go," I said nervously.

Our plan was simple: sabotage the spell array, then get the hell out of there. Zylas had agreed this wasn't the time of *dh'ērrenith*. We needed to wait until Ezra could fight with us.

The demon went first, slinking along the road toward a lumpy shadow right at the shoreline—the remains of the SeaDevils' guild headquarters. Police tape circled the burnt wreckage, and aside from a pair of oversized dumpsters, cleanup and reconstruction had yet to begin.

Water lapped noisily at the rocks, North Vancouver's lights glowing cheerfully on the other side of the harbor. The gently rippling water reflected the city's glow—as well as spots of flickering orange light that didn't belong among the modern lights.

We circled the building's remains, and the helipad came into view. Ezra had said it was large, but my mental picture hadn't come close. It had to be at least seventy yards long—over two-thirds the size of a football field. Set up in a square around the platform's center were four standing torches, their firelight dancing across the concrete.

My nerves pinged with adrenaline at the sight of three human silhouettes in the platform's center.

"Torches?" Amalia muttered, following Zylas's lead as he crouched behind the burnt shell of a car. "Are these guys purists or what?"

"They aren't chancing anything interfering with the portal," I whispered. "Zylas, any sign of Claude or Nazhivēr?"

"No." He canted his head. "I hear the sorcerers. They are speaking your spell language."

An incantation? Not good. "We need to hurry."

"Then we go now."

He scooped me under his arm, and Amalia squawked as he grabbed her too. He launched into a sprint.

The concrete lot ended and the rocky shore rushed to meet us. Zylas sprang over the black water and landed on a thick steel support—not the walkway at the other end of the pad, but a connection point between the platform and a concrete anchor on the shore.

He raced the length of the steel, then leaped again. His feet met the concrete pad—and indigo light flashed.

He jumped straight up, and a volley of glowing spikes peppered the ground. Landing in a one-footed skid, the demon tossed me and Amalia away from him.

I came down on my feet, stumbled, and regained my balance. Amalia fell to her knees with a curse, then scrambled up.

Phantom talons glowing from his fingertips, Zylas charged the twin sorcerers striding to meet him, their armbands gleaming in the firelight. At the center of the helipad, their father had his arms raised as he chanted an incantation.

"Come on!" I yelled to Amalia.

We sprinted toward Saul. I knew the moment we'd crossed the edge of the array—power sizzled into my heels and jolted up my legs. Lines and runes crisscrossed the concrete, etched half an inch deep.

I spotted a large ceramic bowl sitting on a hexagonal node and veered toward it. Midway through kicking the dish, I saw it was empty—the ingredient consumed by the spell. That meant we needed to either interrupt the incantation or damage the array.

One of those tasks was much simpler than the other, since we hadn't brought a jackhammer and Zylas was too busy to explode a chunk of the platform with his magic.

Light flashed—the two sorcerers defending against the attacking demon. As I glanced toward them, a twin fell, Zylas's deadly claws flashing. The other shouted an incantation and silver light blazed, throwing the demon off—but he rolled to his feet in an instant, the spell's effect reduced by Amalia's special gear.

Amalia and I ran toward the old sorcerer as his voice rose in pitch. The buzz of building power rippled through the air. I grabbed Amalia's hand as I thrust out the infernus chain, my artifact dangling beside the pendant.

"*Ori eruptum impel—*"

Light appeared beneath my feet.

I stumbled and almost fell. Every line of the portal array, spanning thirty feet, had lit with white magic. Power burned through the spell.

Pale eyes turning to us, Saul held out his left hand. In his other hand was a silver dagger. He slashed it across his palm, and blood spilled over the center point of the spell.

A circle, eight feet across, took on an eerie, deep pink glow. The stain spread outward, snaking along the array's lines and tinting the runes.

Saul pointed his dagger at me and Amalia. "*Ori astra feriant.*"

The blade rippled with yellow light and a spray of glowing two-inch half-moons blasted out of the tip. I threw my arms over my face. Tearing pain lanced my forearm. Beside me, Amalia screamed.

I staggered backward, half lowering my arms as wetness soaked into my sweater. My leather jacket had blunted the strikes, but one had cut my arm deep.

Saul flipped his dagger over, the opposite edge of the blade pointed skyward. "*Ori ignes sid—ori duo!*"

He bellowed the new incantation, and a rippling barrier formed in front of him an instant before a spinning disc of crimson magic struck it. The attack rebounded across the platform—toward Zylas, who in the middle of his own fight had thrown a spell to help me and Amalia.

"*Ori sex!*" one of the twins shouted.

I whirled at the shouted incantation—number six. A spell I hadn't seen yet.

Zylas lurched, almost falling. Bands of green magic were tangled around his lower leg, wrapped on top of his protective clothing, and the ends had fused to the ground. The spell locked him in place, stealing his best advantage—his speed.

The twins, ten feet away on either side of him, raised their right arms. "*Ori novem!*"

Four-foot-long harpoons of violet light formed in their hands. They drew their arms back and hurled the weapons.

Zylas!

"*Indura,*" he snarled.

The harpoons struck his torso and the abjuration magic shattered against his cantrip-protected garments. The twins exchanged shocked looks, then raised their hands again.

"*Ori decem.*"

Their tenth spell.

Blue light flashed in their hands, then solidified into pale blades, two feet long and blazing with light. They lunged for the trapped demon, and I knew his cantrip garments wouldn't stop those blades.

Daimon, hesychaze!

The blades slashed as Zylas dissolved into red light. The sorcerers' weapons caught on the cantrip clothing, whipping it sideways as the demon's body dissolved. His power streaked toward me, hit the infernus, and bounced out again.

Zylas formed beside me, gasping. Blood spattered the ground.

A slice ran across his chest, parting his leather gear and scoring the plate on his chest—an impossible feat for blades made solely with abjuration Arcana. A matching slash across his lower back wept blood.

Panic squeezed my throat and I grabbed his arm.

"*Ori quinque!*"

A silvery blast hit our backs. Zylas hurtled forward and I was yanked with him, our arms tangled. He landed in a roll, pulling me against his chest, and we came to a stop with him poised protectively over me.

The concrete pad shivered as the pink glow of the array brightened. The heavy buzz of arcane power in the air was thickening, clogging my lungs. Saul wasn't chanting anymore; he'd completed his job. The spell was active. The portal was opening.

Despair choked me more than the magic. We couldn't defeat the sorcerers. We hadn't stopped the spell. We'd failed.

Not yet, vayanin.

Zylas's gleaming red eyes met mine. A crimson-and-shadow presence swept into my mind, sharp with wild ferocity and intense determination. He hadn't survived by surrendering. He hadn't lived this long by handing victory to his enemies.

If he still breathed, he could still fight. He could still win.

Vh'renith vē thāit, he whispered in my mind. *Victory or death.*

Alien warmth scorched my center as power flowed into my body. His determination infected me, and my doubts disappeared.

He rolled, sweeping me with him as he lunged onto his feet. I landed beside him, my fingers curling as heat burned through them. Crimson power snaked up Zylas's arms, reforming his phantom talons.

The three sorcerers circled us, ready to cast their neutralizing or reflective spells. Nothing Zylas could cast would penetrate their defenses.

I stretched my arm out, fingers spread. Shock widened the brothers' eyes at the sight of my hand—at the crimson power radiating from my fingers and veining my wrist.

His mind threading mine, Zylas steadied the image I was drawing forth, his experience in this form of casting bolstering my lack. A simple rune took shape in front of me, formed in an instant—and as tall as me. The crimson lines glowed eerily.

"*Ventos!*" I yelled.

"*Ori tres!*" the twin facing me roared.

My demonic cantrip flashed and a gale of wind exploded outward. Green sparkles formed in front of the sorcerer—the spell that could erase Zylas's demonic attacks. The howling wind hit it.

The sorcerer was blasted off his feet. He flew ten yards and slammed down on his back.

"No!" the other twin shouted.

I grinned tightly. Abjuration was limited. It had to be tailored to the magic it was defending against—and my magic was neither demonic nor Arcana. It was both.

Zylas coiled his body, then sprang. I spun, already knowing where he was going, what he intended. The link between us was a bright line of instinct as he analyzed everything around him. The ground. The sky. The movements of his enemies. The subtle language of their bodies—darts of eyes, flares of nostrils, minute flexing of muscles.

He judged his targets, predicted their movements, and reacted without thought—following years of practice, of muscle memory, of experience.

As he closed in on the second twin, I stretched my hand out again. Another cantrip spanning five feet instantly appeared—right under the sorcerer's feet.

Zylas slashed as the sorcerer barked an incantation. The demon's claws raked the shield as he darted sideways.

"*Rumpas!*" I shouted.

The concrete under the twin shattered. He stumbled, arms pinwheeling. Zylas pivoted on one foot, grace and power. His crimson claws flashed.

The sorcerer fell.

"Braden!" the other twin screamed as his brother hit the ground, blood pooling in the fissured concrete. He flung a hand toward Zylas as his father shouted another spell.

"*Ori quinque!*"

"*Ori novem!*"

Daimon, hesychaze!

As Jaden's and Saul's incantations rang out, Zylas blurred into red power. It streaked to my chest and he reformed in front of me—but the sorcerers weren't done.

"*Ori septem!*" they both shouted.

Blue rings flashed for him, and with a lithe twist, he evaded both. As they whipped past and struck the concrete, a thought flitted from Zylas to me, too fast for words, but I caught the meaning—his observation.

He sprang away from me, charging toward Jaden. I whirled in the opposite direction, toward Saul—just as Amalia crept up behind him, a long red scarf in her hands. She flung the cloth over Saul's head and yanked it tight.

"*Igniaris!*" she cried.

The cantrip-embroidered scarf burst into flame. Amalia yanked her hands away as Saul howled in agony, clawing at the fabric.

I summoned a new cantrip, aiming it at the sorcerer as Amalia dove for the ground. "*Impello!*"

If anyone had asked me a few weeks ago if the simple "push" cantrip, the building block of all *impello* artifacts, could be terrifying, I would've laughed. It was worth a stumble, maybe a fall. After all, who could carry around a cantrip large enough to do real damage?

But who would've thought I could create massive cantrips in an instant?

The blast from the rune catapulted Saul into the air. Trailing flames like a rippling banner, he hurtled across the platform, out over open water, and splashed into the dark ocean.

"*Ori unum! Ori duo! Ori unum!*"

At the platform's other end, Jaden spat incantations nonstop as Zylas darted around him, claws slashing. Voice rising with desperation, the sorcerer flung his hands out.

"*Ori decem!*"

Blue swords formed in both hands and he slashed at the demon.

A fatal mistake.

His abjuration was a nearly unassailable defense against a demon, fast and impenetrable. But in combat? No human could beat Zylas in direct combat.

With smooth grace, the demon ducked the wildly swinging blades. His phantom claws swept up, passing through flesh and bones. The abjuration blades spun away and disappeared.

The sorcerer staggered backward, gaping at his severed fingers, only his thumbs left. The crimson talons on Zylas's left hand dissolved, and he grabbed the man by the throat. His other hand drew back for the killing strike.

Something midnight black and vicious burned through the link between me and Zylas, then the connection snapped off—the demon shoving me out of his head.

He rammed his claws into Jaden's chest, bones crunching. Jaden's agonized scream filled the air as Zylas twisted his hand, then ripped it back out. The man went limp, head lolling.

Zylas dropped him, then opened his hand. A fistful of gore landed beside the dead sorcerer with a wet thud.

My stomach heaved, but I stiffened my spine, remembering Yana Deneva, the aspiring actress, and the other young women Jaden and his family had destroyed. Kidnapped. Tormented. Raped. Killed.

Saul, Braden, and Jaden would never kill again.

The slosh of waves seemed so quiet after the cacophony of battle and death. Firelight from the four torches flickered across the platform and reflected off Zylas's armor.

"Robin …"

Amalia's whisper was almost lost to the breeze. Turning, I found her a dozen paces away, staring at a spot near my feet. Blinking, I looked in that direction.

Pink light glowed all around me, the spiraling lines and sharp geometric shapes of the array interspersed with foot-wide runes. The center of the spell, a few long steps away, wasn't glowing. The core node, that eight-foot circle, had turned pitch black. So black it sucked in the light.

Or … *was* it lightless?

I inched closer, peering at the inky circle. Faint white sparkles dusted the black, glittering delicately in sweeping ribbons. An icy wind teased my face, blowing in the opposite direction of the cold sea breeze. Instead of salt water, the scent of dirt and sand and something wholly unfamiliar tickled my nose.

I stared at the starlike sparkles … and realized what I was looking at: a night sky, as perfect and crisp as a reflection in a mirror.

Except wisps of cloud streaked the familiar sky overhead, while that circle showed a clear but moonless night.

The scuff of a footstep. Zylas's arm brushed mine as he stopped beside me.

"The scent," he whispered. "It smells like …"

Cold deeper than the winter breeze, icier than the sand-scented wind emanating from that black circle, settled in my bones. Terror bubbled through my veins.

"It smells like home."

My fingers closed compulsively around Zylas's wrist, my stare locked on that circle of darkness three yards from my toes.

The portal was open.

25

THE EERIE PINK GLOW of the array shimmered gently as terror hammered through me. Within the portal, stars of another realm dusted a foreign sky. Cold radiated from the darkness, the fitful wind far icier than this Vancouver winter night. The misty wetness clinging to the platform had turned to white frost around the edge of the circle.

Beside me, Zylas leaned forward, nostrils flaring as he drew in the familiar scent of his home.

A tremor ran through me. My mind was empty, devoid of his shadow-tinged presence. I'd barricaded my heart, wrapping it in bands of steel so it could survive what would come next.

With more effort than it had ever taken to move my fingers before, I unclamped my hand from his wrist. My arm fell limply to my side.

He dragged his stare off the portal and looked at me.

"Go."

Someday, I might acknowledge how much it hurt to speak that word.

Zylas didn't move.

"*Go!*" I cried, gasping back the tears stinging my eyes. "Before it's too late!"

His head turned toward the ebony circle, then back to me.

"What are you waiting for?" Anger sparked in my chest, a welcome reprieve from the building grief. Why was he hesitating? Why was he making this harder? "Isn't this what you want? To go home?"

He faced the portal. His tail slid slowly across the ground.

"Go," I choked. "The portal won't last."

He took a slow step toward the starry sky of his home. I clenched my hands into fists, breathing fast through my nose. He didn't belong in my world, I reminded myself. He had no place on Earth, where his very existence was a crime. This was what he wanted. What he *needed*.

What I needed didn't matter—even if what I needed was him.

My demon, my protector, took another step toward the portal. His tail snapped again, more forcefully. He stepped again.

Now he stood at the portal's edge. Now he was crouching, peering into the strange vision of an upside-down sky. Blood from his wounds dripped onto the concrete and froze in the arctic chill emanating from his world.

He stretched out his hand, reaching for the portal.

My throat closed, cutting off my air, and I couldn't speak. Couldn't form words. Couldn't say goodbye.

Zylas.

A gleaming red eye tilted toward me.

Thank you … for everything.

He gazed at me, his face in shadow, eyes unreadable, then returned his attention to the portal. His hand dipped lower. He hesitated one more time, shoulders shifting as he inhaled the scent calling him back to his homeland.

His tail went still. Then he leaped up and backward.

"*Vayanin*, stop the *vīsh!*"

I took half a step away. "Wh-what?"

He retreated from the portal. "Close the circle! Hurry!"

"But—but don't you want to—"

He froze again, fingers curling as his claws unsheathed. "It is coming!"

His tone confused me until I realized what it was. I'd never heard that kind of fear from him before.

The deep pink glow of the arcane array shuddered, and the vision of stars darkened, blocked by an opaque shadow. A strange rushing sound reached my ears, as though the wind were rising and falling with unnatural rhythm.

The array blazed and crackled. The edges of the portal rippled like a stone striking a pond—and the surface of darkness broke.

A—a *shape* pushed out of the portal. Dark, ridged, strangely shiny. My brain couldn't make sense of it as it rose, then rotated. It split, bending apart. Opening.

Jaws opening.

The shape—it was a massive head on an equally thick neck. Vaguely salamander-like, but an endless row of spiky fangs protruded from its lipless snout at a forty-five-degree angle.

As it pushed up through the portal, the spell shuddered. Fuchsia sparks exploded from the glowing lines—and the monstrous creature lurched, jaws gaping.

It screeched.

The sound was a screaming jet engine and nails on a chalkboard amplified a thousand times. My knees hit the ground as a scream tore from my throat, my hands clamped over my ears.

Zylas fell to his knees beside me, hunching forward as he covered his ears. Light fizzled and flashed—and a loud *crack* shook the platform.

Another *crack*. Chips of concrete spat into the air. *Crack crack crack*. More flying debris, and I realized it was pieces of the helipad. The array was breaking apart, shattering under the magical forces flowing through it.

The creature shrieked again and tried to retreat into the portal, but the edges were wavering, the pink glow bubbling in places while other parts of the array went dark. The monster writhed—then lunged upward.

Huge clawed feet slammed down on the platform and ripped into the concrete. Its massive body slid through the portal. As it passed, black liquid sprayed out—rips in its slimy hide. The portal was tearing it apart as it came through.

With its loudest shriek yet, the creature heaved its bulk out of the otherworldly gateway. Its hind legs tore the edges of the portal away, and as its long tail lifted out, the array rippled and went dark. The gateway disappeared, replaced by concrete— with the tip of the creature's tail still in it.

Jaws gaping, it leaped away. Its tail ended in a stump that poured black blood.

The creature landed on the back half of the platform and the whole pad dipped under its weight like a boat in rough seas. I fell forward, catching myself on my hands.

Zylas grabbed my arm and hauled me backward. Blood ran from his ears, and I touched my own. My fingers came away slick and wet.

The creature raised its head. Bulbous yellow eyes, liquid and pupilless like egg yolks implanted in its hideous skull, stared in opposite directions, and dark pits behind each eye added to the freakishness of its face. It panted, huge mouth gaping and a thick white tongue spilling out. Its lungs pumped, chest expanding. Powerful legs supported its lizard-like body—low slung, legs positioned on the sides of its abdomen, long toes and curved claws as long as my arm.

With a final snorting breath, it closed its jaws, teeth coming together like the cilia on a Venus flytrap so that, instead of lips, its mouth was a bristling nightmare of crisscrossing fangs.

Then that bristling face turned toward us.

Zylas's fingers bit into my arm as he forgot to be gentle. "*Vayanin*, we must run away."

"What is it?" I whispered, my voice almost soundless.

"*Īnkav*, it is called."

The word sounded familiar. It was almost like … like *īnkavis*, the demonic word for a murderer who enjoyed dealing death.

"It is a demon killer." He stepped back again. "It will eat me."

Black blood wept from the creature's skin where the portal had torn it. Jaws parting, it inhaled, the air whistling across the ridged roof of its mouth.

"It smells my blood." Zylas dragged me backward. "It is mostly blind. It could not see the portal. It was following my scent."

"Zylas—"

"We must run!"

As he threw me over his shoulder, the *īnkav* launched off its hind legs. The entire platform rocked violently.

"Wait!" I screamed, grabbing at his arm.

Claws tearing into the concrete, the monster propelled itself toward us with insane speed for something so huge. Zylas sprinted for the platform's edge and sprang over the dark water. I thought we would plunge into the icy ocean, but he caught a braided steel cord that ran from the helipad to the metal support anchoring it to the shore.

The *īnkav* slid to a stop, one foot going off the edge and splashing into the water.

"Zylas!" I yelled. "Amalia is still on the platform!"

His eyes widened as he realized his oversight.

The *īnkav* hesitated, thick head turning as it peered at the water.

"Will it follow you?" I whispered, clutching him. "If it can't see—"

"It has second vision like demons." Zylas clung to the cord with one hand, holding me with his other arm. "It sees shapes in hot and cold."

Sucking in air—and the scent of Zylas's blood—the *īnkav* shifted back from the edge. It didn't want to go into the cold water. Its head turned. Those terrifying, hideous jaws parted.

Body curling sideways, it turned its bulk away from us—focusing on a new target.

"It's going for Amalia," I gasped. "Zylas, we have to—"

He heaved us up, got his feet on the wire, and sprang onto the steel beam. Pushing on my hips, he swung me around him. I clamped my legs around his waist, clinging to his back.

Zylas, I whispered silently.

A quiver in his muscles. The rasp of breath through his clenched teeth.

His fear flooded me. A hundred thoughts blazed through my mind in an instant. *Īnkav.* A creature of his world feared by all demonkind. Strong enough to crush demon bones. Skin tougher than demon magic. Always hungry for demon flesh.

Never go to the warm swamps, where sour water wells from the ground. Never go near the water, never never. No demon, not even First House, would test those places.

Not strong enough. Can't win. No dh'ērrenith. This is death.

Run. Run away.

I pressed my face into the back of his neck. "Zylas."

He panted, fighting his terror of this nightmare creature. Another flash from his mind to mine.

A demon that looked very much like Zylas warily approached a still slough, the water coated in green sludge. The horizon glowed with the light of the setting sun, illuminating a landscape of swampy marsh, the foul water broken by a rough path of rocky islands and rotting clumps of vegetation.

Dangerous, dangerous. Not safe to cross. Don't go.

The demon hesitated a long step from slimy rocks at the water's edge, senses straining. He looked back—red eyes glowing in the fading light—then faced the swamp and stepped closer.

The surface of the slough exploded. A maw of spiky teeth surged out of the water, gaping and hungry.

Zylas's memory flashed, surged, whirled too fast for me, but one thought, one feeling dominated—the result of that demon's sudden death.

Alone. Alone now.

My fingers dug into his shoulders. I put my mouth against his ear, his blood smudging my lips. "You're not alone."

He sucked in air.

"I'm here with you. We'll do this together."

His face turned toward mine, eyes wide, nostrils flared as he breathed deep. His frantic thoughts quieted. Calm slid from me to him and back, our determination blending.

Together, we looked toward the helipad.

26

WAVES LAPPED AGAINST THE PLATFORM as it rocked with the *īnkav's* movements. So much had flowed between Zylas and me, but mere seconds had passed. The creature had only taken a few steps, its back to us as it moved away.

Zylas coiled. I tightened my limbs around him.

He launched into a sprint. We flashed across the platform, and I stretched my hand out. Heat scorched my center, leaping from him to me. Crimson burned from my fingertips up my arm.

A rune formed behind the *īnkav's* tail, the stump end leaving a trail of black blood. Zylas leaped onto the cantrip.

"*Surrige!*" I cried.

The levitation spell flung us upward. We soared above the creature as its head swung up.

A few paces ahead of it, Amalia was on the ground, frozen with terror, her glassy stare on the monster and her mouth hanging open in a silent scream.

We plunged down. Zylas's feet smashed into the platform, knees bending, hands reaching. He grabbed Amalia and launched away.

Massive jaws slammed shut with a clap like thunder, barely missing his tail. Zylas landed and slipped on the damp concrete, struggling for balance with the two humans he carried.

The *īnkav* lunged, mouth gaping and neck stretching out.

Flinging my hand backward, I squeezed my eyes shut to picture the cantrip. Crimson gleamed through my eyelids.

"*Impello!*"

A thud of air, and the platform pitched. Zylas sprinted away, aiming for the pathway that connected the helipad with the shore.

An earsplitting shriek shattered the night.

Whether it was his legs that buckled or the slippery concrete, Zylas went down. We crashed to the platform and skidded wildly. Amalia tumbled in a roll and went off the edge with a scream that ended in a splash. I clung desperately to Zylas's back as he slid, his claws scraping the concrete. Thunder filled my ears.

The *īnkav* charging.

A forefoot so large it spanned Zylas's entire torso swung at us. A crushing blow. Spinning. Zylas hit the platform a second time, taking the impact on his elbows and knees, sparing me the bone-breaking collision.

He leaped away and teeth snapped, the creature's hot, reeking breath buffeting our backs. It was so close—too close— and I realized we'd lost our chance. We couldn't get away. The *īnkav* was right behind us, and it wouldn't let us escape a second time.

The only way to survive was to kill it.

Impossible. I can't.

My jaw clenched. *Together, we have a chance. Just stay ahead of it, Zylas.*

He raced forward, just faster than the giant lizard—but the platform was too small. His runway was rapidly vanishing, and the ocean was no escape. If the *īnkav* decided to brave the cold, it was an even more efficient hunter in the water.

Zylas didn't have time to draw on his magic—it would take too many precious seconds to conjure a spell powerful enough to harm the massive creature—but I didn't have to worry about sprinting and evading. I concentrated. Heat burned through me as I drew on his power. My skin was burning. My innards were burning. My human body wasn't built for his power—but if Ezra could survive it as a demon mage, I could survive it too.

Zylas swerved. *Robin!*

I switched the rune I was about to manifest. A levitation cantrip appeared in our path, but the *īnkav* was on Zylas's heels, cutting off his turn.

He leaped onto the glowing cantrip.

"*Surrige!*" I shouted.

The spell shot us into the sky, the *īnkav*'s jaws snapping as we soared out of its reach. I could see the whole platform, could see the creature's true scale. I could see the small figure staggering along the floating pathway toward the shore— Amalia, fleeing the helipad.

As we reached the apex of our leap, Zylas and I extended our hands, glowing with identical magic. Rune circles spiraled up his arms, pulsing with power.

Crimson glowed over my fingers, and on the platform, a huge cantrip took form—bigger than anything Zylas or I had ever created. It spanned the center of the helipad from top to bottom, the *īnkav* in its middle.

Power blazed through Zylas.

Evashvā vīsh!

"*Igniaris!*"

Curved blades in the shape of a cross formed in front of Zylas's palm, then blasted downward. Beneath the *īnkav*, the fire cantrip erupted. A roaring inferno exploded into the sky, the swamp beast vanishing in the hungry flames. Its enraged screech rent the air.

We plummeted—falling straight toward the fire. Heat buffeted us, then frigid cold washed over me as Zylas drew on the heat to replenish his magic. We dropped.

Gaping jaws surged out of the crackling fire.

Zylas twisted in midair, the spiked teeth just missing his legs as he kicked off its snout, propelling us away. The creature twisted after us.

"*Impello!*" I cried, flinging my hand back, but I was too hasty, panic fogging my head, and the crimson rune wavered.

The *īnkav* burst through my attempted cantrip, its slimy skin scorched but not even blistered. A cross-shaped slice marred its back, but the wound had barely broken its tough hide.

The failing portal had done more damage to the creature than either Zylas or I could do.

Zylas slammed down and pushed into a sprint, but we'd landed too close to the platform's edge. He had to veer, and the *īnkav* cut us off.

The demon leaped. Snapping jaws. Slashing forelegs with huge talons. The world spun. I didn't know what was happening, couldn't create a rune, didn't know where to cast it—

Zylas's claws bit into my leg, tearing into my skin. He wrenched me off his back and flung me away.

I clamped my arms over my head an instant before I crashed into the concrete feet first. A snap in my ankle. Screaming, I tumbled to a halt, brain locked with agony. Darkness crowded my vision, unconsciousness threatening.

Then I heard Zylas cry out.

I wrenched my head up, terrified of what I would see.

The *īnkav* had caught Zylas in its jaws, and the only thing saving him from death was his shoulder armor, the plates caught between its teeth, preventing its powerful jaws from closing all the way.

Zylas twisted desperately, trying to pull free of its jaw. Muscles flexed in the creature's huge head.

Terror hazed my mind. *Daimon, hes—*

His armor shattered.

He screamed. Zylas, who'd been ripped open, torn apart, and broken by his enemies, all with hardly a sound, was screaming as those jaws crushed his shoulder and those teeth buried deep into his body.

I was screaming too. I couldn't summon him back into the infernus now—couldn't risk that it would kill him. Forgetting the pain in my ankle, I shoved up, my hands slipping in water.

No, blood.

Braden's body had somehow escaped the inferno of my giant cantrip. I grabbed his limp, cold arm as, ten yards away, the *īnkav* dropped Zylas. He hit the ground, unmoving, silent.

Zylas!

Nothing.

312 ◆ ANNETTE MARIE

I gripped the dead sorcerer's artifacts. "*Ori decem!*"

A ring flashed. Power surged in my hand and I raised it in time for my fingers to close around the hilt of a shimmering blue blade. The handle felt like sizzling air against my palm, solid but not.

I swung it down. It cut through the sorcerer's arm. I didn't notice the blood or gore as I grabbed the sword artifact off his severed forearm. Looping the bloody steel ring around my wrist, I ran for the beast, blade clutched in my hand. My gait was lopsided, my ankle wobbling, but I didn't stop.

The *īnkav* lifted its nose away from the motionless demon. Its massive head started to turn, a bulbous eye swinging toward me. I was too slow, too weak. It would bite me in half before I could swing the sword.

Zylas, a dark shape on the ground, moved. His hand lifted. Dim red light sparked on his fingers, and he flung a blazing orb of power into the soft underside of the creature's jaw.

The *īnkav* jerked back, its nose swinging toward the demon, that bulbous eye sticking off the side of its huge head.

Blade angled, I took aim. With the momentum of my sprint, with every iota of strength I possessed, I drove the glowing blue blade not into its huge yellow eye but into the pit just behind it.

I didn't know if it was an ear hole or an organ for detecting heat signatures, but I knew it was a weakness. A tiny gap in the beast's armor-like skin. And the arcane blade—the only true weapon in the sorcerers' terrifying arsenal, designed to cut through a demon's metal armor—plunged into the creature's skull.

My hand followed, shoving into the hole. Shoving into soft tissue. Shoving that blade as deep as I could get it.

The *īnkav* flung its head up, lifting me off my feet. My arm came free with a squelching sound, and I fell, landing hard on my butt.

Staggering, the beast swung its head back and forth. Its lower jaw sagged open. Black blood poured from the gory wound, then spilled from around its yellow eye.

It stilled, legs braced, sides heaving. Then it collapsed, belly hitting the platform with a dull thud. Its head smacked the concrete, pale tongue lolling from its slack jaws. Firelight from the single surviving torch flickered over its glistening hide.

Breathing hard, I tried to stand. My ankle buckled and I choked on a scream. Tears streaming down my face, I crawled toward Zylas, following the sound of his hoarse, panting breaths. My hands slid through dark, warm blood. Blood everywhere.

Eyes black as pitch stared at me, hazy with pain. Shadowed with fading life.

"No," I whispered, kneeling beside him. I pressed my hands to his cheeks. "Zylas, heal yourself. Quickly!"

His breath rasped in and out. A small voice in the back of my head reminded me that his dark eyes meant he was too weak. There was no time to replenish his strength with heat. He would die before he recovered enough strength and power to perform the complicated healing magic.

Assuming he could even heal wounds this terrible.

My whole body shook. I'd been prepared to lose him to his home world. I would've watched him walk away from me, knowing he was going back to the life my uncle had stolen from him. Maybe it was a dark, violent, lonely life, but it was his. His choice.

But I couldn't lose him like this. I couldn't.

"Zylas," I choked.

His lips moved, making no sound, but I heard his whisper in my mind.

Vayanin … Robin.

My mouth trembled. My heart broke. This couldn't happen. I needed to save him. Somehow, I had to. I straightened, gaze slashing across the platform in a desperate search of help.

Cold fingers curled around my wrist. *Stay with me.*

"I'm here," I whispered. "I'll stay with you. I'll never leave you alone."

His dark eyes lost focus. His hand slid from my wrist, falling to the blood-coated concrete.

"Robin!"

Amalia's frantic shout cut through the anguish strangling me. My head jerked up.

Footsteps slapped against the ground. Amalia appeared from the darkness, sprinting toward me. And behind her was—

"Out of the way!"

I scrambled backward as Ezra slid to a stop and dropped to his knees beside Zylas's crushed shoulder and mangled chest. Dressed in combat gear, scuffed and scraped, he bent over the dying demon.

Crimson lit his left eye—then sparked across the right. Both eyes blazing with potent power, the mage spread one hand over Zylas's chest and put the other on his crushed shoulder. Circles and runes sprang into shapes under his glowing fingers.

Amalia knelt beside me. Her clothes were drenched, her hair plastered to her face. We didn't speak as Ezra—or rather, Eterran—worked. Healing spells rushed out from his hands, bright and pulsing. Magic filled Zylas's wounds, sinking into his body. Eterran cast the next spell, and that too sank into the demon.

Pausing in his cast, Eterran straightened Zylas's shoulder then resumed. Slowly, the crushed parts of the demon took on their proper shape. Slowly, the wounds began to close.

Finally, there were no more gouges. No more bits of bone showing. No more malformed limbs.

The glow in Eterran's eyes had dimmed, and only a faint spark remained. The concentration in his face faded. He blinked, and his eyes were human again. Ezra sat back on his heels with a weary sigh.

"Is he okay?" I asked hoarsely. Zylas's eyes, black and empty, were half-lidded. He hadn't reacted to the healing, showing neither pain nor relief.

"You need to warm him up—as quickly as possible." He pushed to his feet. "Call him into the infernus."

"That's not dangerous when he's so weak?"

"Not at all. It's something demons do when they're injured and need to recover safely."

Not bothering to ask if he was suggesting anything like an infernus existed in the demon world—or why a demon would willingly possess one—I clutched the pendant around my neck. *Daimon, hesychaze.*

The semiconscious demon dissolved into light and streaked into the infernus.

"There's a gray SUV parked in the lot with its lights on," Ezra said. "The keys are in the ignition. Take it and go home."

With Amalia's help, I levered to my feet, keeping my weight off my ankle. It'd gone numb, which was probably a bad thing—and probably wouldn't last.

"What about you?" I asked.

"Eterran has a bit of magic left." His gaze turned to the dead beast. "Enough to get *that* into the water before someone sees it."

As though in response to his words, the distant sound of sirens echoed through the night.

"Get him home," Ezra told me. "Warm him up. Feed him once he's ready to eat."

I nodded weakly.

"I'll contact you soon."

"But Ezra, did you find—"

"Go!" As the sound of sirens grew louder, he pivoted to face the *inkav* corpse and straightened a steel-plated glove. Crimson burned across his fingers.

Amalia tugged on me. "Let's get out of here."

Letting her support me, I limped away from the demon mage. As we moved across the pathway that spanned the water, I pushed my legs a little faster. Urgency pounded in my head. I needed to get Zylas home. I needed to warm him up.

I couldn't lose him now.

27

I SAT ON THE EDGE of the tub, one shoulder braced against the wall. My leg was stretched out, my ankle splinted with two rulers and a tensor bandage, and my arm throbbed where Saul's spell had cut me, gauze taped over the wound. There was no point in seeking medical attention when Zylas could erase my injuries faster than any healer—once he'd recovered.

He lay in the tub behind me, water cascading over him. Steam swirled through the bathroom and I'd opened the door to let fresh air in.

Amalia leaned across the jamb. "Hey."

I smiled weakly. "How're you feeling?"

"Bruised and hurting and exhausted." She limped onto the linoleum and passed me a glass of water and a bottle of painkillers. "Pop those pills, then get some rest. I put three cans of soup in the slow-cooker to warm for when Zylas is awake."

"Thanks."

"Sure." She searched my face. "You all right?"

"I'll be better once Zylas wakes up."

As I unscrewed the cap on the pill bottle, her gaze drifted to Zylas.

"He came back for me," she murmured, her expression softening. She refocused on me. "Get some sleep, okay?"

With a final worried glance at us, she retreated from the bathroom. I put two fat gel caplets in my mouth and washed them down with water. Grunting as I stretched my arm out, the motion triggering all sorts of twinges and aches, I slid the glass and bottle onto the bathroom counter.

The shower poured down, but it wasn't enough to drown out the memories of that fight. The sorcerers' shouts. Saul roaring as his head was engulfed in flame. Jaden screaming as Zylas ripped out his heart. The *īnkav*'s horrific screech.

The crunch of Zylas's shattering armor. His tearing cry of agony as the creature's jaws crushed him.

I turned my hands up, staring at my pale fingers. Remembering the crimson magic flowing over them. Remembering Jaden's blue blade in my grasp. Had I really plunged a magical sword into the *īnkav*'s skull?

Shivering, I twisted toward Zylas. His head was slumped against the back wall of the shower, face slack.

I could see him crouched beside the portal, reaching toward the starry sky of his home.

My heart twisted, ached, the cracks of grief splitting wider. I slid along the tub's edge, careful to keep weight off my ankle, and reached down. Taking his hand, I pulled it into my lap and held tight. For a long time, I sat there, holding on to him in the only way I could right now.

His fingers twitched, startling me from a pain-filled doze. I looked down.

His eyes cracked open. Dark irises stared at me.

"*Sahvē*," I murmured, using the same demonic greeting he'd once given me, weeks ago on another occasion when he'd been recovering under the hot water.

"*Sahvē*." He blinked slowly. "I am not dead."

"Ezra arrived right as ..." I couldn't bring myself to reference Zylas's near death. "Eterran healed you."

He frowned. "Saved by a Dh'irath? I do not like it."

His chest moving with slow breaths, he closed his eyes. I squeezed his hand, worried that his skin felt cool despite the hot water splashing over him.

I inhaled deeply. "Zylas ... tell me about *Ivaknen*."

"*Ivaknen*? Why?"

Zylas crouched at the portal's edge. Reaching for it. About to leave me.

"Because I want to know."

"Now?"

"Why not now?"

Grumbling, he straightened his legs as much as he could in the tub. "When a *Dīnen* is summoned, his *vīsh* ... the power of *Dīnen*, it thinks he is dead. It goes to the next *Dīnen*. If he returns home, the *vīsh* will not come back to him. He cannot be *Dīnen* again, but he cannot swear to new *Dīnen*."

My mouth quirked down.

His dark eyes slitted open. "*Ivaknen* are older than *Dīnen*. They have respect, because they survived. They have had victory over the *hh'ainun*. To be *Ivaknen* is to have pride and power."

"That … doesn't sound so bad," I suggested, struggling to interpret his grim tone.

He tilted his head toward the spray of water, letting the hot droplets run down his face. "*Ivaknen* have respect, but they have nothing else. No place to be, no House, no *purpose*."

The word sparked in my mind, as though I should understand something about the way his husky voice ground through the syllables.

"Some *Ivaknen* find a purpose. They have sons or give advice to new *Dīnen*. But other *Ivaknen* wander. They wander and wander, nowhere to go, nothing to do."

My hand curled around his forearm. "But you still want to go home? Even though you'll no longer have a House?"

"*Var.*"

"Why?"

His dark gaze slid to me. "What else can I do?"

My breath caught. I could see my neat handwriting on a notebook page, a translation of Myrrine's journal entry: *He looked at me with sadness, with a resigned heart, and asked, What else is there?*

I forced myself to breathe. Ignoring my crumbling heart, I pressed his hand between mine. "If you want to go home, I'll make it happen. If those sorcerers could open a portal, so can I."

"Their *vīsh* did not work properly. It tore the *īnkav* and then it broke."

"Something wasn't working right," I agreed. "But we'll figure it out."

He studied me for a long moment, then relaxed against the tub and closed his eyes. His fingers curled around mine, and I held his hand against my stomach, trying not to wonder how long this closeness would last before he was gone ... forever.

I STOOD OVER MY LINK CHART. Socks had knocked the flashcards askew, but they were close enough to their original positions. Claude's name sat in the middle, the short list of facts I knew about him mocking me.

I lifted his card out of the arrangement and set my pen to it. Jaw tight, I added new notes.

> Stole grimoire pages to open a portal.
> Forced Zylas into a contract.
> Involved with something called "the court."
>
> What is his goal???

I underlined the last line three times, then added a star for good measure.

Claude's goal. His ultimate aim. Whatever it was, it was driving everything that had happened to me since my parents had died. My fear now was that Claude was getting close—dangerously close—to achieving his goals, and I still had no idea what his plans were.

Whatever he was up to might not have anything to do with me. Maybe our paths had only crossed because of the grimoire, but the grimoire was *my* responsibility, and he was using the stolen pages. Not to mention he'd killed my parents, and I wasn't about to forgive and forget.

I replaced the card in the center of the chart, then pressed my pen to the one where I'd detailed the albino sorcerer, who'd turned out to be three sorcerers. Feeling vaguely sick, I drew an X across the card. They were no longer threats, though we might have eliminated them too late. The "missing piece" they'd devised to fill in the gap Anthea had left in the portal spell hadn't worked well, but it'd worked well enough.

If Claude had that missing piece, he could open the portal again.

Rising, I lifted my arms over my head in a stretch, and a yawn popped my jaw. I'd stayed up most of the night watching over Zylas, and it'd been nearly dawn by the time he could heal my ankle. I'd slept a few hours after that, but fatigue was clogging my brain.

Stifling another yawn, I traipsed into my room. Zylas was sprawled across the bed, sleeping off his exhaustion. His eyes opened as I heaved out the grimoire's metal case and murmured the spell to unlock it.

"*Vayanin?*"

I slid the grimoire out. "I want to see if the portal array the sorcerers used last night is in here somewhere."

"*Hnn.*" He rolled onto his back. "Tell me if you want help."

"Help?"

His eyes hooded with drowsy lassitude. "I remember things I see, *na?* Better than a *hh'ainun.*"

"Right." I smiled, feeling strangely warm and fuzzy at his offer. "I'll check for likely matches, then you can help confirm them. Rest for now, and I'll wake you later."

His eyes drifted closed. He'd stripped off his armor and leather, leaving only the cloth of his outfit. My gaze lingered on his chest before sliding down across his abs.

He cracked an eye open again.

Flushing, I hurried out of the room. Retreating from him wasn't necessary. If I went back in there, I could do more than admire his physique. I could touch him if I wanted.

After all, we'd already ... he'd ... and I'd ... My blush deepened as I sat on the sofa and set the grimoire on the coffee table. With effort, I made myself think the words: I had ... *kissed* ... my demon.

I swallowed hard. Had it really been just yesterday afternoon that I'd offered him a bite of strawberry in bold invitation? The thought alone made my head spin.

I'd kissed a demon. A demon who didn't plan to stick around, who wanted away from my world—and me—as soon as he could manage it. It was insane, and I knew *exactly* how Myrrine had felt when she'd wondered whether she was losing her mind.

The heat in my cheeks reached radioactive levels as I replayed everything that had happened between us yesterday afternoon—discovering that our contract had never bound him, my shy invitation, his response. Then I replayed it all again, dwelling on each moment as though analyzing it would provide me with greater insight. It was an entirely scientific analysis. Yes. Scientific.

At a glimpse of movement, my exhilarating reverie evaporated. I looked up.

Zylas stood in the bedroom doorway. Hair mussed from sleep, half naked as always. He pushed off the frame and glided toward me with slow, silent steps.

Predatory steps.

He stopped at the sofa, towering over me while he surveyed my pink cheeks.

I blinked up at him, intimidated despite myself. "Why are you up? You should be resting."

"You are thinking very loud."

"Thinking …?" My mouth dropped open. "You said you couldn't hear those kinds of thoughts!"

"I couldn't before." He canted his head, a wicked glint in his eyes. "Now I can. Maybe you want me to hear."

"N-no—I mean—I didn't think—" My cheeks threatened to combust from the buildup of heat, and I buried my face in my hands. "Oh my god."

He'd heard *all* of that? All my breathless reminiscing?

A warm exhale stirred my hair—then knuckles rapped lightly against my skull. "*Zh'ūltis.*"

Parting my fingers enough to see past them, I glared up at him.

He leaned down. "You are being *zh'ūltis, vayanin.*"

I scooted sideways on the cushions, opening more space between us. "I thought we were past the insults."

He put a knee on the sofa, moving into the spot I'd vacated. "Don't be *zh'ūltis* and I will not call you *zh'ūltis.*"

Shuffling farther along the cushions, I increased my glower. "And how am I being stupid?"

"You need me to explain?"

He was on the sofa, and I was scooching across it as he followed, that predatory gleam in his eyes intensifying. My shoulders hit the armrest—nowhere left to retreat. My breath rushed through my lungs.

Now he was kneeling over me, hands braced on either side of my torso. I stared up at him, eyes wide. I was trapped.

His slow smile returned. He lowered his head, and I pressed back into the cushions. His nose grazed my cheek—then he abruptly sat up, his attention turning to the door. Annoyance flitted across his features.

A thudding noise—running footsteps. A key clattered in the lock. I looked up at Zylas. He gazed down, daring me. Did he really think I wouldn't do it?

His eyes narrowed.

Daimon, hesychaze.

He dissolved into red light and vanished into the infernus around my neck. The glow had just faded when the door swung open and Amalia flew inside, her face flushed and eyes bright. She waved a wad of papers, a brown envelope with its top torn open tucked under her elbow.

"I got it!" she crowed.

I pushed off the sofa. "Got what?"

"*This,*" she declared dramatically, holding out the papers like a trophy, "is a patent approval for a hex clothing line!"

"What? No way!" I rushed over to her, and she proudly handed the papers over, the MPD logo standing out boldly in the top corner. "Wow, this is official-looking. 'Hex clothing, hereby defined as casual-wear garments that incorporate cantrips for the purposes of self-defense.' That's awesome!"

"Isn't it?" She kicked her shoes off. "I had to prepare a whole proposal and present it to a patent official at the MPD office. They even called me back last week to explain how my hex clothing was different from wearable self-defense artifacts like medallions or bracelets. I guess I convinced them my designs deserve their own patent."

I turned the page to find a diagram of the shield-hex sweater she'd made for me. "What does the patent mean for you?"

"MPD patents don't stop other mythics from copying you, but if anyone sells anything that falls under my patent, they have to pay me a cut." She sat on a bar stool, an excited grin stretching her cheeks. "Now that my design is protected, I can start approaching guilds to sell to them."

"I can't believe you did all this—all while we were dealing with Claude and sorcerers and stolen grimoire pages. You even went to the MPD?"

She grimaced. "Yeah. I was so nervous. My dad hammered it into us as kids to never draw MagiPol's attention, but I figured I could chance it. It's not like we were ever suspected of any crimes, and even then, the patent office is—well, it's in the same building as the agents and investigators, but it's on a different floor. So there's no reason at all that—"

Bang bang.

We looked at the door. A loud knock sounded again, and cold foreboding settled over me like a winter chill. It couldn't be …

"Who is it?" Amalia shouted, her hand clenched around her patent papers.

"MPD," a male voice called, muffled by the wood. "Open the door."

28

AMALIA'S JAW DROPPED with horror. So did mine.

Pulling herself together, she strode to the door and wrenched it open. Two people stood on the other side: dark-haired, bauble-decorated abjuration expert Lienna Shen and her tall, handsome partner, Kit Morris.

"Agent Shen," Lienna said brusquely, flashing her badge. "This is Agent Morris. May we come in?"

The agent might've been asking politely, but it was clear she didn't need our permission. Amalia silently stepped back.

Lienna strode into our apartment, and Kit strolled in after her, glancing curiously around our home. Almost too quiet to hear, he was humming to himself. That tune ... was it the *Friends* theme song?

"Amalia Harper?" Lienna confirmed. At Amalia's nod, the agent turned to me. "And Robin Page, of course."

"Is there a problem?" I asked cautiously.

"We're following up on last night's report."

Report? What report?

"MPD procedure requires we interview all relevant parties in bounty cases involving one or more deaths." She opened the folder she held. "As reported by Ezra Rowe at 11:23 last night, the Crow and Hammer's official investigation into the suspicious deaths of human civilians Georgina Brandis, May Carter, and Yana Deneva required a guild team, which comprised Ezra, Robin, and Amalia, to track three suspects to the SeaDevils' guild. There, you interrupted the suspects in the midst of conducting unknown Arcana. They resisted capture and were killed in the ensuing battle."

Her sharp gaze rose to me. "Is that correct?"

"Yes," I said quickly, and Amalia nodded.

"Normally, we would question you in more detail about how those events played out, but"—she tapped the papers in her folder—"you and Amalia have not yet submitted your reports. I expect those within forty-eight hours."

I bobbed my head earnestly.

"We're still recovering evidence from the crime scene—"

"—which has been tricky," Kit added unexpectedly, "seeing as how the helipad is under twenty feet of water."

My mouth fell open. I snapped it shut. "Oh. Yes, of course."

"We aren't entirely clear on how the platform sank," Lienna added, her assessing gaze on me. "Ezra speculated in his report that the suspects' unknown spell damaged it."

"My thought too," I lied.

Lienna noted that in her folder. "As for the unidentified remains found in the water—"

"I only know the sorcerers' first names," I interrupted nervously. "We didn't—"

"Not *those* remains." Kit arched an eyebrow. "The *other* remains."

"Reconstructing the suspects' array on the platform may be impossible." Lienna snapped her folder closed. "But our preliminary findings suggest the reptilian remains belong to some kind of fae."

"*Fae?*" I blurted.

Kit fixed those bright blue eyes on me. "Definitely fae."

"You agree, don't you, Miss Page?" Lienna was also giving me an intent look.

I blinked. "Y-yes. Of course. Fae."

"Good," she said primly. "Make sure that's included in your report. You don't need to add any speculation on the array carved into the platform. It's too damaged to reconstruct."

"Fae beasty, no guesses on what that spell was for," Kit summarized, glancing between Amalia and me. "Let's not stress our poor overworked MagiPol boss-people with any mentions of portals and otherworldly monsters, mmkay?"

Lienna tensed, then rolled her eyes so hard her pupils disappeared. "Does the word 'subtlety' mean *anything* to you, Kit?"

"Sure, but Robin here didn't seem to be getting it. No offense," he added, flashing me a grin.

I was too anxious to be insulted. "I've got it."

He slid his hands into his pockets. "Good. So, let's all forget about Arcana Flamingostra—"

"Fenestram," Lienna growled.

"—and not turn Vancouver into an episode of *Buffy the Vampire Slayer*."

Amalia folded her arms. "Dunno what you're talking about. We killed a couple sicko murderers and their freaky pet fae. That's it."

"*She* gets it," Kit told Lienna.

Another dramatic eye roll. "Let's go before you start spilling agency secrets."

He followed her to the door. "It wouldn't matter what I said if the MPD had Neuralyzers like *Men in Black*. There's got to be a magic equivalent to—"

"Or you could just be more careful with what you blurt out …"

Her voice trailed off as Kit swung the door shut.

Amalia and I stood in silence for a full minute after the agents had left. Finally, I let out a long, exhausted breath.

"Well," Amalia drawled, "that was interesting."

"They don't want anything about portal magic in our reports," I mused, nervously adjusting my glasses. "They came here just to make sure our story would match Ezra's."

"The question is why they want to push that fae bullshit instead of finding the truth." She waved a hand. "Not that I'm complaining. We don't want them investigating us."

"Unless they are … unofficially."

We exchanged worried looks.

"Have you talked to Ezra since we left him last night?" she asked.

"I've texted him four times asking him to call me. No answer." I grimaced. "Sounds like he's been busy, though. I guess reporting what happened was the smart thing to do. Someone would've eventually noticed the helipad had sunk and looked into it."

"Still, would've been nice if he'd given us a heads-up." She checked the time on her phone, stuffed it back in her pocket, and scooped up her patent paperwork. "I'm going to start getting ready."

"Getting ready? We don't need to leave for over an hour."

"Yeah, but this is Zora's 'welcome back' party. It's her first time at the guild since she was hurt! We can't be late for *that*." She gave me a chiding look as though I were the one who never arrived on time for anything, then headed into her room.

Smiling at her new concern for promptness, I returned to the sofa. Since my beauty routine involved a straightening iron and a tube of lip gloss, I only needed a few minutes to prepare.

The grimoire sat on the coffee table, and beside it was Zylas's book of landscape photography. The top corner was a mess of dog-eared pages. Bemusedly, I slid the book onto my lap and flipped through all the photos he'd marked. Wildebeest herds on the African savanna, the precariously narrow mountains of Hunan Province in China, a waterfall across black rocks in Iceland, snow-crusted mountains of the Antarctic, California's breathtaking Redwood forests, towering sea cliffs on Scotland's coast.

As I gazed at the last one, my imagination added Zylas and me to those cliffs. Looking out across the iron seas, the cold wind whipping at us. His awe and delight—and mine. Sights neither of us had seen. An adventure I could never imagine attempting on my own, but with him …

I shook my head. What was I thinking? Zylas wanted to go home, not tour the planet. He'd already almost left me.

My chest tightened.

Heat vibrated through the infernus. Zylas appeared in a crouch on the sofa and immediately reclined against the cushions, one foot propped up. Those crimson eyes watched me, and I wondered how much of my thoughts he'd heard.

The ache inside me grew, and I closed the book. We wouldn't see those places together. He wanted to go home—

and that's what I wanted too. I wanted my normal life back, where I wasn't an illegal contractor constantly fearing for my life. I didn't want to share my home, my life, and my mind with a demon. I didn't want to be bound to him forever.

I didn't … but my chest still ached.

"What hurts, *vayanin?*"

Flinching, I ducked my head. So he wasn't privy to my current thoughts—but he was picking up on other signs. Unwilling to delve into the confused maelstrom of feelings I was experiencing at the prospect of his departure from this world, I gave him a scowl.

"Do you *have* to keep insulting me, Zylas?"

"I am not insulting you."

"Maybe you don't think calling me clumsy is an insult, but—"

"I did not call you *clumsy.*"

"You keep calling me *vayanin.*"

"I told you, it is not an insult."

"Then what does it mean?"

He grinned, amusement brightening his crimson eyes.

I bristled self-consciously. "It might not be an insult, but you're still making fun of me."

"I am not *making fun.*"

Despite his claim, I could see the laughter he was holding back, and hurt slashed me. Maybe he wasn't being mean-spirited, but if he thought it was funny, it couldn't be anything pleasant. Why would he use everyone else's name, but not mine?

Huffing to hide my distress, I shoved off the sofa and took a stomping step away.

A hard tug on my sweater. I fell backward, landing on his lap. Before I could think of leaping off him, he wrapped his powerful arms around me, pulling me tight against his chest.

"*Vayanin* is not an insult," he murmured, his warm breath teasing my ear. "Your language does not have this word. You do not know it."

"Then why do you keep calling me it?"

"It is a good word for you."

I gritted my teeth, too aware of all the places our bodies were touching. "Explain it to me, then."

"*Hnn* ... that is not fun." He sighed. "*Vayanin* means ..."

For a moment, he was quiet. Gathering his thoughts or deciding whether to speak at all?

"Night is a time of danger." All amusement left his voice, his tone low and husky. "It is the time when we hunt. When we are hunted. It is dark and cold, with no way to recover *vīsh*. All night, we watch the horizon."

I held still in his arms, my breath snared in my lungs as I listened.

"When the first light reaches the land, and the sky turns to yellow, and the warmth comes, we are safe for another day. The moment when the sun touches you after the cold night— that is *vayanin*."

My pulse thumped in my ears. My chest tightened again, but not with the sorrowful ache of earlier. A different sort of ache. Twisting in his hold, I craned my neck back to stare at him in disbelieving wonder. "I thought ... This whole time, I thought you were insulting me."

His somber gaze turned toward me—and his wolfish grin flashed. "I know."

334 ◆ ANNETTE MARIE

I blinked. *That's* why he'd always looked so amused when I'd demanded to know what *vayanin* meant? He hadn't been entertained by his clever insult, but by my assumption about its meaning? Instead of telling me, he'd let me think it was an insult. It'd been his little joke, a secret he'd never intended to explain.

I was still reeling, my head and heart a complete mess, when Amalia breezed out of her room, carrying two slim sweater-dresses.

"Robin, which do you think I should—" She broke off at the sight of me trapped in Zylas's arms. "Oh my god, seriously?"

My face burned.

Amalia tossed her dresses toward her bedroom, stomped over to the sofa, and mashed her hand over Zylas's face. Shoving him backward, she hauled me off his lap with her other hand. I stumbled away, blinking dumbly.

"You have an infernus, remember?" she barked at me. "Use it once in a while! And *you*." Hands on her hips, she glared at Zylas. "You're an obnoxious pig! Don't make that face. If you knew what a pig was, you wouldn't think it's funny!"

Choking on a laugh, I scooped up the grimoire and hurried into my room, Amalia's angry lecture carrying after me.

"Holding Robin down is just gross, and you need to get it through your thick horned skull that civilized men don't—" A pause. "I didn't say you were a human, but you can do better than behaving like a beast!"

I swung my door shut before she heard my stifled giggles. Shaking my head, I stopped at my closet, figuring I might as well pick out my outfit for the party. I was looking forward to seeing Zora again—and she would have a million questions about what had happened with Claude and the sorcerers.

"Oh yeah?" Amalia shouted. "Just try me! I'll steal pieces from your puzzle and *burn them!*"

Snorting with laughter, I almost dropped the grimoire. Before I could damage it, I crossed to my bed and pulled out its case. I laid the book in its nest of brown paper, my fingers brushing the leather cover with reverence.

People put their souls in books, my mother had always said. Had she left a remnant of her soul behind in the grimoire? What about Myrrine and Melitta, who'd added impassioned words to its pages? How many of my ancestors had put a piece of themselves into this tome?

I gently straightened the book's torn clasp. Every time I picked up the book and turned its pages, I thought of my mother's hands picking it up and turning the same pages. I knew it was nostalgic whimsy, but I felt like she was with me, guiding me, every time I worked on the translations.

Since discovering Myrrine's journal entries, I'd felt like she was leading me too—a smart, bold older sister braving the way. As Myrrine had protected Melitta, she'd guided me with her insights, showing me a path I might have rejected otherwise.

Smiling, I folded the protective brown paper over the grimoire and closed the steel lid. As I pushed the box under my bed, my phone buzzed in my pocket. I slid it out and woke the screen to find a new message. My heart rate jumped at the sender: Ezra Rowe.

We need to talk ASAP. In private.

I bit my lip. Was there a reason we couldn't talk on the phone? What was so urgent?

With five taps on my screen, I sent a reply: *Why?*

Standing rigidly beside my bed, I waited. My phone grew heavier in my hands as the seconds crawled past. Amalia and Zylas's argument had petered out, and the silence pressed down on me.

My phone buzzed against my palm. His reply appeared on the screen, four words that sent a fear-tinged thrill down my spine.

It's time to trade.

ROBIN'S STORY CONCLUDES IN

DELIVERING EVIL FOR EXPERTS

THE GUILD CODEX: DEMONIZED / FOUR

www.guildcodex.ca

ABOUT THE AUTHOR

Annette Marie is the author of YA urban fantasy series *Steel & Stone*, its prequel trilogy *Spell Weaver*, romantic fantasy trilogy *Red Winter*, and sassy urban fantasy series *The Guild Codex*.

Her first love is fantasy, but fast-paced adventures, bold heroines, and tantalizing forbidden romances are her guilty pleasures. She proudly admits she has a thing for dragons, and her editor has politely inquired as to whether she intends to include them in every book.

Annette lives in the frozen winter wasteland of Alberta, Canada (okay, it's not quite that bad) and shares her life with her husband and their furry minion of darkness—sorry, cat—Caesar. When not writing, she can be found elbow-deep in one art project or another while blissfully ignoring all adult responsibilities.

www.annettemarie.ca

SPECIAL THANKS

My thanks to Erich Merkel for sharing your exceptional expertise in Latin and Ancient Greek. Any errors are mine.

THE GUILD CODEX

DEMONIZED

Robin finally has some answers, but too many questions remain.
Why are Twelfth House demons immune to contracts? How did
summoning begin? What was Anthea Athanas hiding? However,
Robin does know this: the lost amulet *is* the key to everything.

DISCOVER MORE BOOKS AT
www.guildcodex.ca

THE
GUILD CODEX
SPELLBOUND

Meet Tori. She's feisty. She's broke. She has a bit of an issue with running her mouth off. And she just landed a job at the local magic guild. Problem is, she's also 100% human. Oops.

Welcome to the Crow and Hammer.

STEEL
&STONE

When everyone wants you dead, good help is hard to find.

The first rule for an apprentice Consul is *don't trust daemons*. But when Piper is framed for the theft of the deadly Sahar Stone, she ends up with two troublesome daemons as her only allies: Lyre, a hotter-than-hell incubus who isn't as harmless as he seems, and Ash, a draconian mercenary with a seriously bad reputation. Trusting them might be her biggest mistake yet.

GET THE COMPLETE SERIES
www.annettemarie.ca/steelandstone

SPELL WEAVER

The only thing more dangerous than the denizens of the Underworld ... is stealing from them.

As a daemon living in exile among humans, Clio has picked up some unique skills. But pilfering magic from the Underworld's deadliest spell weavers? Not so much. Unfortunately, that's exactly what she has to do to earn a ticket home.

A destiny written by the gods. A fate forged by lies.

If Emi is sure of anything, it's that *kami*—the gods—are good, and *yokai*—the earth spirits—are evil. But when she saves the life of a fox shapeshifter, the truths of her world start to crumble. And the treachery of the gods runs deep.

This stunning trilogy features 30 full-page illustrations.

GET THE COMPLETE TRILOGY
www.annettemarie.ca/redwinter

Made in the USA
San Bernardino, CA
28 May 2020

72443824R00224